THE DOOR OPENED
AND NATALIE CAME IN

Adam froze. He could feel his heavy pulse accelerate as he scrutinized her. She still had her hair up, exposing the long column of her neck and her naked shoulders. The deep mauve negligee accentuated every curve, and the lace bodice revealed tantalizing amounts of cleavage. When she moved, the long skirt seemed to caress her erotically.

His heart was hammering so hard that he could barely breathe, and when he was finally able to speak, his voice was low and textured by a smoldering sexuality. "Nice. Very nice."

She was trembling and uncertain, but her gaze was riveted on him, her eyes dark and smoky. Leaning forward, Adam caught her wrist and gathered her against him. Holding her like that felt so good, but he wanted much more....

ABOUT THE AUTHOR

Amid the chaos in her Calgary household of four
teenagers, a husband and two cats, Judith Duncan
has created her fifth Superromance. Her many fans
will be thrilled to find that, as always, Judith's
writing is warm and sensitive, the romance intense,
and the compelling story sure to bring laughter
and tears.

Books by Judith Duncan

HARLEQUIN SUPERROMANCE

51—TENDER RHAPSODY
77—HOLD BACK THE DAWN
114—REACH THE SPLENDOR
143—WHEN MORNING COMES
196—INTO THE LIGHT

These books may be available at your local bookseller.

Don't miss any of our special offers. Write to us at the
following address for information on our newest releases.

Harlequin Reader Service
P.O. Box 52040, Phoenix, AZ 85072-2040
Canadian address: P.O. Box 2800, Postal Station A,
5170 Yonge St., Willowdale, Ont. M2N 6J3

Judith Duncan

INTO THE LIGHT

Harlequin Books

TORONTO • NEW YORK • LONDON
AMSTERDAM • PARIS • SYDNEY • HAMBURG
STOCKHOLM • ATHENS • TOKYO • MILAN

Published January 1986

First printing November 1985

ISBN 0-373-70196-9

CHAPTER ONE

THE REST STOP at the side of the road overlooked a narrow green valley wedged between two mountain ranges, the distant jagged peaks now muted by a soft purple haze. Coniferous forests clung tenaciously to the steep slopes, their growth rooted in shallow infertile soil, their survival dependent on heavy rainfalls. Farther down the valley, avalanche trails lay barrenly exposed, their never-changing paths scoured clean during countless winters by thundering snow slides.

The destructive forces of nature were dormant now, their ravaging power sedated by the potency of the summer sun. But even in the summer, this remained a hostile wilderness, cloaking itself in a menacing stillness.

She stood alone, her arms resting on top of a cairn as she stared across the valley. At first glance, there was an almost puritanical plainness about her. Her ash-blond hair was pulled back from her face and twisted into an austere chignon, and she wore little, if any, makeup. She was dressed in a long-sleeved white silk blouse and a pair of steel-gray slacks, and had a matching gray cardigan draped around her shoulders.

Everything about her was subdued, but there was something unusually compelling about her, too. As she stood there motionless, her eyes fixed on some distant point, a lone eagle skimmed overhead, its eerie screech echoing in the silence of the noonday heat. She looked up, one hand shielding her eyes against the brightness. As she watched the soaring, wheeling flight of this magnificent bird of prey, her impassive expression dramatically altered and a look of elation blazed in her eyes. And for that split second, it was as if she and the eagle were one, and she was experiencing the same untamed freedom, the same soaring flight. There was another echoing scream and the golden bird plummeted from sight, its talons outstretched as it prepared for a kill.

As quickly as it came, her excitement died, leaving behind a haunting emptiness that darkened her wide gray eyes. As if a shadow suddenly crossed her face, her expression changed. Her finely sculpted features were marked by tension and her soft mouth compressed into a taut line. She shivered and pulled her cardigan more snugly around her. Her trial by fire had begun.

Natalie Carter leaned against the cairn and dispassionately looked out over the valley. It was not as she remembered it. The ugly bald scars left by excessive logging were no longer evident, and where there had once been only graying stumps, young forests were beginning to flourish. And the air, once polluted by the foul haze belching from the stacks of the pulp mill, was now clean and unspoiled, free of the acrid stench she remembered so well. It had always been there it seemed, that stench. Heavier than the thin alpine air, it had been trapped in the valley by the mountains that surrounded the town.

Folding her arms in front of her, she tried to stifle the dread that was settling like a rock inside her. She had left eleven years ago, and she had never been back. And if it wasn't for Doc, she would have never come back to Canada, let alone to this remote area of British Columbia. If it wasn't for him, she wouldn't be within a hundred miles of this isolated valley in the wilderness. But he needed her now, and no matter how deep her apprehensions were, she could not turn her back on the man who had salvaged a scrap of humanity so many years ago—the man who had become a father to her during the ensuing years. He had given her a means of escape, and she owed him her life for that.

After Natalie's mother had died, Doc had taken her to his widowed sister in California, and from that day, Aunt Bea and Doc had become her family. They had given her a secure home, provided for her and educated her, and she cared for them more than words could ever express. But especially Doc. She owed him everything. He had been her guardian, her mentor, her provider. But now, at sixty-eight, he was suffering a stretch of very bad health. He'd had to be hospitalized a few weeks earlier, and Aunt Bea had come. His doctor had told Bea that Doc's severe problems with high blood pressure and diabetes were acutely compounded by an improper diet. He was very frank; Doc was not looking after himself, and if he didn't start, his condition would worsen rapidly. He was, in sober terms, playing with his life.

Deeply concerned about his welfare, both Natalie and Aunt Bea tried to pressure him into moving to California, but he refused to even consider it. He said that he could never rip up the roots he had put down in the dying, depression-struck town that had once been the thriving center of this narrow valley. He could never leave the lush forests of his beloved mountains; he could never leave the people who had been his friends for forty years. He was like an old Douglas fir, he said—he would die from transplant shock if they tried to move him to new soil.

Even though she didn't share his feelings about the valley, Natalie could understand them. He had been a vital part of the community for a long time. He was a pharmacist by profession and had opened up the first drugstore in that part of British Columbia shortly after he emigrated from Ireland. In the beginning there wasn't a doctor within a hundred miles, so he was automatically the authority everyone turned to for advice if there was a sickness. It was only a matter of time until Patrick James Alexander Patterson was known to everyone simply as "Doc."

But in a different way, this man had served an even more essential role in the town. He had been the kind of man anyone could go to in times of trouble, and no one would ever know for certain how many dozens of people he and his wife had quietly helped over the years. And most of those people remembered the Pattersons' kindness. When his beloved Nell died fifteen years ago, people had come from all over the country to attend her funeral.

Natalie knew Doc's many friends would never neglect him, but it worried her to death when Aunt Bea had come back home and he was left alone. As soon as she could arrange it, she took her four weeks of holidays and two weeks' leave of absence. She had come to take care of him, but while she was there, she was also going to try to persuade him to go back to California with her, at least for a few months. She could not stand the thought of his being alone and uncared for.

The cool mountain breeze finally penetrated her sweater and Natalie sighed and straightened, then turned and started back toward her car. Her unwillingness to complete the final leg of her journey was becoming more and more intense. She had known that going back to the town that had been her childhood home would be an ordeal, but now that she was actually facing it, she realized it was going to be much worse than she had anticipated. Somehow she had to find the courage to get back in the car and force herself to drive down that winding road, a road she had not traveled since that chilling rain-slashed night more than a decade ago—a route she swore she would never travel again—one that would lead her back to that which she most desperately wanted to forget.

She met only two transport trucks on the road, one following the other, their diesel engines straining with the loads they were hauling from the coast. Navigating a hairpin turn, Natalie crossed a trestle bridge that spanned the rushing waters of a river. Shadows from tall spruce stretched across the pavement as she passed through a dense stand of trees, then rounding a sweeping turn, she entered an open area and the pulp mill came into view.

It was closed now, the weathered buildings deteriorating in their abandonment, the steel link fence locked against intruders. Shrinking international markets had had dire effects on the lumber industry in

British Columbia, and since the mill had been the major source of employment in the valley, its closure had hit the town very hard. But somehow the town and its people had managed to survive. Many of the younger workers had left, hoping to find better opportunities for employment elsewhere. But most of the older ones had stayed, a few finding work in the independently owned sawmill at the edge of town, some taking laborer jobs with the railway or the Department of Highways, some eking out a living on traplines, and some of the luckier ones landing good-paying jobs in a mine that had been reopened forty miles away.

Slowing to obey the speed limit, Natalie shut off the air-conditioning in the car and rolled down her window. A distinctive fragrance wafted in. The scent of rain-dampened forest, freshly sawn cedar stockpiled by the railway, crisp mountain air all mixed together in a fresh, clean bouquet. She had forgotten how beautiful, how invigorating that fragrance was. She crossed the river again, only now its wild downhill rush had slowed and she was able to see the rocky bottom through the crystal-clear water. The road led across a railway crossing, then made another sweeping turn.

Before her was Main Street.

In all those years, it had hardly changed. The two-story hotel had been painted and a new neon sign advertised Goldie's Bar, but there were only a few other alterations: new aluminum siding and a minor remodeling job on the town office; a set of traffic lights at the main intersection; a new post office. It was as though time had stood still, and Natalie didn't like the feeling. It threatened her with familiar impressions, familiar memories—and she didn't want to remember any of it.

Turning on her signal light, she waited for a half-ton pickup to pass, then made a left-hand turn at the Sears Catalog Order Office. That was something else she had forgotten about. The area was isolated and it was several hours' drive to a major center, so catalog shopping was a way of life in the valley. From clothes to winter tires, to material, to appliances—the catalog had it all, and the order office used to do the steadiest business in town. Brides had been married in Sears wedding dresses, babies had been brought home in Sears blankets and nearly every kid who started school had started in a new Sears outfit. The Christmas *Wish Book* was the ultimate in catalogs, and was probably fully memorized by every youngster in the valley.

The lines of anxiety on Natalie's face were softened by a look of amusement. Catalog shopping was a little like playing Russian roulette. There was always that chance that the girl she disliked the most would show up at school one day in the same outfit. But then, it had the added advantage that she and her best friend could get identical clothes, and dressing the same was the visible evidence of their absolute loyalty to each other.

Natalie turned down a street that led toward the river and smiled slightly when she approached a group of children gathered at the side of the road. It was still the same—summer holidays, and it was up to the kids to amuse themselves. There were no elaborate sports complexes to provide equipment and facilities, nor were there any specially trained recreational directors to develop a long list of structured activities. But maybe that wasn't the terrible disadvantage Natalie once thought it was. Maybe the kids here had retained that wonderful sense of adventure she had grown up with.

She drove past the small white church and a house with a For Sale sign stuck haphazardly in a patch of grass by the front walk, then slowed as she approached a yard surrounded by a slightly overgrown hedge. Natalie pulled into the graveled driveway and parked behind the small four-wheel-drive station wagon. This must be the new vehicle Doc had raved about in his most recent letter. He loved nothing better than investigating all the old abandoned logging roads in his never-ending search for the ultimate in trout streams, and she knew this new car was his concession to that passion. She suspected he bought a four-wheel-drive because he'd had to walk out of the bush once too often, stubbornly refusing to believe there was a road anywhere in the valley he couldn't navigate.

A sudden bout of nervousness hit her, and Natalie closed her eyes and made herself take some deep, even breaths. She most definitely did not want to be here. If only Doc had agreed to come to California. But that was such pointless thinking, and it changed nothing. He didn't want to go, she was here and that was that. She'd better make the best of it. Resolutely lifting her chin, she picked up her purse and got out of the car.

She found Doc in the garden at the back of the house staking up some delphiniums that had blown over in the wind, and she smiled when she heard his familiar Irish brogue as he muttered to himself,

"These damned intolerable flowers aren't worth Paddy's spit."

Her drawn expression changed to one of deep affection as she watched him wrestle with the tall stalks. "If you hate them so much, why don't you just chop them off?"

There was an obvious struggle with stiff muscles and an arthritic back as he straightened and slowly turned around. His eyes mirrored his disbelief when he saw her standing there, then his craggy face creased with profound pleasure. As he made his way across the large garden he fumbled with the side of his sweater and managed to find his pocket and shove in the wad of twine he'd been holding. He was so flustered by her unexpected arrival that he plowed through a row of peas and trampled his precious strawberry patch in his haste to get to her.

With his arms open wide he exclaimed loudly, "Faith and begorra! I never expected to find you planted in my garden."

As he enfolded her in a hearty bear hug, she fought back a sudden rush of tears, then said unsteadily, "Well, since you wouldn't come to us, I decided I'd better come to you."

"Bless you, lass, bless you. You are a sight for these tired old eyes." He held her away from him. "Here, now let's be havin' a look at you." Pursing his lips, he nodded his head in approval. "You look fine. Just fine."

"You'd say that even if I was covered with warts."

There was a touch of devil in his faded blue eyes as he chuckled. "And you'd look just fine with warts, too."

Natalie made a face at him, then slipped her arm through his as they started walking back toward the house. "You lie with such finesse."

He patted her hand. "I'm sure you'll manage to do a passable job yourself. I can't wait to hear the load of rubbish you're going to feed me when you start explaining why you're here."

She laughed. "Would I do that to you?"

"Unquestionably, if you thought you could get away with it."

"I just came for a visit."

"Balderdash. You came to boss me around and to play nursemaid."

"I came," she said firmly, "to make sure you're following doctor's orders and to see that you're sticking to your diet."

"Same thing."

She thought about it for a minute, then answered, "You're right. It is the same thing."

Doc chuckled as he opened the screen door for her. "I can see my sister's hand in this. My guess is you have orders to bring me to heel, come hell or high water."

Natalie grinned. "Well, she never mentioned anything about hell or high water."

He snorted. "Damn woman. She does love to meddle."

"You love it and you know it."

He didn't answer, but Natalie saw the twinkle in his eyes as he stomped through the sun porch and opened another screen door that led into the living room.

When Doc had built the house for his new bride decades before, he had constructed it to take advantage of the spectacular view of the river his property afforded. Consequently, the whole design was basically back to front, and one entered the living room through the back door.

As a child, Natalie had loved this house, and walking into it was like coming home. She had to wait a moment for her eyes to adjust to the dimness of the interior before she could take it all in. He had a few pieces of new furniture—a sofa and two easy chairs—but there was still much that she remembered. His old leather easy chair, an ancient rolltop desk, the beautiful old cherrywood dining-room suite, his favorite floor lamp with the brass stand. And on the table by his chair was a humidor and a rack of pipes. The familiar smell of his tobacco permeated the room, and Natalie inhaled deeply. She loved that smell.

"Would you like a cup of tea?" he asked as he took off his garden shoes and put on his slippers.

"I'd rather have something cold, if you have it."

There was a flash of dry humor. "Then how about a cup of cold tea?"

She laughed as she set her purse on the desk. "Sounds great."

Still smiling, she followed him into the kitchen. Hugging herself against the cool breeze from the open window, she leaned against the cupboard and watched him fill the battered copper kettle. His white hair was still thick, and as usual, it was in a disheveled mess. He was tall and thin, and for some reason, he always reminded Natalie of a stork. Maybe it was because of his long neck and his long legs. Or maybe it was because of the way he marched along with his head thrust forward. The exact reason was forever elusive.

As she scrutinized him, she realized something she had never been consciously aware of. Doc was aging. With each passing year he was getting a little more stooped, a little stiffer. She hated the thought of him getting old, but she took comfort in the fact that he still moved with the briskness of a man who liked to walk. And Natalie knew that he still walked a great deal. Doc knew the high country like the back of his hand, and she doubted if there were many trails around that he hadn't hiked at one time or another.

Knowing that he took heated exception to anyone commenting on how he managed in his home, Natalie watched him fix her tea in silence. But she had to bite her lip to keep from laughing. Doc's idea of iced tea was to use the dregs of what was still in the pot from lunch, pour it over some crushed leaves ripped from the potted mint plant on the windowsill and throw in a few chips of ice. He slapped the drink he'd prepared on the counter, as if he was silently daring her to try it. Natalie took a wary sip. Expecting it to taste like mint-flavored lye, she was surprised by the refreshing flavor, and without thinking, she nodded her head in approval.

"Surprised you, didn't I?"

She grinned. "Never."

He snorted and waved his hand toward the living room. "Let's go sit in there."

"What about your tea?"

He gave her a disgruntled look, then responded tartly, "My new nursemaid can fix it for me when the kettle boils."

Natalie managed to keep a straight face, but her dancing eyes gave her away as she stared back at Doc. He muttered something about her being cheeky as he sat in his comfortable old chair. He pretended to ignore her as he selected a pipe, but she could see the corner of his mouth twitch as he filled the bowl. It was an old game they played, this father-daughter routine, but there was an element of truth to it. No daughter could have loved him more.

Doc's expression became deeply thoughtful as he carefully tamped the tobacco. There was a lengthy silence before he lifted his head and stuck the stem between his teeth. Natalie sat on the hassock in front of him and took a long drink from her glass, then set it on the table by his chair.

Watching her steadily over the rim, he put a burning match to the bowl and continued to draw in until the tobacco glowed red, then he shook out the flame and dropped the burned match in the ashtray. "I never expected to see you sitting at my hearth, Natalie," he said quietly.

Tucking her hands beneath her thighs, she watched the thin thread of smoke spiraling up from the charred match, her face showing signs of strain. When she finally met his gaze, her gray eyes were solemn. "I never intended to come back, Doc. You know that."

"But you came back because of me."

She held his steady gaze for a second, then nodded.

Leaning forward, he reached out and laid his bony hand on her shoulder. "That means a great deal to me, lass—knowing that you'd do that for me."

The affection she saw in his eyes touched her deeply. She tried to smile at him, but unshed tears suddenly burned her eyes and she abruptly looked away. "You're my family," she said simply.

"I know that, lass. I know that." Grasping her shoulder, he gave her a reassuring little shake, then leaned back in his chair and reflectively puffed on his pipe. Several quiet moments passed before he spoke again. "How long are you staying?"

She swallowed against the tightness in her throat, then looked up at him. "I've a month's holiday and I've taken a two-week leave of absence."

He pursed his lips together and studied her with wry amusement. "With orders from Bea to bring me back with you."

Natalie managed a smile. "Come hell or high water."

He chuckled, then fell silent as he nursed his pipe, lost in reflection. Cradling the bowl in his hand, he stared into space, his brogue touched with melancholy. "'Tis been my home for forty years, lass. I cannot leave."

There was empathy in her eyes as she said softly, "I know you can't, Doc. I don't think either Bea or I ever really believed you would. You can't leave here for the same reason Bea can't leave there."

"Except her ties are even stronger. All her children and grandchildren are there." He raised his finger in a gentle admonishment. "You're not to worry about me, Natalie Carter. I'm content with my life." He took another pull on his pipe, then said absently, "Do you know, lass, I've always hated California in the summer." He spoke in a tone of voice that held a certain bafflement, as though he knew he was out of step with the rest of the world and didn't understand why. "I couldna abide to live there, you know."

There was a spark of humor in her eyes as Natalie responded in a flawless Irish lilt. "Bea would rip your heart out, lad, if she heard such blasphemy cross your lips."

His shoulders shook with silent laughter as Doc nodded in absolute agreement. "That she would, lass. That she would."

Natalie smiled at him with affection, then restlessly stood up. She wandered around the room, stopping to study the collection of photographs on the piano, pausing to examine a group of paintings on the wall. But there was an air of distraction about everything she did. Slipping off her cardigan, she hung it on the back of a chair and went to the window. Staring out, she didn't say anything for the longest time, then folding her arms tightly in front of her, she said softly, "I can't believe I'm actually here."

Doc watched her with concern as he rested the stem of his pipe against his bottom lip. "Perhaps it won't be as bad as you think. You've been gone a long time."

"I wish I could believe that." She leaned her shoulder against the window frame, her head resting against the cool pane. It was a long time before she could make herself ask about the past, and her voice was strained when she spoke. "What did you tell everyone...after I left?"

With studied care, he laid his pipe in the enormous ashtray by his elbow. Sighing heavily, he lowered his head and laced his fingers across his chest. "I simply told them you were in the car when your mother had the accident, only you were thrown free. It was obvious you couldn't possibly be at her funeral because you'd been so badly injured yourself."

"Did anyone ask why I never came back?"

A hard glint of Irish ire appeared in Doc's eyes and his voice had a bitter ring to it. "It was obvious you had nothing to come back to after your stepfather burned the house to the ground. In the drunken state he was in, it was a wonder he didn't burn up with it." Doc's hands were trembling and an unhealthy flush darkened his face. "I know she couldn't cope with all the pressures after your father died, but I'll never understand what she saw in that scoundrel of a Carl Willard."

Natalie suddenly had to fight for breath as a heaviness pressed upon her chest, and her knuckles turned white as she clenched her fists against the terrifying feeling. "Don't, Doc," she pleaded desperately. "Don't even mention him."

The grandfather clock in the corner sounded out the half hour, and Natalie made herself focus on it, the familiar chime echoing in the charged silence of the room. It was very strange, but the chime of that grandfather clock was one sound that was crystal clear in the confusion of Natalie's jumbled memories. She could recall it so clearly. And it was a memory that held no menacing overtones. It was a safe one to hang on to.

It seemed like an eternity passed before Doc broke the silence. "It's all in the past, Natalie. No one ever knew the real reason why you left."

Without thinking, she responded with a grim smile. "And no one cared."

"That's not true, lass, and you know it," he scolded her gently. "The lad was near frantic when he couldn't find you. It was a terrible hurt you inflicted on him."

"I had no choice—"

"You should have at least told him about the babe," he interjected. "You'll live to regret that, lass. You denied him the right that was his. And you denied the boy his father."

She took a deep, unsteady breath before she spoke, her voice low and taut. "I know what I did was wrong, Doc, but I couldn't face him then." Her voice broke, and she pressed her hands tightly together. "And because I didn't face him then, I could never do it now."

Doc sighed. "I know, lass. I know. It's easy for me to say what was right and what was wrong."

Her eyes darkened by tormenting memories, she nervously fingered the chain around her neck, trying to scrape up the courage to ask. "Have you heard anything about him recently?"

Doc hesitated, then said, "There was a write-up about him a few months ago in a news magazine—I've got it tucked away in some cranny. He was about to leave for South America to start filming another wildlife documentary." Doc wearily rubbed his eyes, then tipped his head back. "I sometimes wonder what would have happened if your mother hadn't had that accident."

She turned to face him, her expression suddenly inflexible, her face ashen. "Her death was no accident, Doc."

His age seemed to have doubled as he slowly lifted himself out of the chair and went to her, his shoulders more stooped than usual. With compassion lining his face, he put his arm around her and drew her against him, trying to give her some measure of comfort. "We'll never know what was going through her mind that night, lass," he said gently. "And it will serve no purpose if we start wondering now."

Her body was stiff with tension as she stared numbly out the window. He was right. What good would it do to know for certain that her mother had abandoned her by taking her own life? All she wanted to do was put that nightmare out of her mind, once and for all. Maybe by coming back, by facing the past, she would be able to put those old ghosts to rest. Maybe. She closed her eyes as she slowly massaged her temples with her fingertips, trying to erase the dull ache that throbbed in her head. With a heavy sigh, she turned to look at him. "One reason I've dreaded coming back was because of all the questions."

There was a sudden haggardness about him as Doc dragged his hand across his face. "If anyone starts asking, tell them you don't remember."

She gave him a grim smile. "I *don't* remember." Her eyes were like ice as she turned and again stared rigidly out the window. "At least I don't remember anything after I was admitted to the hospital. I doubt if I'll ever forget what happened before."

"You must quit tormenting yourself, lass," Doc said gently. "I sometimes think that beneath the disgust and ugliness of it all, you unconsciously keep blaming yourself for what happened, and it wasn't your fault."

There was a heavy silence as both of them became lost in their own thoughts. When Natalie finally spoke, her voice had lost some of the bitterness. "In my logical mind, I know that. But whenever it all rises up to haunt me, there's always guilt associated with it. There's always that awful feeling I must have done something, that somehow I was to blame for everything that happened. If it hadn't been for me, mother wouldn't have done what she did."

"You can't think like that, Natalie," he said firmly. "What happened was out of your hands." Sensing how much this conversation was disturbing her and knowing nothing would be gained by continuing it, Doc wisely changed tack. "I hear the kettle boiling. Come make my tea and tell me how that fine lad of yours is doing and how you're doing. Bea wrote and said you had another promotion."

Grateful for his insight, Natalie was more than willing to follow his lead. Turning from the window, she gave him a look that was laced with perverse humor. "It seems to me that you've adapted to the idea of a nursemaid awfully fast."

He chuckled. "If the truth be known, lass, there isn't a man alive who doesn't like to be pampered now and again. But being the strong, hardy providers we are, we aren't supposed to let anyone know it."

Natalie knew his game and didn't take the bait. Picking up her glass from the table and following him into the kitchen, she retorted dryly, "This could be interesting. I've never looked after a sixty-eight-year-old boy before.''

''A new challenge, lass. Look upon it as a new challenge.''

''I don't need any more challenges in my life. Patrick gives me plenty of those.''

''He's a fine lad, lass. He'll do you proud.''

Natalie smiled ruefully. ''If he doesn't do me in first.''

''He has some life in him, that one. His letters always make my day.'' Doc rinsed out the teapot. ''One of my favorites was the one he wrote telling me about his big adventure when he went deep-sea fishing with . . . what was his friend's name? Gary, wasn't it? I laughed for days over that.''

Natalie smiled and nodded as she opened the cupboard door Doc pointed to. ''He was so excited about going that he nearly drove me crazy. He had his suitcase packed two weeks in advance.''

''I'm glad that boy had a chance to go along. He'll remember that weekend for a good many years.''

''He really will. He had a fantastic time.'' Setting two mugs on the countertop, she passed Doc the canister of tea, and added absently, ''Gary's father took a picture of Patrick hauling in his very first catch.'' She grinned. ''Seeing there's a fish in the picture, I thought you might like to have a copy, so I got the negative and had an enlargement done for you.''

''That's a fine gift, lass. I'll be putting it on the piano with the others.'' Doc flung some tea in the pot and slapped the lid back on the canister. ''How come he didn't come with you?''

Natalie shot her mentor a quick glance, but his expression was bland. She knew very well that he was skirting the question he really wanted to ask. For years Doc had wanted Natalie to let Patrick spend part of his summer vacation with him, but Natalie would never let him come. She was afraid her son might be put in a very awkward situation and asked questions he didn't have any answers for. And Natalie didn't want that to happen. This time, though, she had relented to Patrick's badgering, but she still had some very deep misgivings about it.

Her tone was introspective when she answered, "He's going to come later. I'd promised him he could go to camp this year with some of his friends, so Aunt Bea's going to put him on a plane as soon as he gets back."

Doc bowed his head and frowned, his face creased with concern. Natalie studied him intently for a moment, then glanced away. "What is it, Doc?"

He kept turning the teapot lid over and over in his hand, then he looked at her and sighed. "His coming will raise a few eyebrows, lass. I would have dealt with the gossips if he had come alone, but with you being here, you could be put on the spot, you know."

"Eyebrows can raise all they want, Doc," she said tersely. "Patrick is the one thing in my life I'll never ever apologize for."

"As long as you realize what's apt to happen."

She gave him a warped smile. "Oh, I know." And she did know. Yet as skeptical as she was about Patrick's coming, her guilt had finally outweighed her reluctance. It didn't seem fair to deny the boy the chance to spend a summer vacation with his adopted grandfather because of her own apprehension. Her voice was low when she said, "He's so excited. He's wanted to visit you for ages."

"Good. I've wanted him to come. Now I can take him fishing."

She gave Doc a pointed look. "You can take *me* fishing."

He chuckled and nodded. "As good as done, lass. As good as done. We'll explore all the old spots."

For some reason his comment hit a nerve, and Natalie kept her head averted so he couldn't see her face. She didn't want to explore the old spots. She didn't want to do anything that might arouse old memories. But her mental barriers had been weakened. The picture of Patrick she brought for Doc took shape in her mind, and even though she tried to block it out, another image slowly superimposed itself on Patrick's. And a deep ache started to unfold. There were memories she wanted to forget, and there were others she didn't dare remember.

CHAPTER TWO

THE NEXT FEW DAYS slipped by quietly. Doc took her for several drives along some of his favorite logging roads, and if the mood hit them, they did a little fishing along the way. Mostly though, they stayed at home. Doc had a housekeeper who came in twice a week, so there was little for Natalie to do in that respect, but meals were another matter altogether.

Natalie was determined that Doc's health was not going to deteriorate any further because of sheer neglect. She thoroughly studied all the information about the strict diet Doc was supposed to be on, and with him grumbling about bossy women, she implemented a dietary regime that would make a nutritionist cringe. His days of eating what he felt like eating were definitely over, and he accepted that with a certain acerbic equanimity that made Natalie want to laugh.

It had not all been sunshine and roses for her, though. They had gone downtown twice: once for groceries and once to get some fishing gear for her. And both times they had run into neighbors. Without consciously being aware of it, she had been very cool when questions about her mother and stepfather had arisen. In both instances the women realized that she didn't want to talk about it and had tactfully let the matter drop. Natalie honestly didn't know how she would have handled the situation if they hadn't, and that uncertainty unsettled her nearly as much as the meetings had. She would give anything if she could simply avoid further confrontations, but that was going to be impossible. Especially with the major local event that was planned for the upcoming week.

The town council had organized a homecoming to celebrate the seventy-fifth birthday of the town, and the entire community had become involved. The businesses had awarded prizes for the most beautified storefronts, the streets had been decorated and the Chamber of Commerce had organized a parade. The celebrations were to take place the second weekend she was there, and the kickoff event was a community dance that was to be held in the hockey arena on Friday night. She desperately wanted to steer clear of the whole thing, but she knew that Doc was counting on her to attend with him, and she could not let him down.

Right from the beginning, the homecoming had all the makings of a roaring success. Former residents were coming back by the scores. By late Friday afternoon, tents, truck campers, holiday trailers and motor homes were everywhere, and the usually quiet streets were bustling with activity. It didn't seem like the same town.

Natalie felt a near giddy sense of relief when it dawned on her that if she was going to come back, she couldn't have picked a better time to do it. Everyone assumed she had come back for the reunion, and there were so many other people who had returned for the same reason that she ended up safely lost in the crowd.

This was a celebration. No one cared about what had happened eleven years ago; they were too intent on making the best of a good time now. And it wasn't long before she was actually enjoying herself.

She was even looking forward to the dance. Natalie was tour coordinator for a national travel agency and her job demanded a certain amount of socializing, but except for those instances, she seldom attended adult functions. Aunt Bea's two sons and their families considered Natalie and Patrick part of the clan, so most outings were family oriented. Maybe she was simply caught up in the general excitement and enthusiasm, but whatever the reason, she found herself in youthful high spirits as she dressed that evening.

She took extra time choosing her clothes and applying her makeup. She always wore her hair up and drawn severely back in a chignon because it was neat and easy to manage, but without consciously realizing it, she had selected a style that suited her perfectly. The dramatic simplicity did incredible things to her face. It gave a classic look to her delicate features and sharply emphasized her wide eyes and long slender neck. But tonight she spent more time on her hair, and instead of the simple bun, she did it up in an elaborate woven style, which highlighted her blondness. On Natalie, it was sheer elegance.

The dress she chose added to the effect. It was made of a fine cotton, the simple design a perfect style for the gauzy material. It had long, very full sleeves that were caught at the wrists in wide cuffs, and a full skirt that was topped by a wide belt, which accentuated her narrow waist. The wispy fabric made her seem even more slender and willowy, but what added the ultimate touch was the color. It was a deep pink that was shot with mauve, and it intensified the color of her eyes and added a faint blush to her skin. She was utterly femimine and looked as delicate as an orchid.

When she entered the living room, Doc stopped filling his pipe and stared at her. After a long silence he said, "You look lovely, lass. You do me proud."

She smiled at him. "You aren't so bad yourself. You look very spiffy." Doc was wearing gray flannel slacks and his navy-blue legion blazer with its red, white and gold silk crest embroidered on the left pocket. And he did indeed look spiffy. The collar of his white shirt was slightly twisted, and Natalie stepped behind him to fix it. She smoothed the lightly starched fabric down over his tie, then brushed a piece of lint from the shoulder of his jacket as he turned to face her.

"Tell me, do I pass inspection or do I look like I dressed in the dark?"

She laughed and patted his shoulder reassuringly. "You most certainly pass inspection. And I don't even have to check behind your ears or see if your fingernails are clean."

There was a large crowd already gathered when they arrived at the arena, and Natalie glanced around as the young man at the door took Doc's tickets and stamped the backs of their hands. Some of the tables and chairs had been cleared out of the combined lounge and cafeteria, leaving an enormous space for an informal reception area. Glancing through the row of windows that separated the outer room from the sports complex, Natalie could see that the floor of the arena had been covered with boards for the event.

Doc had told her that the steering committee had decided to organize a Community Showcase. It would feature various arts and crafts from former and current residents of the community. Through the crowd, she caught a glimpse of the displays set up at the near end of the arena. At the far end a space had been kept clear for a dance floor, which was already jammed with people. She could see the live band on a make-shift stage, and over the din she could hear the beat of a snappy polka. The party was in full swing.

Even in the crush of milling people, she could pick out several familiar faces, and Doc raised his hand in greeting as someone in the crowd called to him. For some strange reason she experienced an acute nervousness, but she buried that feeling behind a smile as Doc guided her toward a large group.

"For gawd's sake, it's Natalie Carter!" A buxom woman worked her way through the crowd and raised her arms in an expansive gesture of welcome.

Natalie's face lit up as the redhead moved toward her. Stella Ralston. She most certainly had not changed. If anyone else had ever dared to dress the way this woman did, it would look cheap and garish, but for some weird reason, Stella Ralston managed it with a very earthy kind of style. Her slinky black dress had a slit up the side that revealed a startling amount of thigh, the plunging neckline exposed a daring amount of cleavage and what little there was of the satin material clung graphically to every curve.

Somewhere in bygone years, Stella had cultivated a mind-boggling walk that made her full hips roll provocatively. Her shoes, which had two rhinestone-studded straps across the toes and extremely slender high heels, exaggerated her hip-swinging strut. As always, she wore her coppery red hair piled on top of her head in an elaborate upsweep that was stiffened with hair spray and adorned with rhinestone combs. Her theatrical makeup was liberally applied, the crowning touch being incredibly long, thick false eyelashes that weighed her eyelids down in a sensuous droop. The whole effect was a lush and lusty sensuality. And that was exactly the effect that Stella wanted.

The redhead finally reached her, and with an extravagant sweep of her arms, clutched Natalie against her voluptuous bosom in a smothering embrace. Natalie laughed and hugged her back.

Releasing her, Stella took Natalie's face in her beringed hands and gave her an affectionate shake. "Gawd, don't you look marvelous! It is so damned good to see you!" Grasping Natalie's hand, she turned to Doc. "Why didn't you tell me she was coming?" she scolded testily, one hand on her thrust-out hip.

Stella's perfume was a bit overwhelming and Natalie moved downwind as she laughingly interceded on Doc's behalf. "He didn't know. It was a surprise." She squeezed Stella's hand, her eyes sparkling. "You look terrific, Stella. You haven't changed at all." Stella did look terrific. Her age could have been anywhere from thirty to fifty, and Natalie was one of the selected few who knew the truth. Nearly eleven years— it didn't seem possible, but this woman was in her early fifties. Knowing her old co-worker the way she did, Natalie was willing to bet a month's salary that she was publicly swearing she was still thirty-nine.

Stella managed not to look too pleased as she snorted, "Gawd, child—I'm ten years older. Of course I've changed. My boobs are sagging down to my—"

"Stella!" blustered Doc. "We don't want specifics of your anatomy here and now!"

Stella grinned and patted him on the cheek with an airy gesture that showed off her long scarlet nails. "Don't be such a prude, Doc. You'd think you were a virgin the way you huff and puff."

It was impossible for Natalie to keep from laughing as she watched the two of them in action. Stella had worked in Doc's drugstore for years, and she always seemed to get some sort of perverse enjoyment out of trying to shock him. She might have the compassion of an angel, but she also had the vocabulary of a truck driver, and with frequent and deliberate regularity, Stella would scandalize her boss. Doc, on the other hand, always seemed to enjoy tormenting Stella with tantalizing bits and pieces of gossip. While she was going to high school, Natalie had worked part-time for Doc, and she had idolized the flashy and glamorous Stella with an adolescent awe. But beneath her exterior glitter, Stella was a warm and caring person who viewed life with a mixture of skepticism and dry humor. And she was loyal to the core. Natalie was genuinely glad to see her.

Stella turned back to Natalie and pursed her mouth in a skeptical twist of humor. "Why in hell did you ever come back to this dump, Natalie? What ever possessed you to leave the high life, tinsel town, the razzle-dazzle dazzle, the gorgeous male bodies on the beach for this godforsaken country?"

Natalie's amusement was written all over her face as she tilted her head toward Doc. "He's been misbehaving again, so I thought I'd better get back here and whip him into shape."

Stella gave Doc a pithy look. "Good luck. That should keep you busy for the rest of your life."

"Don't talk as if I wasn't here, Stella," Doc responded loudly. Then muttering to himself, he added, "I should have fired her twenty-five years ago."

Stella made a face at him and grinned as she slipped her arm through Natalie's. "How long are you here for, Chicken?"

"Six weeks, unless I can persuade Doc to go back with me."

"Did you bring Patrick with you? I'm dying to meet this kid of yours."

Natalie's expression became suddenly guarded as she shot Doc a questioning look. He nodded his head, wordlessly reassuring her. Stella hadn't missed the silent exchange and she raised one eyebrow in an expression that was mildly disdainful. "Really, Natalie. Of course he told me about the kid. I mean, I could hardly miss the several hundred photos he has stuffed in his wallet, could I? He brags about him so much it's disgusting. He's ten times worse than a real grandfather, you know."

Natalie laughed, but her discomfort was visible and she had trouble meeting Stella's steady gaze. "I'm sorry, Stella. I don't know quite how to handle this, I guess."

"Honey, you don't owe one damned person in this hellhole an explanation," Stella said firmly. "What you've done or not done with your life is none of their damned business." She tightened her arm around the younger woman's waist and gave her a bolstering hug. "If anyone gives you a hard time, you tell them to go to hell." She gave Natalie another squeeze and grinned. "Now tell me about this boy of yours. Am I going to get a chance to check this kid out?"

"He'll be here later on. He's in camp right now."

"Well, as soon as he gets here, I want to meet him." The effervescence beneath Stella's breeziness faded and she became serious. She lowered her head, a small frown appearing as she absently toyed with her gaudy rings. When she finally looked up, her eyes were unsmiling and she stared at Natalie with a strange intentness. "If you need a friend or need to talk, Natalie, don't hesitate to call on me," she said quietly. "I'm always available."

Natalie had the strangest feeling that Stella had a certain insight that she lacked and that there was something darkly significant about her offer. It was disconcerting. But Stella never gave her time to dwell on it as the redhead grabbed Doc and Natalie by the arms and swept them off in a whirlwind of socializing.

For the next hour Stella was firmly in charge and acted a little like a mother hen, never letting either one of them out of her sight. They were shepherded from one group to another until Natalie was lost in an avalanche of names and faces and was beginning to feel slightly giddy. Needing a bit of a breather from all the commotion, she unobtrusively slipped away from yet another mob and went into the arena.

The Community Showcase had been well organized and the caliber of homegrown talent that was featured was surprisingly good. There was everything from paintings to needlework, from woodworking to silversmithing, and as Natalie moved slowly from one display to another, she became more and more engrossed. She had a deep respect for anyone who had the ability to create, probably because she had a strong creative streak herself. But because of the demands and financial responsibility of being a single parent, what talent she possessed had never been nurtured. At one time, long ago, she had dreamed of enrolling in art school, but that was just another dream that had died from neglect.

Natalie approached the final exhibit but the display was obscured by a crowd of people. Not wanting to push her way through, Natalie was about to bypass it and go back to Doc and Stella. As she moved behind the audience, she caught bits and pieces of what the woman behind the table was saying, and with mild curiosity, she paused to listen. "It was very generous of him really. He donated all these books, and the entire proceeds from the sale of them goes toward our library fund."

That awful feeling of having walked into a bad dream washed through Natalie, followed by a chill of premonition. She wanted to run but was drawn by an overpowering need to know. With certain dread, she slipped through the crowd. The voices around her faded into a distant drone, and her heartbeat was spurred to a frantic gallop as she screwed up enough courage to pick up a book from the top of the stack. It was one of those expensively bound, carefully produced showpieces of photojournalism that allowed the reader to view the subjects and the scenes through the eyes of a master craftsman.

She didn't even need to open it. She could recognize one of his photographs among a thousand others, and the incredible shot on the dustcover of a lynx poised on a rocky overhang was distinctively one of his. The shock of finding a display of his books in the Community Showcase was paralyzing. It shouldn't be affecting her this way. It wasn't as though his work was unfamiliar to her; she had seen several of his wildlife documentaries on TV, and she'd bought two of his books for Patrick. But she had never once considered coming face-to-face with a new volume of his work here.

And that was stupid and unthinking. After all, this was where his career was launched, where it had all began.

With trembling hands Natalie opened the book and felt suddenly suffocated by the overwhelming potency of the photograph on the inside fold of the cover. It was one of those rare pictures that fully captured the vital element of the subject, creating a powerful study of the man. He was leaning against a tree with one hand resting on his hip, the other holding two cameras by the straps. The wind was ruffling his hair. One foot was balanced on an exposed root, and he was gazing off in the distance, intent on something in the sky. Even in repose, his muscled athletic body hinted at the animal power that was not unlike the sleek wildcats he so often photographed. His aura was dynamic, virile, magnetic, but there was something more, something indefinable. It was a candid black-and-white shot, and the lights and shadows across the chiseled masculine face created an illusion of strength and sensitivity. The photo exposed his raw vitality, but it also subtly revealed a deeper, darker element, something very poignant, something haunting. Something that filled her with profound sorrow.

In a weak attempt to avoid confronting the feelings that were beginning to smother her, she made herself concentrate on reading the author's profile. "Adam Rutherford began his illustrious career as a photographer of wildlife in the Canadian Rockies when he was still a university student..." But the list of his impressive credits was lost on Natalie. Buried memories were painfully unearthed. She remembered only too well how his career had been launched.

He'd had a summer job with the provincial government on a reforestation project. A carelessly attended campfire had started a forest fire that had raged out of control for days, razing thousands of acres of prime forest. He had been working on a firebreak along a small lake, and he had taken a single roll of film of animals taking refuge in the water from the roaring flames and the blinding smoke. They were sensitive, gripping pictures that had eloquently captured the terror and destruction. The local newspaper had run some of his shots, which were eventually picked up by a national wire service. One thing led to another, and within a matter of months, those same photographs were used for a massive public awareness campaign for the prevention of forest fires. His genius had been discovered, and from that point on, he had never looked back professionally.

But all that happened so long ago. More and more memories came flooding back, and the nearly forgotten grief slammed into her with such force that she didn't think she could endure the pain.

Forgetting the volume she had clutched against her, she whirled, desperate to elude the old feelings that were bombarding her, but her path of escape was blocked. She glanced up and suddenly every muscle in her body was paralyzed, and for an instant she couldn't breathe. She was trapped, and Adam Rutherford was watching her with steely eyes, his expression inflexible. And she could tell by the look on his face that he had been watching her for some time.

WHEN STELLA REALIZED that Natalie was no longer with them in the lounge her anxiety became plainly visible and she scanned the crowd. A frown appeared on Doc's weathered face as he watched her. He knew Stella very well; if she was anxious, she had every reason to be. "What is it, Stella? What's troubling you?"

She pursed her lips in exasperation, still searching with a worried desperation. "Adam Rutherford is here. I saw him earlier in town, and I saw him come in the door a few minutes ago." She placed her hands on her hips and stared at Doc, a shrewd look in her eyes. "I don't know the whole story, Doc, and I figured you had damned good reasons not to tell me, but any bloody idiot can add." She gave him a wry smile. "I don't think I'd be taking a big risk if I bet my life that Natalie's kid is also his. And I don't think I'd be taking much of a risk if I said he doesn't know a damned thing about it, either."

Doc gravely studied her for a minute, then slowly shook his head. "No, he doesn't."

"Well, isn't that just peachy keen," she muttered. "This could turn into a real stinker if he finds out. You know what he was like after she disappeared. He was ready to tear this whole damned town apart."

He sighed heavily, his sudden weariness weighing heavily upon him. "I know, Stella, I know. Now all the things she's refused to deal with have finally come home to rest. She can't evade the past forever." His brogue was thick with sadness as he stared off over Stella's shoulder, caught by some deep reflection. "Natalie's been living in a vacuum for years, Stella— pushing the past into the dark recesses of her mind. She's become a shell of what she once was because of it. I've seen it coming for a long time, this moment of truth. It fills me with dread, but I know that she's reached a crucial point in her life. She can't get on with her life until she deals with what went before." There was a deep sorrow revealed in the old man's eyes as he finally met Stella's compassionate gaze. "She's caught in a terrible maze, Stella. She cannot go forward any further until she goes back the way she came." He shook his head sadly as she stared across the room. "And the terrible truth is, she has to do it alone."

CHAPTER THREE

HE STOOD IN THE SHADOWS of the darkened vestibule of the side exit to the lounge, the ever-present camera and equipment bag slung over his shoulder. There was an air of introspection about him as he folded his arms in front of him and leaned against the wall. He stared at the crowd within, his expression unfathomable.

He was no stranger, yet he was. Gone was the free and easy youth; in its place was the cool and collected man. He had the quiet confidence and polish that comes with experience, and it was apparent to even the most casual observer that this man would be as much at ease in an exclusive country club as he was here. His clothes were expensive; his light brown shirt and slacks were complemented by an off-white suede jacket, and his suede boots were handmade. His shirt was open at the neck, exposing corded muscles and a deep tan. His dark blond hair, which was heavily streaked by the sun, was brushed back from his chiseled face. Broad cheekbones accentuated dark hazel eyes. Overwhelming masculinity enhanced the image of success and sophistication, but there was an underlying hardiness about him that warned the image was only a veneer and that this man was as tough and rugged as he looked.

But there was an emotional upheaval taking place in Adam Rutherford that was eroding his calm veneer. It was insane how her memory had come back to torment him after so many years. There had been long periods of time when he'd gone for months without thinking about his youth, but for some incomprehensible reason that had all changed within the past year. Now something as insignificant as the words of a song would summon up disturbing memories of her. And those memories would haunt him until, out of sheer desperation, he'd immerse himself in his work and drive himself so hard that he'd eventually hit a point of exhaustion where he couldn't think at all.

There had been a time when Adam honestly thought he could substitute success for happiness, but he finally came to terms with the fact that all the success in the world could never fill the vacuum in his life. And his life was indeed empty. After Natalie, he'd initially been very guarded about the types of relationships he developed with women, vowing he'd never let anyone get that close again. But eventually the pain had eased, and when he'd been able to get on with his life, he found that his work was of primary importance, and he simply didn't want a permanent relationship tying him down. There had been plenty of women during the past few years, but no one really special. Nobody he could see himself spending the rest of his life with. Nobody who could fill the emptiness. Nobody like Natalie.

And that was a little unnerving, to think that maybe he had been unconsciously making that kind of comparison all along. His only logical explanation for his recent preoccupation with her was that he had, in fact, burned all his bridges. He'd reached a point in his life when he'd started doing some very serious evaluating. He had attained all his professional goals, and what lay ahead held few challenges. There was nothing in his future but more emptiness. Maybe that's why he was preoccupied with the past; his life had been so full and promising in those golden days.

With all the old memories reactivated, he knew he was taking a tremendous risk when he decided to come back to his hometown, but he was impelled by some self-destructive force that overrode his common sense. His parents had moved from the valley five years ago, and after they left, he'd had no reason to return. He had tried to justify his coming back now with the excuse that this was the best possible location for the filming of his proposed television documentary on the cougar. But now that he was here, with her memories all around him, he realized there was a damned sight more to it than that. Ever since he had come back from South America, he'd been fighting against an inexplicable compunction to return to his boyhood home. And as he stood in the shadows, he knew it was her ghost that had drawn him back.

To his way of thinking, there was something abnormal about this obsession with faded memories of a sixteen-year-old girl, especially when he hadn't laid eyes on her for eleven years. It was as though it was an insidious disease he had no immunity against. He strongly suspected that there was some deep-seated flaw in his personality that prevented him from recovering from that first poignant affair. Yet he knew with absolute certainty that if he was ever going to find any peace of mind he would have to drag up those

ghosts—and that meant he was going to have to talk
to Doc. He was hoping that once he finally dealt with
all the unanswered questions, he could put her and
everything associated with her out of his mind for
good. Maybe then he could stop being the cynical
bastard he was and finally get on with his life. Maybe.

And then maybe not. His facing it didn't seem to be
making one bit of difference now. The moment he had
arrived at the arena, he was swamped with stifling
recollections of her. He had been fighting with himself for the past hour, but he was getting nowhere.

Shaking his head in self-disgust, Adam straightened and entered the hall. For a brief moment he stood
at the edge of the crowd and stared out the row of
windows at the arena floor. That was a big mistake. It
seemed as if it were impossible to escape her ghost in
this place, and everywhere he looked he was reminded of her. Even when he let his glance sweep
across the shifting crowd, his attention was immediately drawn to a blond woman—the color of her hair,
her slenderness, the way she held her head—it was all
too damned familiar. And if it hadn't been for the fact
that he had promised the steering-committee chair-
man he'd be available to autograph copies of his book,
he'd have gone back to his trailer and drunk himself
into a stupor.

With an uncompromising set to his mouth, he went
into the arena through one of the sets of double doors
and worked his way down the steps to the floor, heading in the direction of the display area where his books
were. He'd get this over with as fast as possible so he
could get the hell out of here. As determined as he was
to clear his mind of memories, he couldn't keep his

eyes off the blonde as he wound his way through the crowd. Drawn like a moth to the proverbial flame.

She stood out so distinctly from the rest of the crowd, like some fragile mountain flower clinging to a rocky windswept slope. A subdued elegance, an unstudied grace, that incredible glossy silver-gold hair—she looked like a delicate, lithesome dancer in that dress. He had a sudden image of her twirling in slow motion, her pliant body arching like a ballerina's as she slowly raised her arms, the deep pink fabric flaring out around her like a gossamer cloud. Adam felt as if he were trapped in a bad dream. She too closely resembled the real thing, and her likeness awakened all the disturbing feelings he had been trying to forget. He was about to turn away when the person beside her moved and he was able to get a good look at her profile. The shock of recognition hit him with a devastating force.

This was no dream.

For a moment he felt completely removed from reality. But as he stood there staring at her, a newly ignited resentment about the past slowly spread through him. Nearly eleven years and he'd never really gotten over the stunt she'd pulled. Those long, unbearable months after she disappeared when he'd tried to convince himself that it was only an adolescent infatuation, that it was only his injured pride that wouldn't let go. Those months of trying to deal with the knowledge that she had been able to dispassionately walk away without so much as one single word. Eleven long years, and feelings were emerging that he thought he had put behind him. He didn't like it one damned bit.

When she lifted her head and saw him, she froze, her eyes widening with shock as the color drained from her face. For a moment he thought she was going to faint, then she whispered, "God, no."

For some reason her response riled him. When he realized how much his presence had rocked her, he experienced a weird disconnected sensation that only added to the conflicting feelings warring within him. There was a part of him that wanted to turn around and walk away, but there was another part of him, a long-forgotten part, that desperately wanted to touch her.

Her lips parted as if she was going to speak, but instead she closed her eyes and took a deep unsteady breath. When she looked up at him, she had regained a thin veneer of control, but it was obvious that she was badly shaken. Taking another deep breath, she clutched the book even tighter. "I—Adam, I—"

"Hello, Natalie. I never expected to see you back in this part of the country." His voice was cool and impersonal as he stared at her, his expression impassive.

She was gripping the book so tightly her knuckles were white, and the pulse in her neck was throbbing frantically as she avoided his gaze. For a moment Adam expected her to simply escape this exceedingly difficult confrontation and disappear into the crowd, but she held her ground. Her body was stiff and unnatural, and there was a nervous tremor in her voice when she answered evasively, "I hadn't planned on coming to this... It was more circumstance than anything." She hesitated, and as though bracing herself to face some formidable ordeal, she hauled in a shaky breath and looked up at him. "Your work is incredible, Adam. I didn't think it was possible, but it's even better." She swallowed hard, then unable to hold his gaze any longer, she looked down, her movements jerky as she fingered the volume. "I know how much you wanted this and how hard you've worked. And I just wanted to tell you that I think you really deserve your success."

A nerve in his jaw twitched as Adam stared down at her lowered head. After so many years, why would she think it mattered to him what she thought? He didn't want to continue this pointless, awkward conversation; there was nothing she could possibly say that would interest him in the slightest. His manner was one of complete indifference. "Thank you." He motioned toward the table where his books were displayed. "Now if you'll excuse me...." With one last stony glance, he turned and walked away. He was halfway across the arena before he realized how angry he was. He was filled with resentment. He had never expected that seeing her again would arouse such hostile feelings. He didn't think she had that power over him anymore. But she did. Damn it, she did.

ADAM DIDN'T COME OUT of his trailer for the next two days. He had lost count of how many bottles of rye he'd gone through, but no matter how much he drank, he could not erase the fact that she was here. Whether he liked it or not, that was an unalterable fact.

With his shoulder braced against the metal frame and a drink in his hand, Adam stood in the doorway of his trailer staring out, his haggard, unshaven face ravaged by tension and fatigue. The sky was tinged with the first streaks of dawn, silhouetting the jagged top of the forest against the deepening shades of mauves and pinks. The exquisite color made him think of Natalie's dress, and clenching his jaw against the sudden twist of pain, he slowly drew in a deep breath to try to ease it.

What was it about her that had such power over him? In the space of a few minutes she had eradicated the years that separated them, and he was experiencing the same devastating sense of loss, the same sense of betrayal, the same frantic helplessness he had felt when she had disappeared. And that was utter madness. He couldn't let her screw up his life again, especially when there was a damned good chance she had probably taken off sometime during the past two days. Disappeared again.

Somehow he was going to have to attain a certain degree of objectivity about what had happened. Somehow.

His eyes became bleak as he thought about their meeting. She hadn't changed much. She was slimmer and she had a certain maturity and poise about her now—but that inner sparkle was gone. He wondered why. He tossed back the remainder of his drink, then angrily crushed the plastic glass in his hand. This was getting him nowhere.

As if suddenly doused in cold water, a random thought cut through the fog of too much booze and too little sleep. There was a very real possibility that she was married and had a family, and that disturbed him more than he liked to admit. He frowned, trying to recall if she'd had rings on, but he couldn't form a total image. He could picture only her stricken face, and that image was one he wanted to forget.

His frown deepened as he went over the details of the confrontation in his mind and uncovered something he hadn't recognized before. There was more behind that look than shock. When he stopped to think about it in the cold light of day, he could also identify a deep apprehension, an apprehension that bordered on panic. It was almost as if she were afraid of him, and that made him wonder. What did she have to fear? But there could be another explanation for her alarm: what did she have to hide?

Swearing softly through gritted teeth, he slammed his hand against the doorjamb in frustration. This was so damned senseless. This marathon of sleeplessness had netted him nothing, except he had definitely decided to drive into town to see Doc. He didn't know what purpose that would serve, but it was something he had to do. And feeling as though he was beaten before he started, Adam wearily straightened and went into the trailer.

It was midmorning when he finally drove down the quiet street to Doc's house. He felt like hell and didn't look much better. He desperately needed a few hours of uninterrupted sleep, but he knew he wouldn't get a moment's rest until this was behind him. Adam wasn't looking forward to this meeting with the old druggist for more reasons than one.

Ever since he could remember, he and Doc had hiked the back country together. They both had the wilderness in their blood, and in many ways, Doc had been a mentor and teacher to Adam. He had trusted Doc and honestly believed that there was a solid bond between them. But that adolescent confidence was brutally shattered when Natalie disappeared without a trace. Adam suspected that Doc knew far more than he let on, and he had gone to him on more than one occasion trying to find out what had happened. But Doc would tell him nothing, and to a twenty-year-old kid whose world had just come crashing down, his silence was like salt in an open wound. Adam had viewed it as an outright double cross, and he had sworn he'd never forgive the old man for that. The whole mess had ended with one nasty scene in the drugstore when he'd told Doc exactly how he felt.

Subdued by those unpleasant recollections, Adam silently vowed that no matter what transpired today, he would not lose his temper like that again. He slowed as he approached the hedge, prepared to pull into the driveway. But there was already a small car parked there with California plates, so he drove past and parked his mud-splattered Bronco on the street beside the front walk.

Hunching forward, Adam rested his arms on the steering wheel and stared out the window. Obviously Doc had company, and under the circumstances, Adam really didn't want an audience. Now was not the time, it seemed, nor the place. He was just about to turn on the ignition and drive off when the white-haired man came out the side door of his garage carrying a spade. Without giving himself a chance to reconsider, Adam quickly climbed out of his truck.

Doc turned when he heard the door slam, and with a solemn expression etched into his wrinkled face, he watched the young man walk up the gravel driveway toward him. It was apparent that the old gentleman was not at all surprised to see him there, and that struck Adam as very strange. Why was he expecting him? There was something about the way the old man was watching him that made Adam suspicious. What was going on here?

A knot of apprehension settled in his gut, but somehow Adam managed to keep his voice devoid of all expression. "Hello, Doc."

Doc tipped his head in acknowledgment as he stretched his hand toward the newcomer. "Hello, Adam. I heard you were in town."

Adam shook the pharmacist's thickly veined hand, mildly surprised by the firmness of the grip, then stuck his hands in the back pockets of his jeans. A sudden gut feeling hit him, and without taking time to consider it, he played out his hunch. "I'd like to talk to Natalie, if you don't mind."

Doc didn't say anything as he looked away, his face set as he squinted against the sun. From the older man's calmness, Adam deduced his hunch was wrong. Then Doc turned his attention back to him and spoke. "She's in the house." He seemed to be weighed down by some invisible burden as he slowly turned and motioned toward the back door. "I'll take you in and tell her you're here."

The unexpectedness of this evoked a host of conflicting feelings that really caught Adam off balance, but he had long since mastered the ability to mask every trace of emotion. When he met Doc's worried glance, his expression was completely unreadable, and he said nothing.

As he followed his old companion up the steps and into the porch, he found himself questioning the rationale behind this visit. What did he hope to gain by all of this? It wasn't as if he could look back on their time together dispassionately. His feelings had been too strong. On the other hand, it had been made acutely clear to him that Natalie's feelings had been pretty damned shallow; if she had cared about him at all, she never could have done what she did.

Catching the screen door so it wouldn't slam shut behind him, Adam entered the living room. Doc motioned to a chair. "Have a seat, lad. I'll get her. She's in the kitchen."

Adam acknowledged the offer with an abrupt nod, but remained standing as Doc left the room. His edginess left him feeling like a caged cat. Needing something to focus on, he went over to the piano and idly glanced at the framed photographs arranged on top. There were quite a few: two old ones of Doc's wife, another large faded photo of a group of young men wearing World War II air-force uniforms and standing beside a Lancaster bomber, and a couple more of people he didn't know. But the one that arrested his attention was a studio pose of Natalie. His expression hardened as he stared at it for a moment before deliberately focusing on the two remaining photographs. They were encased in brass frames that were hinged together, and driven by some sort of morbid curiosity, Adam picked the unit up.

One was a candid shot of Natalie standing under a tree, holding a small boy in her arms. The other was a color photo of the same boy, only in this one, he was several years older. A sensation similar to claustrophobia suddenly washed through him, and he was only vaguely aware of the sound of Doc departing by the other door.

There was no doubt about it—the kid was Natalie's. The eyes were a dead giveaway. He set the frame down with a slam and went to stand rigidly before the window. He stared out, his face cast in harsh lines. He had sensed she had something to hide. Now he knew what it was. He had a nearly uncontrollable urge to drive his fist through the wall as his anger took on a new dimension. He intended to bloody well find out what her story was. And the way he was feeling, he didn't give a damn what he had to do to get it out of her. The questions would all be answered, one way or another.

"Doc said you wanted to talk to me."

Adam took a minute to get a grip on his temper before he turned to face her. When he did, his hazel eyes were as brittle as emeralds. "I thought it might be a good idea." He moved toward the piano, and his cutting tone was dripping with sarcasm as he went on. "There are one or two things about your disappearance I've been mildly interested in."

"Adam, I—"

He indicated the photographs. "Your son, I take it?"

Natalie went deathly pale. Again he sensed the apprehension that bordered on panic, and he pressed the issue. "Well, is he your son?"

She folded her arms tightly in front of her as though she was suddenly cold, her eyes darkening. In a nearly inaudible voice she answered, "Yes, he's my son."

Adam picked up the pictures and studied them. "You work fast, Natalie," he said curtly. "I'd say he was nine or so."

She didn't respond and he looked at her as he replaced the pictures, his eyes narrow. She had started to tremble; her fear was visible. Adam had seen that same fear in wild animals that had been cornered. By some sixth sense he knew she was still hiding something. It was pretty obvious from the age of the boy that she'd become involved with someone shortly after she'd disappeared. The idea of that happening ignited his fury and a streak of ruthlessness emerged. He wanted confirmation of her duplicity, and he wanted it now. "How old is he, Natalie?" he ground out.

She still didn't answer, and he glanced at her left hand. No rings; she wasn't married. He knew Natalie well enough to realize that even if her marriage had collapsed, she very likely would still wear a wedding ring, especially when there was a kid involved. So what did that mean?

He studied her intently as he tried to make something out of all this. What was she hiding? His voice was ominously soft as he repeated the question. "How old is he?"

Her voice was barely a whisper. "He's ten."

Ten. That meant she'd had to pick up with someone else within a matter of weeks after she left, and the thought sickened him. There was, however, another possibility. She could have been involved with someone else even before she disappeared, right after he'd left his summer job to go back to university. That thought really rocked him. He had been so much in love with her, so sure of her, and he'd never once doubted how she felt about him. Not until she disappeared. A sense of betrayal nearly choked him. "When did he turn ten, Natalie?"

She had a trapped look about her, and he could sense her desperation. And he knew. Before she even answered, he knew that she had violated his trust long before he'd thought she had. He braced himself for her answer. Her voice was wrought with tension when she finally choked out, "His birthday's in April."

Adam stared at her, his anger overridden by disbelief. Born in April. Conceived in July. He felt as if she had just yanked the rug out from under him, and he continued to stare at her. Not once in all the time that had passed between then and now had he ever considered this as even an outside chance. But he knew by the look on her face that his deduction was right.

The kid was his.

The shock of it numbed him, and with his face looking as if it had been carved out of stone, he turned back to the window. His mind was in a turmoil. He had been so damned careful with her—except that very first time—that first time when their feelings overwhelmed every shred of common sense, and an uncheckable passion carried them off like leaves in a storm. The memory of that very special afternoon clawed through his numbness and unearthed a deep, empty ache. The consummation of that passion had been so intense, so incredible that he'd never been able to erase it from his mind. And it was then that she'd conceived . . . his son.

And she never even had the decency to tell him. He had a son who was ten years old, a son she had deliberately kept from him. Anger began to build in him until he felt as though he couldn't contain it. There wasn't one single reason she could give him that could even come close to justifying what she'd done. His wrath was infused by a cold, calculating vindictiveness. He'd be damned if she'd walk away again unscathed. This time he'd call the shots, he thought bitterly, and one way or another, he was going to even an old score. He'd hurt her as much as she'd hurt him, and he knew exactly how to do it.

He continued to stare out the window as he spoke, his voice low and grating. "Why in hell didn't you tell me? Why didn't you have the decency to tell me you were pregnant?"

Her voice was very low. "I didn't . . . I wasn't sure until after I left."

Natalie had never been able to lie worth a damn, but knowing that she wasn't telling the truth really didn't matter now. There were other things that were far more important. "I want to see him."

She didn't answer and he turned around, his eyes filled with contempt. She was sitting in a big leather armchair, her body hunched forward, her head lowered so he couldn't see her face. He felt nothing but fury. "I said I want to see him."

She looked up at Adam, her eyes dark and tormented. Then, as if daunted by the look on his face, she quickly glanced away. She swallowed hard before she whispered brokenly, "He's at camp for the summer—"

"That's not good enough, Natalie. I want to see him, and I won't be put off by some damned lame excuse." His voice was like ice as he gave her an ominous warning. "You'd better bloody well produce him, lady, or you're going to regret it."

She lifted one hand in a beseeching gesture, her eyes pleading with him as she whispered unevenly, "Please don't involve him in this, Adam. Don't hurt him because of me—''

"Don't play games, damn it!'' Adam went to stand before her, his voice shaking with rage as he bent over the armchair. "He's mine, Natalie, just as much as he's yours. And if you don't cooperate, I'll have you in court so fast it'll make your head swim. I'll bring in the best damned lawyers in the country, and I'll challenge you. Just give me an excuse and I'll do anything I have to to gain full custody of him.'' With his eyes narrowed menacingly, he pointed his finger at her, his tone harsh and threatening. "And don't try anything cute. Another stunt like your last one, and I'll track you down, Natalie, and I'll make damned sure you never see him again.''

He was breathing heavily, his pulse pounding from the violent anger that was consuming him. She had kept the knowledge of his son from him for ten years, and if he hadn't met her again through sheer chance, he very likely would have never known about the boy. And the fact that she had made that conscious decision, that she had withheld that piece of information from him, enraged him like nothing ever had. For years he had been trapped in a web of lies. He had remembered only her gentleness; until she'd vanished he'd known nothing of her deceptiveness. He turned and went back to the window, and with his expression steeled by rage, he braced his arm against the window frame and stood glaring out.

A son. His own flesh and blood. A son he knew absolutely nothing about. How could she be so damned hard, so damned unfeeling? It was a long time before the strangling feeling of full-blown fury eased, and his pulse rate slowed to an even beat. Adam slowly drew in a deep breath in an attempt to regain a semblance of control before he faced her again.

His voice was devoid of emotion. "I don't even know what his name is."

Natalie lifted her head and looked at him, her eyes dark, her ashen face scored by strain. "Patrick. I named him Patrick—" Her breath caught as a tremor quivered through her. She clenched her hands tightly together, her knuckles turning white. "Don't do anything to hurt him, Adam." Her voice broke and she looked away. "Don't punish him because of what I did."

Adam stared at her for a moment, then snorted in disgust. "Do you really think I'd stoop to those kinds of tactics?" His smile was twisted by malice. "But be forewarned, Natalie. I have every intention of taking him away from you, but by the time I'm finished, it will be Patrick's decision to leave. You won't have a damned thing to say about it."

"Adam—"

"Drop it, Natalie. You just make damned sure he gets here." His voice took on a sinister tone. "And don't try any tricks. You'll be sorry if you do."

There was a tense silence, and she knew he meant every word. Her face seemed paralyzed when she whispered, "He's finished camp this Friday. He'll be arriving in Calgary on a direct flight from Los Angeles on Sunday."

He studied her suspiciously, his fury abating. "Why Calgary? Why not Vancouver?"

"I work for a travel agency, and I could get a much cheaper rate with the Calgary flight." Her level gaze held his, and he knew she was telling the truth.

"What time does the flight arrive?"

"I'll have to check to make sure it's on time, but if it is, it's due late in the afternoon."

Absently stroking his bottom lip, Adam assessed her with cold detachment. He had no intention of letting her pick up the boy alone—he didn't trust her for a minute. It was a little more than a six-hour drive to Calgary, which meant they could leave in the morning and still be there in plenty of time to meet Patrick's plane. He watched her like a hawk as he spoke in a tone that dared her to argue. "We'll both go to get him."

That was the last thing she wanted and he knew it, but she also knew he had her backed in a corner, and she didn't have the energy or strength to fight her way out. It seemed to take a massive effort for her to nod in unwilling assent. Her hand was shaking badly as she brushed back a loose tendril of hair, and it was this unsteady movement that drew his attention to the long ragged scar along the left side of her jaw. That hadn't been there before. He frowned slightly as he scrutinized her. There was something else that hadn't been there before, and that was the finely veiled tenor of fear. The scar was probably from the accident she'd been in when her mother was killed, just before she dropped out of sight. Where, he speculated silently, had the fear come from? His hostility and anger faded as he stared at Natalie intently. There were other scars, he sensed, scars that went deeper and were more disfiguring than the one on her face.

Irritated by the direction his thoughts were taking, Adam tore his eyes away from her stricken face and directed his attention to the pictures on the piano. His expression softened. He was a good-looking kid, he thought with the first glimmer of paternal pride. The boy had the kind of face he liked to photograph: good bone structure, an animated expression, an engaging smile. A flicker of recognition punctured his thoughts, unmasking a staggering revelation. The smile, he realized, was a carbon copy of his own. This one identifiable likeness drove home the irrefutable fact that this was, without a doubt, his child.

He wanted to ask her what he was like, to find out everything about him, but anything she told him would have little meaning. She had denied him the knowledge of his own son, the special memories, the chance to be an important part of his child's life. She had denied him all that, and he could never reclaim that which was lost to time. He could never forgive her for that.

A peculiar heaviness settled in his chest as he stood totally self-absorbed, trying to cope with the host of new feelings that were slowly unfolding. The incredible miracle of conception and life were biological phenomena that filled him with reverence and awe, and knowing that a part of him had gone into the creation of this boy meant more to him than anyone would ever know.

As if drawn by a force that was too powerful to deny, he reached out and touched the pictures of his son with an unspoken longing, his finger slowly outlining the shape of the boy's face. There was something in that one lingering gesture that hinted of an immeasurable hunger, a certain poignancy that provided insight into the man. He was a complex, sensitive human being; he was also a solitary figure, alone and bitter. Unwittingly he had allowed his defensive barrier to slip, exposing the deep feelings and the even deeper passions of the man he had become.

"He's very much like your family," Natalie said softly.

An unaccustomed tightness in his throat made it difficult for him to talk, and his words were strained when he finally spoke. "In what way?"

Adam's question was met with a tense silence and he turned toward her. She was watching him with dark, fearful eyes, and he realized her comment had been an impulsive response. It goaded him, knowing that she held the only key to his finding out about the boy, and his anger reignited with a vengeance. But as quickly as his fury flared, it died. He loathed himself for letting her get to him. And he loathed her even more for having the power to do it. He jammed his hands in his back pockets as he stared at her, his jaw set in rigid lines. She stared back at him, her finely sculpted features as colorless as wax. She knew how close he'd come to losing control. And that knowledge had obviously frightened her, but for some strange reason, he sensed his reaction hurt her a hundred times more than it scared her.

Adam experienced a certain amount of grim satisfaction, but that feeling was pathetically short-lived. The pain he had inflicted on her was obvious; she abruptly turned her head, tearing her eyes from his riveting gaze. But he had already seen the awful anguish in those gray depths.

As if by some telepathic osmosis her pain became his, and Adam was suddenly swamped by the most intense need to shield her from whatever was tearing her apart. Again his memories betrayed him. As though it were yesterday, he remembered how intoxicating it was to hold her supple body tightly against his and to envelop her slender form in his strength. He remembered her warmth, her softness, the fragrance of her, how she moved beneath him in the night. And he remembered in living detail the scorching fever of needing her.

His response was overpowering. He didn't try to analyze it, he didn't try to rationalize it. Instead he fought to stifle it, but it was unrelenting. His bitterness and anger were being seduced by ghosts that had haunted him forever. Feeling dangerously exposed, Adam turned away, his hands curled into tight fists.

It felt as though his chest was in a vise and he couldn't breathe. Damn it, what was happening to him? His feelings were so volatile, so unpredictable, and they were boomeranging from one end of the emotional spectrum to the other. The anger he understood, the bitterness he understood, and he certainly understood the whole range of responses in between, from loathing to a sense of betrayal. But what was throwing him more than anything was this feral protectiveness she still aroused in him. That was not expected. Nor did he understand it. Especially after the gaping hole she'd left in his life; especially after finding out she'd chosen to keep the existence of the boy from him for so many years. He should feel nothing but anger. Anger was a clear-cut, definable emotion, one with definite parameters. And it was an emotion he could control and nurture with black memories. But the feelings he was experiencing now were uncontrollable; they had a will of their own.

Adam was unconscious of passing time, and he had no idea how long he had stood staring numbly out the window. But the long shadow from the garage had shrunk to a thin line by the time he finally dragged his thoughts from his personal turmoil. It took a lot of self-discipline for him to grasp some semblance of dispassion. It had been a long time since he'd lost his cool like he had, and he couldn't afford to lose it again. Now, more than ever, he had to use his head. Threatening her had been a stupid move, and the only thing he was apt to accomplish with threats was to drive her back into hiding. And she was the one existing link to his son. His son.

Turning slightly, he rested his shoulder against the wall and looked at her. His tone was low and expressionless when he finally spoke. "Are you going to try to stop me from spending some time with him?"

It was a challenge she could have probably evaded if she'd wanted to, but Natalie didn't even attempt to dodge the issue. Instead she met his piercing gaze with unwavering directness. "No." There was a haunting bleakness in her eyes that seemed to reach down to her very soul, and Adam detected the glisten of tears before she lowered her head. "I know you aren't going to believe this, but I never wanted to keep him from you, Adam." He saw her try to swallow, and it seemed to be very difficult for her to speak when she finally continued in an uneven whisper. "There was never a conscious decision not to tell you."

Adam narrowed his eyes as he studied her, silently searching for some tiny clue that would either support or refute her sincerity. But he was unwilling to trust his instincts. A gut feeling warned him that now was not the time to delve into her reasons for doing what she did. Not when the accessibility of his son was at stake. This time he was forced to give her the benefit of the doubt, whether he liked it or not. His calm, rational mind told him that it had all happened a long time ago, and that she had been little more than a child herself when she'd been faced with an unexpected pregnancy. Then there had been her mother's fatal accident on top of it. Who was he to sit in judgment?

But his rational self was submerged beneath a part of him that did not respond to logic. He had been torn apart by her callous rejection, and there was no explanation on earth that could ever excuse what she'd done.

The emotional battle was draining him of what little energy he had, and Adam was suddenly bone tired. Wearily rubbing the back of his neck, he went to the armchair nearest Natalie's and sat down. He slouched his shoulders, stretched his long legs out in front of him, then rested his elbows on the wide arms and laced his fingers together across his chest. Those feelings that tied him to the past would have to wait. What he had to do now was make sure she wouldn't balk at letting him see the boy. And until that was assured, he was totally within her power. He didn't like it, but that's the way it was.

He studied her as he tried to assess all the angles. One thing he had going for him was that Natalie had always been a lousy liar. As long as he asked all the right questions, he should get all the right answers. He frowned slightly as he considered his best line of attack, then spoke in a deliberately passive tone. "I'm not asking you to tell him who I am right off the bat, Natalie. All I'm asking is a chance to spend some time with him. I think you owe me that."

She was huddled in the large armchair with her feet tucked under her, her profile muted by shadows. She had always sat like that when she was troubled about something, and the sudden exposure to that long-forgotten mannerism of hers jarred him more than he liked to admit. In some ways, she had changed so little.

There was a slight softening in Adam's expression as he solemnly watched her. She was the same, yet she was a stranger. Physically, she had changed little, but there was a remoteness about her now that was utterly foreign to the girl he remembered, and there was that element of fear he had sensed. And something else that he couldn't quite put his finger on. It was almost as though some inner flame had gone out and part of her had died. He found that analogy grimly disturbing.

Abruptly realizing that his idle reflections were leading him toward treacherous ground, he forcibly closed his mind against her. He could not, no matter how strong the temptation, lose sight of the cold hard fact that she had deceived him once, and she'd do it again if given the chance. There was now too much at stake to take any risks. Even being fully aware of the kind of person she was, it took every ounce of self-discipline he had to drag his attention back to the issue of Patrick. Somehow he managed to marshal his resolve, and when she lifted her head and looked at him, his face was without a trace of emotion.

She seemed to have nothing left to fight with—no energy, no spirit, no desire—as if she was completely spent. Her voice was lifeless. "I won't try to keep him from you, if that's what you're worried about." She finally looked at him, her eyes as lifeless as her voice. "The only thing that I ask is that you give me some time with him before I tell him...who you are. I'd like to prepare him a little."

"Has he ever asked about me?"

"Yes."

"What did you tell him? Or did you take the easy route and tell him I was dead?"

Natalie wearily leaned her head against the high wing of the chair, an air of absolute defeat about her as she stared into space. "No, I didn't tell him you were dead," she said quietly, her voice a monotone of resignation. "But I've never encouraged him to ask too many questions."

Adam silently considered her response, trying very hard not to let his emotions gain the upper hand; he couldn't risk making a mistake because his temper got the best of him. It was imperative that he shut down any avenues of escape she may have. "I plan on going with you when you go to get him, Natalie," he said flatly.

She looked at him, anxiety etched in her face. "It would be best for Patrick if I could spend some time alone with him before you see him."

He gave her a cynical smile, his eyes riveted on her. "It won't wash, Natalie. I'm not as blind and trusting as I used to be. There would be absolutely nothing stopping you from picking him up and taking off.'' His voice was cutting with sarcasm. ''You are, after all, very good at disappearing.''

She met his disdainful look, silently begging him to relent as she raised her hands in an imploring gesture. ''I promise I'll bring him back, Adam. Just let me go get him alone.''

He snorted derisively. ''Do you honestly think I'm stupid enough to let you out of my sight? I've everything to lose and nothing to gain.'' He folded his arms across his chest, his expression unyielding. ''You know damned well I don't have any kind of information on you. It would take a while to track you down if I let you get away from me. And you also know that my only source of information would be Doc—and we both know he won't open his mouth if you tell him not to.'' He gave her another cold smile that was warped with bitterness. ''You forget that I've been through all this once before with you.''

Natalie managed to remain unmoving beneath his hostile gaze for only a moment, then she stood up abruptly, her body unnaturally stiff. She moved to the piano and gently touched the photos of her son. Adam never took his eyes off her. He sensed she was struggling with a decision concerning his demands and he watched her through narrowed eyes, trying to read something from her expression. She turned, and with her face drawn by tension, she went over to the ancient rolltop desk and opened a handbag that was lying beside a stack of books. She took out something and came back to where Adam was sitting. Deliberately avoiding his gaze, she held out her wallet to him.

At first he didn't comprehend, then the significance of what she was doing registered; she was handing him the most concise source of information about her life that any detective could hope to find. Glancing up at her face, he wordlessly took the wallet from her and opened it.

Her driver's license, one general credit card and one for an oil company, a card for medical insurance, two pink insurance slips for her car, one of which was out of date. There were other pieces of identification relevant to her day-to-day living—a wallet-size copy of her birth certificate, a library card, a picture of Patrick—all revealing a great deal about one Natalie Anne Carter.

In a side pocket Adam found several of her business cards, and on the back of one was written a name, an address and two telephone numbers; beneath these details was a printed record of some dates and locations. His edginess eased a little when Adam realized he was holding all the information about Patrick's camp in his hand. So now, at least, he knew where the kid was. He couldn't have asked for more.

Natalie opened her mouth to protest when he slipped the picture of Patrick, the expired copy of her car insurance and the business card with the details of Patrick's camp in his shirt pocket. He could tell by the horrified look in her eyes that she realized she had unwittingly trapped herself. Not only did Adam have access to her vehicle registration, her home address and her place of employment, but he now had something she had no intention of giving him—Patrick's present whereabouts. With an insolent smile, he gave her a level look that dared her to challenge him. She hesitated, then abruptly turned away, her eyes filled with stark comprehension. They both knew he had her cornered. If she didn't play his game, he could get to Patrick, on his own.

Feeling adequately defended against anything she might have considered, Adam started replacing everything he had taken out of her wallet. As he went to slip her plasticized birth certificate back in a side pocket, an identically sized card separated from the back of it. "The Province of Alberta, Division of Vital Statistics." For a moment he thought it was a duplicate of her birth certificate, but when he looked at it more closely, he realized it was Patrick's. Adam frowned as he glanced at the statistics. Place of birth: Calgary. Why Calgary? He read it again, only this time he noticed every detail. And he was in for another shock, one that would haunt him for many nights to come. Registered name: Adam Patrick Carter.

His son carried his name.

CHAPTER FOUR

FROM THE TIME HE LEFT Doc's until he parked the Bronco at the campsite, Adam wasn't aware of anything—not of driving through town, nor of turning onto the old forestry road. Nothing. The accidental discovery that Natalie had named the boy after him had really shaken him. He couldn't figure out why she'd done it. It seemed to him that naming the kid after a lover she had left without a backward glance didn't make much sense. But then, nothing was making much sense.

Adam was contemplative as he climbed out of the truck and slammed the door, then turned toward the river. He kept searching for explanations that didn't exist, kept digging for the slightest clue when there wasn't one, and the more he mulled it over, the more tangled his thoughts became. He was reaching for answers but was only uncovering more questions. If only he could summon up the energizing fury he had felt earlier. Without it, he was so damned exhausted he could hardly think—and he had to think. He had a lot to sort out.

For once oblivious to the siren's call of the untamed country that surrounded him, Adam walked along the rocky riverbed until the river narrowed and the dense bush crowded against the mountain stream as its rush to the sea became more turbulent. A huge chunk of granite had been heaved up by some ancient force of nature, it's stony mass warmed by the heat of the sun. Sitting down beside it, Adam leaned back against the smooth face of the rock, his forearm resting on his raised knee as he stared across the sparkling water, squinting against the glare.

When he'd first found out about Patrick, Adam had been trapped in a war of opposing emotions. But now that he had a chance to look at everything in a more rational light, he found he was doing some very heavy soul-searching. He felt oddly out of touch, as though some force had altered the course of his life and he was left scrambling to catch up. For the past few years he had been a man alone, a man on the move, but still a man who had an ever deepening and unsettling awareness of his own mortality.

But now, in the space of a few hours, all that had changed. He learned he had a son, his sole link with continuation, his only provision for the perpetuation of a part of himself. It was a sobering discovery. And he also felt a deep sense of fulfillment, and as he thought about the boy, a strong paternal instinct was unearthed that he didn't even know he possessed.

Now that he was finally able to dissect his thoughts and feelings with some objectivity, he came up with one unalterable conclusion. And that was that he very much wanted this kid. This resolution had nothing to do with vindictiveness, nor did it have anything to do with his feelings about Natalie. It did, however, have everything to do with one of the things he had wanted out of life, and that was a generation to follow him. Now he had it. And he wasn't going to take any chances of losing it. This time he was going to protect his back.

He went back to the trailer and immediately drove into town to make the phone calls. The first was to the headquarters of the summer camp to confirm the information he had found on the business card, and to find out for certain that Patrick was enrolled in the program. The second call was to a prominent lawyer he knew in Los Angeles who represented the television network that aired his documentaries. The purpose was to arrange for a tail to be put on Patrick. By the following morning, the boy would be under the surveillance of one of the best private investigation firms in the country. He was not taking any chances, not with Natalie's track record.

Using his telephone credit card, Adam made the calls from the pay phone that was still located in the cubbyhole he remembered in the deserted hotel lobby. After he completed the calls, he crossed the dingy foyer and entered the brightly lit coffee shop. He couldn't honestly remember when he had eaten last, and he was beginning to feel the effects.

Straddling one of the rust-speckled chrome stools, he sat down at the counter and took the ketchup-battered menu from its place behind the napkin holder. Adam scanned it as a disinterested gum-chewing, pony-tailed waitress ambled over and gave the chipped blue Formica an indifferent swipe, then listlessly waited for him to order. For the first time in days, a spark of humor lit Adam's eyes as he studied her profile in the mirror backing of the glass shelves behind the counter. He would love to photograph her just like that, with the harsh light and the long empty counter providing an unfocused background. She was a perfect study of absolute, utter, total boredom.

He had placed his order and was drinking coffee when someone sat down on the stool beside his. "Are you going to buy me a coffee, or are you going to sit there like a dummy and ignore me?"

He turned to find Stella Ralston, one eyebrow cocked in a mocking expression. He grinned lopsidedly, his eyes lighting up with a warning that he was going to try to get a rise out of her. "Stella," he said in deliberately provocative tones, "I'll buy you anything you damned well want."

She grinned as she signaled for a cup of coffee. "I'll settle for a one-way ticket out of this dump," she responded dryly. Taking a deep drag on her cigarette, she propped her elbows on the counter and stared at him through a haze of blue smoke. "What in hell are you doing here? I thought for sure you'd be one of the smart ones who'd have enough sense not to come back."

The gleam in Adam's eyes grew more mischievous. "I couldn't stay away from you any longer, Stella."

Stella gave him a long level stare, her mouth twisted in a tart expression. "God, you're a lousy actor. If you expect me to believe that crap, you're a damned sight thicker in the head than I thought."

The lines around his eyes crinkled as he laughed and shrugged slightly. "It was worth a try." He paused as he reached down the counter to the bowl of sugar cubes she had motioned to, then met her steady gaze as he passed it to her. "Actually, I was looking for a location to film the next TV segment, and thought some of that country northwest of here might work well."

"So you'll be around for a while?"

"Very likely."

She obviously had something on her mind as she slowly unwrapped the sugar. "I saw you at the arena the other night, but you disappeared before I had a chance to talk to you."

Adam's expression immediately became shuttered as he hunched forward, his attention focused intently on his coffee mug. He absently traced the crack in the handle with his thumbnail. "I didn't stick around," he said curtly.

Stella had been watching him closely, her lips pursed in a thoughtful expression as the silence stretched between them. She took another drag on her cigarette and exhaled slowly, her eyes narrowed in contemplation. "Where are you staying while you're in town?"

He continued to pick idly at the crack. "I haul a trailer when I'm out scouting locations. I'm parked down by the river just off the old forestry road."

"Why don't you come for dinner tonight? I'll cook you a real meal instead of this crap."

Adam finally looked up and gave her a lopsided grin. "That's an offer I can't refuse."

Stella glanced at her watch, then crushed her cigarette in the battered metal ashtray. "I've got to run or I'll miss the bank." She stood up and slipped the strap of her handbag over her shoulder. "I'm still living in the apartment above the drugstore. Make it around seven, okay?"

"Sounds great."

Stella Ralston had a reputation for being one of the best cooks in the valley, and it was a reputation well deserved. But she was also an excellent hostess—funny, entertaining and with a view on life that was definitely ribald. During dinner, she brought Adam up to date on all the happenings in the community, and by the time they reached the liqueurs and coffee, he was more relaxed than he'd been in months. He couldn't remember the last time he had enjoyed an evening more or laughed so much.

They had moved into her living room, and he was sitting on the sofa, his legs stretched in front of him, his elbow propped on the wide arm. Stella was seated in an armchair across from him, absently swirling the brandy in her glass, her expression settling into one of thoughtfulness. She looked at him intently. "What's the real reason you came back, Adam?"

Adam stared at her, then drained his glass. With studied care, he set it on the table beside him, his expression suddenly unfathomable. "Was this entire evening a setup, Stella?"

"Partly."

His gaze narrowed on her, and she gave him a rueful smile. "There are some things I think you ought to know, and there are some things I want to find out." She frowned as she slowly ran her finger around the lip of the crystal brandy snifter. "And you look like you bloody well need a friend right now."

He held her gaze for a minute, then looked away. There was a heavy silence before he said, "I sure in hell need something."

"You saw Natalie, I take it."

His voice was gruff. "Yes, I saw her."

Setting her glass down, Stella drew a cigarette from the inlaid silver case sitting on the table and tapped the end of it on the polished surface. "Look, Adam, I know it's none of my business, but what in hell happened between you two? I would have bet the farm on you kids."

Several moments passed before Adam raised his head and looked at her, his mouth twisted in a humorless lopsided smile. "Don't ask me, Stella," he said stiffly. "I hadn't heard from her for four or five weeks, so I came home from university to find out what was going on."

"Hadn't you heard anything about the accident?"

He continued to stare at her for a minute, then sighing heavily, he looked down at his feet. "My folks were away visiting my sister in Ontario that fall, so I didn't hear a damned thing until I came home. Tim Watson was at the bus depot when I arrived, and he told me her mother had been killed in a car accident a month earlier, and that Natalie had been badly injured. But no one I talked to seemed to know anything—where she was, how badly she'd been hurt—nothing. I damned near turned this town inside out, but I still couldn't find out anything, and to top it off, I couldn't find hide nor hair of Natalie's stepfather."

Adam would never forget the awful helplessness he had felt that day. It was a desperation he had never known before, and it was one he'd never known since.

"How did you find out?"

"I finally tracked Doc down. His neighbor told me he'd been away but that he was due home that night, so I was sitting on his doorstep when he arrived."

Stella toyed with her glass as she dissected this bit of information. She had been away on a buying trip for the small gift shop Doc ran in one section of the drugstore, and she didn't know a thing about the tragedy until she arrived home the day after Jean Willard's funeral. But there had always been something about the whole mess that didn't quite sit right with her. She could never put her finger on exactly what it was that made her suspicious.

She was still frowning slightly as she asked, "What did Doc tell you?"

"Not a hell of a lot. He said that Natalie and her mother were on their way back from Calgary when the car went out of control. Apparently it rolled before it plunged over the edge of the enbankment, and that's when Natalie was thrown clear." His voice was heavily strained when he added, "Unfortunatey Mrs. Willard wasn't so lucky."

Resting his head against the high back of the sofa, Adam stared off into space, his mind caught up in dark recollections. "Tell me about it, Adam."

He glanced at her, then looked away, his face scored by the agony of remembering. His voice was very quiet when he began to speak. "It was a hell of a night, Stella. I borrowed Tim's car, and after hitting nothing but dead ends, I parked in Doc's driveway waiting for him to show. I couldn't figure out for the life of me...I couldn't figure out why someone...why Doc hadn't had the decency to notify me about the accident, especially since Natalie had been injured. She could have been killed and I wouldn't have even known."

No words could ever explain the panic he felt that night. After enduring countless hours of wondering and waiting, Adam had been almost frantic by the time Doc showed up.

Looking back, he realized he had handled that meeting very badly, but he'd been nearly crazy with worry and so damned desperate to find Natalie, he had simply overreacted. It had in fact, been pretty ugly.

"What happened when Doc showed up? What did he tell you?"

Adam sighed and dragged his hand down his face. "Doc told me the details about the accident—when it had happened and where. But when I asked him why Natalie and Jean Willard had been traveling from Calgary in the first place, Doc had said he didn't know. I don't know why, but I started to suspect Doc was holding something back. And I was pretty upset." Which was putting it mildly. But it wasn't until Adam's sense of utter helplessness turned into fury that the situation started to come apart. He had been trying to find out if Natalie had been moved to a hospital in Calgary, or if she had been taken somewhere else when Doc finally leveled with him.

Now that he could look back with a certain amount of objectivity, Adam realized that Doc had tried to soften the blow, but for a twenty-year-old kid who had stars in his eyes, the blow was devastating. Natalie had been discharged two weeks earlier and had gone to live with an aunt somewhere in the United States. Without a word. After all they had shared, she had been able to leave without one single word. Nothing could ever describe how betrayed he felt, but at least now he knew why she'd gone. She had obviously left to keep him from finding out about Patrick, and that was almost as devastating as her betrayal had been.

The redhead watched Adam intently as she lit her cigarette, a frown of concentration furrowing her brow. "When did Doc finally tell you that Natalie wasn't coming back?"

"That night."

"Did you believe him?"

There was a watchfulness about Adam as he met Stella's gaze with a warped, mocking smile that was filled with self-disdain. "It's a nasty habit of mine. I have to bang my head against a few brick walls before I accept the facts, Stella."

Adam's eyes narrowed as he watched his companion's face. "He told me how the accident happened, and he told me Natalie wasn't coming back, but that was it. I still don't know why Natalie and Mrs. Willard were in Calgary in the first place."

Stella exhaled a cloud of smoke, then absently rolled the tip of her cigarette around the edge of the ashtray by her elbow. "I can answer that. Jean was having bad back problems, and there was a doctor in Calgary who had a new treatment. Her doctor here made the appointment for her."

Adam's eyes narrowed even more. "Then what was the big deal? Why didn't Doc tell me that?"

The redhead shrugged. "Your guess is as good as mine. Doc was damned closemouthed about the whole mess."

"What happened to Carl? I tried to track him down that fall and he'd disappeared."

"You knew about the fire, didn't you?"

Adam shifted his position and gave her a quizzical look. "I heard that he'd gone to bed and left a cigarette burning. A stack of newspapers caught fire and they barely got him out before the entire house went up in flames."

"Yeah, well, that's what happened all right. Except he was so drunk, it took him two days to sober up. In fact, I don't think he drew one sober breath after Jean died." She took another long drag of her cigarette before she continued. "He took off right after the fire. That was the last anyone heard of him." It was obvious that she was agitated as she flicked the ash into the ashtray and shook her head in disgust. "Good riddance to bad rubbish. Carl Willard was a louse from the word go."

Adam gave her a warped grin. "Well, he sure didn't like me hanging around."

"He didn't like anyone hanging around," Stella added sardonically. "Carl Willard was nothing but an arrogant, self-centered loudmouth."

Leaning forward, Adam poured himself another brandy from the decanter sitting on the coffee table, then rested his shoulder against the arm of the sofa as he studied Stella. "You said there were things I should know... Or was that just a ruse to get me talking?"

Deliberately avoiding his gaze, she emptied her glass, consuming the potent drink as though it was some kind of fortification.

There was a long, tense silence before Adam prodded her. "Spit it out, Stella."

Her brow creased as she pursed her lips in an expression of consternation, and her bosom heaved as she exhaled sharply. Her eyes were filled with apprehension when she finally looked at him. "Have you been to see Natalie?"

He stared at her woodenly. "Yes, I have."

"Did she say anything to you?"

Adam drained his own glass and set it on the table, then folded his arms across his chest. It was unquestionably a defensive gesture. "Like what, Stella? What was it she should have told me?"

She met his cold glare with a steady calm. "Did she tell you she had a son?"

"I saw his picture."

Stella was finished hedging around, and she snorted in exasperation as she set her glass down with a solid slam. "Just how thickheaded are you, Rutherford? I mean, I can add and subtract. It didn't take a genius to figure it out."

"So?"

She shook her head in disbelief. "So! So since the kid has been such a deep dark secret, I thought maybe she hadn't told you," she snapped, irritated by his offishness. "I thought maybe you didn't even know about him, that's all."

The hardness in Adam's eyes changed to bleakness as he answered quietly, "I didn't."

Stella sighed heavily. She rested her arm on her crossed knee and laced her fingers together. "When did you find out?"

"This morning."

"Wonderful," she said succinctly.

"Yeah." Restraint showed on his face as he sat up and poured himself another drink. "How did you know about him?"

"Doc. He has pictures of him in his office at the drugstore." She picked a piece of lint off her slacks and idly rolled it between her fingers, her mood contemplative. "Are you going to get a chance to see him?"

"He's flying into Calgary on Sunday, and Natalie and I are going to pick him up."

She watched him closely, her shrewd eyes assessing as she tried to read his face. "It must have been one hell of a shock, finding out you had a kid."

"Shock doesn't even come close." His expression became reflective, and there was an air of vulnerability about him as he stared at the glass in his hand. "I was so damned furious at first, I couldn't see straight. A kid—and she never even had the decency to tell me."

Stella butted her cigarette, brushing an ash off the arm of her chair as she asked, "Did she give you a reason *why* she didn't tell you?"

"She said she didn't tell me because she didn't find out that she was pregnant until after she left."

"Sounds like a crock of crap to me."

Adam gave her a halfhearted grin. "It sounded like a crock of crap to me, too." He averted his eyes and the muscles in his face tensed. "Did you know his name was Adam Patrick?"

Instantly alert, Stella responded, "How did you find that out?"

"I saw his birth certificate."

"Does the kid know about you?"

"No."

"Did you ask her why she named him Adam?"

"No."

There was exasperation in her voice when she asked, "Well why in hell didn't you?"

Adam's expression was suddenly guarded as he looked at her. "What difference does it make? Maybe she did it out of guilt—who knows? All I know is that it's going to be a damned sight easier for everyone concerned if we don't even see each other, let alone talk."

"If that's how you feel, your trip to Calgary could prove interesting," retorted Stella dryly.

Adam sighed heavily, as though he didn't have the energy to speak. "I wish I trusted her enough to let her go alone."

Stella frowned and tilted her head to one side. "Why don't you trust her?"

"I really don't know. I just have this gut feeling that there's a hell of a lot she's not telling me. And if she disappeared once because of it, she could disappear again."

Stella thoughtfully tugged at her bottom lip as she mulled that over in her mind, and her eyes narrowed as she murmured more or less to herself. "I wonder what in hell she's hiding?"

SUNDAY MORNING, and the final countdown. Adam had hardly slept during the past few days, and when he had managed to sleep for a few hours, his rest had been punctuated by disturbing dreams. If it hadn't been for Stella, he didn't think he could have made it. As it was, he was sure he couldn't have taken much more of the tension or the endless hours with nothing to do but think.

The shrill drone of his rechargeable razor sliced through the distinctive hush of early morning as he stood in the minuscule bathroom of the trailer, his mind wandering. Patrick's flight was due in at 3:40 P.M. In little more than nine hours he would meet his son, and for the first time in years, Adam had butterflies.

If he had managed to accomplish anything during the past few days, it was to separate his negative feelings about Natalie from his awakening feelings for the boy. He had made up his mind to be careful not to do or say anything that might alienate Patrick. The kid was bound to have deep-seated loyalties toward his mother; it was only natural. And regardless of how Adam felt about Natalie, he would not use Patrick as a weapon to even an old score.

He shut off his razor and replaced it in its case, then pulled the towel from around his neck and tossed it in the sink. Absently rubbing his hand across his naked chest, he stared at his reflection in the mirror, trying to see himself through a stranger's eyes—his boy's eyes. What if Patrick wanted to have nothing to do with him? What then? With a grim expression lining his gaunt face, he swore and turned away.

What he put on was never a big deal for Adam. His wardrobe was certainly adequate, but he wore even his most expensive clothes with the same kind of detachment he did blue jeans and a faded plaid shirt. But today he found himself selecting nis clothes with un-accustomed care. He kept telling himself it was only a kid, but that did nothing to calm the butterflies.

The sun hadn't yet risen over the mountain to touch the valley floor, but that first soft breeze of daylight was rustling through the trees by the time he reached the Patterson house. The neighborhood was still early-morning quiet, except for the far-off barking of a lone dog.

When he had phoned Natalie the day before to make arrangements for the trip, she had once again tried to persuade him not to go with her, but Adam refused to compromise. He did relent when she had asked to take her car. He suspected that was a kind of thin assurance for her that she had some control over what was happening, that she wasn't completely within his control. It didn't matter to him how they got there, only that they did.

Climbing out of the truck, Adam picked up a small duffel bag, a camera case and his camera from the passenger seat, then closed the door. He slung all three straps over his shoulder, and thrusting his hands in his pockets, he walked into the backyard. Doc had a fantastic view of the river, and for a few tranquil moments Adam savored the raw beauty of the panorama that opened up before him.

The breathtaking backdrop of the jagged gray fortress of haze-clad mountains, the impenetrable denseness of the verdant forest, the rushing, crystal-clear stream—it was like a majestic cathedral, more awe-inspiring than any structure built by man. This wilderness was in his blood, and no matter where he went it called out to him like some possessive mistress. He could never rid himself of that relentless attraction.

The sound of a screen door closing shattered his reverie, and he turned. Natalie was coming down the back steps carrying a small soft-sided case and a handbag. She had on steel gray slacks, with a matching cardigan draped around her shoulders, the shade exactly the color of her eyes. There was a glint of silver chains against the pristine whiteness of her silk blouse, and her thick, flaxen hair was drawn back in an austere chignon. Her girlhood loveliness had evolved into a classic beauty and an ethereal remoteness.

His face was unreadable as he moved toward her. 'Good morning, Natalie.''

She had trouble meeting his gaze, and she toyed nervously with the car keys in her hand. "Good morning."

He took her suitcase, aware of her reluctance to let it go, and turned toward the car. She cast him a nervous look as she followed him, her small face drawn with fatigue and strain. He kept his voice impersonal as he asked, "Did you phone Patrick last night?"

"Yes. He was so excited about finally getting to come. He wants to go trout fishing in the worst way."

"I'd like to take him with me when I go back into the high country, if you don't mind." His tone of voice suggested that it didn't matter if she minded or not, he had every intention of taking his son with him.

In an unsteady whisper she answered, "He'll like that."

As they reached the car, Natalie looked up at him as though she was about to speak, then changed her mind. He sensed that she longed to try to dissuade him from going with her, but after seeing the tenacious set to his jaw, she knew better than to try. Adam opened the passenger door of her small car and swung her suitcase, his duffel bag and camera case onto the back seat, then set his camera on the console separating the bucket seats as he climbed in. Adjusting the seat to accommodate his long legs, he did up his seat belt and rolled down the window. He watched Natalie as she took her sunglasses out of her handbag and put them on, then selected the proper key. Her hands were trembling as she put the key in the ignition. This was going to be one hell of a long trip, he thought darkly as he tossed his own sunglasses on the dash. She was a wreck and so was he.

Adam fell asleep within the first half hour, his arms folded across his chest, his head resting against the door. Natalie couldn't have been more relieved. The drive to Calgary along twisting mountain roads was an endurance test at the best of times, but having Adam sitting there in brooding silence would make the six-hour trip nearly unbearable.

And her nerves were nearly shot as it was. Ever since Adam had appeared at Doc's, she had been going through an agony of indecision about how she was going to tell her son about his father. It was a confrontation she was dreading. Patrick had always been very sensitive and troubled about the absence of his father, and when he discovered he had a father like Adam, somebody he'd idolize, she realized he could end up hating her for what she'd done. She didn't know what she was going to do; she didn't know what she was going to say. And she was alone in this. Alone and scared.

To make matters worse, her sleep had been repetitively broken by shadows in the night. Shadows of old memories, shadows of remembered dreams.

When she had first left the valley, she had relived every moment of that incredible summer with Adam so often and with such detail that every second spent with him was indelibly engraved in her mind. In those black days after Doc had taken her away, those beautiful memories had been her salvation. She had been able to block out the horror of her mother's death with those memories. She had been able to block out the ripping pain that filled her whole body as she fought for her life and that of her unborn baby's, and she had been able to block out the revulsion, the loneliness, the grief, the guilt.

But in time, the specialness of those memories turned on her, and she honestly didn't know how she bore the anguish when she finally had to admit that it was truly finished. Those same memories became a self-inflicted torture, and she tried to hold them back. But they always came. If it hadn't been for Patrick, and knowing that he needed her, Natalie knew she wouldn't have survived.

A rough spot in the highway jerked her back to reality, and she made herself relax her white-knuckled grip on the wheel. Her shoulders and arms hurt from tension, and her fingers were numb and unresponsive. Her nerves were as taut as a drawn bow.

Orange warning signs told of construction ahead and Natalie slowed to the posted speed. Around the next curve, heavy equipment was ripping up a portion of the highway and she stopped behind the other vehicles that were lined up, waiting for the flagman to wave them through. Resting her arm on the open window, she turned to look at Adam. The racket outside was almost deafening, but he didn't move a muscle, and his breathing remained deep and even.

He had been twenty when she'd left and he had remained twenty in her memories, but now she had a chance to study him and fully absorb the changes that had matured him.

And there had been changes. The boy in her memories had worn his blond, slightly curly hair fairly long. But that had changed. It had darkened to a rich tawny color that was heavily streaked by the sun, and was shorter and brushed back from his face.

The years had left their mark in other ways. The boyish face had lost its smoothness and had become more chiseled, more weathered, more durable. There were lines around his eyes and creases around his mouth that hadn't been there before, and his cheeks had hollowed out beneath broad cheekbones. His jaw had always jutted forward, but now it had a more pronounced and determined set to it, and his mouth had lost much of its softness. His thick eyebrows had darkened and were bushier, but she could see that his eyelashes, which fanned out against his cheeks as he slept, were still tipped with the remembered gold. It had become such a strong masculine profile, and Natalie realized that she would never be able to call up the image of the boy she had known without calling up this new image, as well. And she felt a haunting sense of loss.

But it wasn't just his face that had matured. Adam had always been muscular, but he had filled out even more. He was wider through the shoulders and broader through the chest, and there was a nuance of sheer brute strength that hadn't been there before. But he still moved with that same fluid athletic grace she remembered so well.

Within this man was the familiar twenty-year-old, but other changes had turned him into a stranger. He had become remote and uncommunicative. And hostile.

Those changes hurt her most of all, and Natalie looked away, blinking rapidly against the threat of tears as her hands curled tightly around the steering wheel. Had she done that to him, or had living the life he had turned him into that kind of man? The line of vehicles started to edge forward, and Natalie put her car in gear and followed, the ache in her chest worsening. One thing was certain. He despised her now, and of all the changes that had taken place in this man, that was the hardest one of all to bear.

With the exception of that brief stop at the construction site, Natalie drove nonstop for three hours, and she was beginning to feel the lack of sleep. There was a mining town up the road a mile or so and she planned to stop there for a coffee and gas. Adam had stirred a couple of times, but he was in a deep sleep and she was grateful for that.

She found that the magnificent scenery was a soothing balm to her distressing thoughts, and she was lulled into a floating detachment, as though she had become suddenly divorced from the trauma of the previous week. She didn't want to let go of this unexpected sense of calm, but the steady hum of the tires on the pavement and the heat of the sun beating in through the window were drugging her, and she had to make a conscious effort to stay awake. It was definitely time for a break.

ADAM HAD OFFERED TO DRIVE after they'd stopped for breakfast, and much to his surprise, Natalie had unresistingly handed him the keys. She had been silently staring out the window for some time and Adam shot her a quick glance. Her head was resting against the door and Adam realized she had fallen asleep. Unaware that a sudden frown lined his brow, he turned his attention back to the road. He had been following a logging truck for several miles, and when the narrow highway finally widened into a passing lane, he swung out to pass.

Propping his elbow on the open window, Adam rested the back of his hand against his mouth, a troubled expression darkening his eyes. This whole thing with Natalie was getting out of hand. He had been half-asleep when they pulled up in front of the coffee shop, and there had been a split second when their eyes met and he nearly reached out and touched her. He'd been caught with his guard down, and he had been more vulnerable than he liked to admit. He had to be careful it didn't happen again, especially when he knew he was playing with an undefendable weakness. His shield of rage was gone. It had come as something of a shock when he realized his anger had burned itself out, and he was left with nothing but a gnawing emptiness....

"Where are we?"

He dropped his hand and looked at her. "Just a few miles this side of Banff."

Straightening, Natalie tucked a loose strand of hair back in place, then glanced at her watch.

He knew she was thinking of Patrick. "Has he ever traveled alone?"

"No. He's always gone with someone. But at least this is a direct flight. He should be fine."

But Adam could tell by the tone of her voice that she wasn't at all comfortable about him traveling by himself. There was a hint of a grim smile around Adam's mouth as he considered Natalie's concern. Even though she was uneasy about him traveling alone, Adam doubted that she would feel any more secure if she found out that Patrick had been under the watchful eye of a private eye for the past week.

"Adam?"

"What?"

"You will give me a chance to talk to him first, won't you?"

Adam's jaw stiffened, his eyes becoming hard behind his sunglasses. She looked so scared. So damned scared. And suddenly there was a very large chink in Adam's protective armor; he no longer wanted to bring her to her knees. He couldn't stand the thought of Natalie being afraid of him or afraid of what he might do. At least not the kind of soul-destroying fear he saw in her eyes. Never that.

There was a tightness encasing his chest when he finally responded. "I said something in anger that should never have been said, Natalie. I don't want to hurt him or confuse him." He met her gaze with forthrightness. "And I won't ever try to turn him against you." His tone was still low, and there was a quality to it that let her know he was not prepared to play any games. "But on the other hand, I expect some cooperation on your part. I don't want to be shut out of his life any longer." He stared at the road, his expression altering as a muscle in his jaw twitched and his voice became flat and emotionless. "Of course, there is the possibility that he won't want to have anything to do with me."

"Adam," she said softly, as though she was chiding him for being so absurd. "That isn't even a remote possibility."

It wasn't so much what she said that surprised him, but how she said it. It was clear that she felt certain Adam would become a major influence in Patrick's life, but what surprised him the most was that she seemed to approve. And that approval put them on neutral ground. Adam felt some of the tension ease from him, and he was finally able to ask, "What's he like?"

Bracing her elbow on the open window, she rested her head against the back of her hand, a touch of amusement in her voice. "He's a little taller than average, he has an energy supply that never seems to deplete, loves sports, hates girls and drags home every stray animal he can find."

Adam grinned lopsidedly. "He sounds like a normal boy to me. Does he like school?"

"So far. He's not allowed to watch very much TV, so he reads a tremendous amount, and he's in the swim club." She smiled wryly, affectionately. "He's a total loss at neatness, but he does excel in math. And for the most part, he's really easy to get along with."

When he spoke again, it was almost as though he was thinking out loud. "It must have been tough, raising a kid on your own."

She laughed softly, a rueful tone in her voice. "It's had its moments. But the travel agency where I work pays well, so that makes a big difference."

"How did you get into that business?"

"I started out as a clerk, but I took night courses and I worked my way through the ranks. Then a little more than four years ago, I was given the job of tour coordinator."

Adam suddenly remembered her always saying that someday she would see the world. "Have you done much traveling?"

"No. I didn't like leaving Patrick, and it wasn't really required of me."

Adam became lost in thought and there a brief silence as he turned something over in his mind. Finally he looked at her and asked, "Did you ever consider giving him up for adoption?"

There was a sudden steeliness about her as she sat up abruptly, defiance flashing in her eyes as she met his gaze. Her response was fiercely adamant. "Never."

For some reason Adam felt compelled to push. "There was nothing stopping you. You could have even decided not to have him. An abortion wasn't unheard of then."

"That was absolutely out of the question," she said, her voice brittle. Adam frowned, unsettled by her obvious agitation. Her body was stiff and her face was unyielding, and she had laced her fingers together in a white-knuckled grip. Adam said nothing more as he vainly tried to focus his full attention on the winding, treacherous road that had been blasted out of the side of a mountain.

What had happened in the past to leave such wounds? It was obvious he had touched a raw nerve, and Adam had the most uncanny feeling that she had been, for one reason or another, heavily pressured to terminate the pregnancy. There had been plenty of gossip about her mother's accident, and it was a well-known fact that Natalie had been with her. Adam considered the possibility that the older woman had known about Natalie's pregnancy, and that knowledge had something to do with the crash. One explanation started to take form in his mind, but it was too grisly to even consider. Surely it hadn't been deliberate.

Keeping his voice calm and devoid of expression, he said quietly, "For what it's worth, I'm glad you made the decision you did—to have him and keep him."

Natalie's eyes flew to his face, and Adam held her gaze for as long as he dared. But he caught the unmistakable glitter of tears before she turned away. If there had been any anger left in Adam, it would have died then. This was a tormented woman. And for whatever pain she had inflicted, she had paid the price many times over.

THE LONG DRIVE had left its mark, and by the time they got off the elevator, Natalie was so pale, she was beginning to look ill. Adam was starting to wonder if it was just nervousness or if there was something really wrong. She had hardly eaten anything when they had stopped for breakfast, and she seemed to be constantly cold. Even as warm as it had been in the car, she had kept her sweater either on or wrapped around her.

The adjoining rooms they had been given were the ultimate in comfort, and Adam laid his camera on the desk, then hung up his jacket as the bellboy opened the drapes and adjusted the air conditioner. After the uniformed young man unlocked the separating doors between the two rooms, Adam tipped him and quietly pocketed both keys.

Adam closed the door, then glanced at Natalie, who was standing at the window looking out, her body a silhouette against the outside brightness. "We have a couple hours before we have to leave for the airport," he said. "Why don't you try to get some sleep?"

She shook her head as she slipped her sweater from her shoulders and dropped it on the small sofa. "I doubt if I can."

"Would you like me to have something sent up from room service?"

She shook her head again. "No thanks." Pensively, she began caressing the chains around her neck and his attention was drawn to her hands—slender and graceful, so delicately expressive—and they still held a deep fascination for him. They could be so gentle, so tender, so unbelievably sensual....

He jerked his eyes away and clenched his jaw as he turned abruptly, trying to beat back the sudden recollection of how it felt to have her hands caressing his naked chest and thighs. He could clearly remember the sensation she induced when she softly stroked him, arousing a pulsating ache that he could barely contain. And he could recall the paralyzing excitement when their bodies were finally welded together in a searing, impassioned need that equaled no other.

The room was suddenly hot and airless, and Adam felt as if he were slowly suffocating. He could feel beads of sweat dampen his skin as he clenched every muscle in his body against the debilitating empty ache of wanting her. His pulse was thundering in his head as he said raggedly, ''I'm going to have a shower.''

CHAPTER FIVE

A LONG LINE OF CABS was parked along the arrival ramp of the airport, and the traffic was heavy. Realizing he'd never get a metered parking spot in front of the building, Adam dropped Natalie off at the entrance doors and made another circuit to the parking lots.

Inside was just as bad. The place was congested with summertime traffic, and the minute he strode through the sliding doors he was caught in a steady stream of holiday travelers. Crowds of people gathered around the luggage carousels on the lower level, and it was apparent by the flight numbers displayed on the huge screens that two flights had just landed, disgorging their loads of passengers among the swarm of people already there.

It took him only a moment to spot Natalie in the crowd. She was looking up at the TV monitors that displayed all the updated departure and arrival times. Adam had phoned just before they'd left the hotel to make sure that Patrick's flight was on schedule, but obviously Natalie wanted to make sure there had been no changes since then. For a moment he stood watching her. Again he was struck by her uniqueness. And once again, he experienced feelings he dared not acknowledge.

He picked his way through a group of travelers to get to her. "Still on time?"

"So far." She glanced up at him, her anxiety beginning to show. "I wish he didn't have to clear customs by himself."

"They aren't going to hassle him," he said quietly. "And besides, a flight attendant will help him through." He glanced at the huge information signs suspended overhead, then motioned toward the escalators. "Let's get out of this crowd. There's an observation deck on the next level. We may as well find a decent place to wait since we have a half an hour before his flight's due in."

"Where's customs?"

"On this level. But we'll have plenty of time to work our way back once they announce the flight arrival." She hesitated a moment, then nodded and fell into step with him.

The second level, where the arrival gates for all the domestic flights were located, was just as busy as the lower level, and they had to pick their way across the congested concourse to get to the spacious lounge on the far side of the terminal.

Adam dropped his suede jacket on an empty chair, then motioned to the coffee bar that was located down the mall. "Would you like anything while we're waiting?"

She didn't meet his eyes as she shook her head. "No, I don't think so."

His expression was contemplative. "You haven't had anything to eat all day, Natalie."

She shrugged, still refusing to meet his eyes. "I couldn't eat anything right now."

Natalie was a fairly readable person and Adam knew she was very worried about telling Patrick the truth; he also knew it wasn't going to be an easy thing for her to do. And in spite of everything, he did want to take the pressure off. His voice was quiet when he said, "I told you I don't expect you to tell him right away, and I meant that. And if you'd rather, I'll tell him."

"No, I'll tell him. It has to come from me." She turned away, and Adam's expression was inflexible as he watched her walk over to the massive windows overlooking the runway approach. Ever since that afternoon, a hole had been punched in his resistance, and it was becoming more and more difficult to remain detached. She seemed so damned defenseless.

Needing something familiar to do to help him relax and regain his composure, Adam checked the reading on the light meter attached to his camera strap, then made some adjustments to his lens settings.

The routine was such a deeply ingrained habit that he never even thought about it. He had packed photography equipment for so many years that his cameras had become an extension of himself, and he very rarely went anywhere without one. Early in his career, his initial fascination with wildlife and landscapes had expanded to other types of photography, and the subject he now found most rewarding was character studies of people. Acquiring exceptional photographs of wildlife took sound knowledge, hard work and painstaking patience. But with people, the most incredible shots could turn up anywhere.

Adam removed the lens cover and focused, and for a reason he didn't stop to analyze, he focused on Natalie. She was standing with her shoulder resting against the glass, her face profiled against the light from the windows. There was something very poignant about this solitary figure alone in the crowd, her pensiveness a nearly tangible thing. She had her head tipped slightly as she watched a flock of pigeons arch skyward, the muted light angling across her finely sculpted features and casting her solemn face in a compelling study of light and shadows.

It was a portrait of aloneness. A haunting study. And even as he shot several frames, Adam was grimly aware that this would be one batch of photographs he should have never taken.

His face suddenly hardened as he slung the camera strap over his shoulder and sat down. Leaning forward, he clasped his hands together and rested his arms across his thighs as he stared at the floor. Only his eyes revealed the bleakness of his thoughts. He didn't like the feeling that he was walking a narrow line of self-control. He didn't like it at all.

The minutes crawled by and Adam must have looked at his watch a hundred times before it was finally time to return to the lower level. Never in his life had he felt the nerve-racking kind of anxiety he experienced as he followed Natalie to the waiting area outside customs. This waiting game was over, and in a few minutes, he'd see his son for the first time. It seemed to take forever before passengers started straggling into the area visible behind the glassed-in partition that separated the Canadian Customs's final checkpoint from the rest of the terminal. Unable to get a clear field of view, he moved forward until he was standing behind Natalie, his body a shield for hers against the

buffeting from the milling people who were beginning to gather around them. She looked up at him,
then with a flustered movement, turned away.

They were standing with their bodies lightly touching when a laughing flight attendant appeared from
behind a partition with a grinning blond-haired boy in
tow. Adam felt Natalie react, and suddenly his butterflies were back. But he only caught a quick glimpse
of his son before the pair disappeared behind another
partition. A short time later they reappeared, and
Patrick was dragging a large suitcase that matched the
one Natalie had brought.

Adam was aware of nothing except this small blond
boy. This was his flesh and blood. A part of himself,
his son.

Just then, Patrick spotted his mother on the other
side of the glass wall, and he grinned broadly and
hiked up his shoulder bag before giving her an excited
little wave. Natalie waved back then glanced up at
Adam, her eyes bright with unshed tears, communi-
cating her wordless appeal. He tipped his head, silently indicating that she was to meet the boy alone.
She only hesitated a moment.

Seeing this kid of his for the first time was having
one hell of an effect on Adam, and he desperately
needed time to deal with these new, intensely gripping
feelings. The boy and the flight attendant came
through the door, and as if compelled by some reflex
action, he automatically reached for the familiar security of his camera. Safe behind the anonymity of his
equipment, he recorded it all: Patrick's face lighting
up as he approached his mother, the sheer joy in Natalie's eyes, the way she fought back the tears as she

knelt and hugged her son. But the photographs were unnecessary; it was a scene Adam would never forget.

It all seemed to happen in slow motion, but finally Natalie gave Patrick another quick hug, then stood up, her eyes no longer bleak as she smiled down at the boy. She spoke to the flight attendant, then laying her hand on Patrick's shoulder, she leaned over and said something to him.

With her hand still against his back, she guided him toward Adam. "There's someone special I'd like you to meet, Patrick," she said quietly, and Adam shot her a sharp look. Surely she wasn't going to tell him here.

Patrick looked up, and for a moment he didn't react. Then his eyes widened and his mouth sagged open in an expression of incredulity. He stared at Adam a moment, then as though he was unsure of what he was seeing, he glanced at his mother. She smiled and nodded, and Patrick looked back at Adam, his face suddenly flushed. He swallowed hard and whispered in awe, "Are you really Adam Rutherford—you know, from 'The Wilderness Beyond'?"

It had never once entered Adam's head that Patrick might be familiar with his wilderness shows, and it came as a bit of a shock when the boy recognized him. Knowing that he wasn't a complete stranger to the boy did, however, help to take the edge off his tenseness. Smiling crookedly, he stretched out his hand and nodded. "Yes, I am. I'm glad to meet you, Patrick."

Still staring at him in wonderment, Patrick dazedly shook his hand. "I've watched every one of your specials, but I like your books even better. My mom bought 'em all for me, and they're my favorites. I like the one about jungle cats the best."

So Natalie had bought his books for Patrick. That was a bolt out of the blue, and Adam shot Natalie another penetrating look. What had possessed her to do that? If she had purposely not told the kid who his father was, why had she purposely chosen to expose Patrick to his work? Natalie deliberately evaded his eyes, her discomfort becoming more pronounced as he continued to scrutinize her, his eyes narrowing contemplatively. None of the information he was receiving seemed to jigsaw together, and he was still coming up with more questions than answers.

Aware that Patrick was watching him closely, Adam managed a smile. "I have a new book out, Patrick. I'll give you a copy."

"Will you autograph it for me?"

The boy's gray eyes were wide with wonder—so much like another pair of gray eyes, and Adam found that very disturbing. His voice showed signs of strain when he answerd, "I'd be happy to."

Another passenger paused to speak to Patrick, and Adam shifted his gaze. The newcomer was a medium-size nondescript man in his early forties, the kind of person who would be easily lost in a crowd. But as soon as Adam got a good look at his eyes, he realized that that first impression was a carefully nurtured image.

"This is Mr. Dickson," explained Patrick. "He sat with me on the plane." Shyly, the boy indicated his mother. "And this is my mom."

Mr. Dickson grinned at Natalie as he ruffled Patrick's hair. "This is quite the boy you have, ma'am.

He was good company.'' He looked down at the boy as he grasped his shoulder. ''You have a good holiday, Pat. And you be sure and catch a few fish for me.''

''I will, sir. You have a good holiday, too.''

Raising his hand in a friendly gesture of farewell, the man turned to leave, but as he turned he very pointedly caught Adam's eye. Adam acknowledged the wordless message with an almost imperceptible nod, and with that silent dismissal, Mr. Dickson's responsibility as the investigator tailing Patrick was completed. Adam suddenly felt like a traitor for hiring him in the first place. It had been a cheap shot and an unnecessary move. He knew that now. Unable to meet Natalie's gaze, he picked up Patrick's suitcase and indicated the doors. ''Why don't we get out of this crowd?''

NATALIE WATCHED HER YOUNG SON rummage through his suitcase, an uneasy feeling grating away at her already shaky composure. Something was definitely wrong. He seemed strangely alienated and had been uncommonly quiet on the drive back from the airport. She'd caught him watching Adam with an intentness that was definitely unsettling, and she suspected that he was trying to figure out why this man was suddenly so involved in their lives. He had given his mother a strange, quizzical look when Adam had slid behind the wheel of the car, and he'd given her another one when they'd arrived at the hotel and it became apparent that this stranger was lodged in the adjoining room.

Patrick took a flat box out of his suitcase and stiffly laid it on the bed, and Natalie's stomach did a sickening nose dive when she recognized it. So Bea had found it. Natalie clasped her arms in front of her, suddenly chilled by a strange reluctance. She should have left it where it had been hidden, in the top back shelf of her closet. Having it here was a mistake—a very big mistake. She glanced at the box, then quickly looked out the window, feeling suddenly trapped. On a foolish impulse, she had asked Bea to send it, and now that it was here, she didn't know what to do with it.

It was a photograph album. A photograph album that carefully chronicled Patrick's life from the time he'd been born to the present. And it had been Natalie's way of evading reality for a very long time. It had been her escape, her consolation, her atonement to Adam.

Because the album was for Adam. Right from the beginning, it had been for him.

And she had taken such comfort in that, especially in the beginning. When she had been almost unable to cope with the horror, the guilt, the utter despair, the photograph album had been her source of comfort. It was her way of clinging to that part of her life that was so very special, and by carefully tending the picture journal of their small son, she was able to hang on to that shattered dream.

When her day of reckoning finally came, when she finally had to face the fact that she'd been living in a warped fantasy and that Adam could never again be a part of her life, she had wanted to die. If it hadn't been for Patrick, she would have never survived.

And now it was here. Lying on the bed.

Trying to take a deep breath to ease the awful ache in her chest, Natalie pulled herself back from the brink of those disturbing thoughts and turned to study her son. His face was pale and the set to his jaw fore-warned her of his mood.

Her own face was drawn as she went over to the bed and sat beside him. Clasping her hands tightly to-gether to keep from turning him to face her, she asked quietly, "What's the matter?"

He didn't look at her. "Nothing."

"That's not true, Patrick. You've hardly said ten words since we picked you up, and that's not like you."

He didn't say anything for a minute, then he finally met her gaze steadily, an accusing look in his eyes. "You never told me you knew him. You bought me his books and everything, and you knew how much I liked his shows, but you never told me you knew him from before."

There was not a single thing she'd said that could have possibly revealed she had known Adam "from before," and her son's unexpected astuteness left her groping for balance. "What makes you think I've known him for very long?" she countered softly.

"I can tell."

Her apprehension became more acute as she real-ized that she would not be able to put off telling him the truth about Adam, even for a few days. The thought scared her to death. Patrick would have every reason to turn on her.

"Aunt Bea packed this box in my suitcase, and she said you asked her to get it from home." Natalie stared at him uncomprehendingly, confused by his change in direction and even more confused by his agitation. His mouth started to tremble as he continued, his voice becoming more strident. "So I looked in it and there was a photograph album and it was full of pictures of me. I've never seen it before, and I wondered and wondered why you had it."

It was as though an invisible hand forcefully squeezed the air from her lungs and the room began to swim as panic crawled up her throat. Her hands were trembling as she reached for him. "Patrick—"

He stepped away, his eyes glistening with angry tears. "But now I know. You had it hidden so I wouldn't find it because it was a big secret. And you never keep secrets, except about my dad. So it has to be for him. He's my dad, isn't he?"

She had never dreamed that he would figure it out on his own, and the awful shock paralyzed her as she stared at him, her face suddenly deathly white, her heartbeat echoing dully in her head.

"Isn't he?" he demanded shrilly.

"Patrick, let me explain—"

He twisted away from her, his hands balled into fists, his white face streaked with tears. "Isn't he?"

Damn, she had wanted to spare him this. Natalie felt like she was condemning him to some horrible fate as she answered in a tortured whisper, "Yes, he's your father."

He stared at her, his small body shaking with suppressed sobs, then he whirled and made a blind dash for the door. "I hate you!" he cried. "I hate you! I hate you!" He was in the hallway before Natalie could catch him, and like a wild thing, he fought his way out of her grasp. He was running blindly.

Adam, who was just coming up from the lobby, stepped off the elevator just as Patrick bolted from his mother, his racking sobs echoing hollowly in the long corridor. One glance at the stricken look on Natalie's face, and he knew something was desperately wrong. Reacting on pure instinct, he crouched, intercepting the boy's wild flight. Holding this sobbing, hurting, angry child in an enveloping embrace, Adam experienced a rush of feelings that went beyond anything he'd experienced before. For the first time he was holding his son in his arms. And for the first time in his life, Adam Rutherford felt the agony only a father can feel.

His voice was shaking badly from this onslaught of emotion as he murmured against Patrick's hair. "It's okay, son. It's okay."

Patrick tried to fight his way free as he sobbed, "Let me go! Let me go! I hate her!" He twisted and struggled, but Adam's hold was unbreakable. Eventually realizing his fight was in vain, he collapsed against his father and wept bitterly, his thin arms in a strangle-hold around Adam's neck. "Why couldn't you come before? Why?"

Why. Forty-eight hours ago, the heartbreaking pain he heard in that one muffled question would have evoked a seething rage in Adam, but now it only made him feel impotent. How could he find the right words to give comfort when he didn't know the answer himself?

He purposely kept his eyes averted from Natalie's as he stood up with the boy in his arms, strangely reluctant to see what kind of anguish Patrick's words had inflicted on her. On one hand, she deserved the attack for deliberately keeping father from son, but on the other hand, Adam was beginning to suspect that something dark and sinister had driven her to do what she had. Her reasons were obscure but they were genuine, and he had a gut feeling whatever they were, they were directly related to her mother's accident.

The heavy door had swung shut behind Natalie when she had gone after Patrick, and they were automatically locked out of the room. Bracing the weight of his son on his thigh, Adam fished a room key out of his slacks' pocket and handed it to Natalie as he talked quietly to Patrick, who had his face buried in his father's shoulder. His deep sobs seemed to be torn from his small body, and Adam felt every sob.

Once inside, he carried Patrick over to the sofa and sat down, the distraught child clinging to him with a desperate strength. Gently stroking his fair head, Adam said softly, "It's okay to cry, Patrick. Get it out of your system, and we'll talk later. It's okay, son." He finally looked at Natalie and nearly winced when he saw the effect this was having on her. And he wondered if Patrick had any idea just how much pain he'd inflicted when he told his mother he hated her.

It took awhile for Patrick's stormy outburst to subside into the occasional deep, shuddering sob. Natalie appeared with a glass of water and a cold cloth and wordlessly handed them both to Adam. His face was taut with worry as he took them, fervently hoping that Patrick would suffer no permanent scars from this. Both his mother and his father carried too many as it was.

He gently eased the boy away, and the tension lines around his mouth deepened when he saw how the violent weeping had ravaged his son's face. His eyes and mouth were so swollen, he looked as though he'd been physically battered. With infinite tenderness he wiped Patrick's face with the cool cloth, then pressed the glass into his hand. "Have a drink, Patrick. Then we'll talk."

Patrick had a sip, then Adam set the glass on the table by his elbow. Hooking his knuckles under his chin, he lifted his son's face and gently forced him to meet his sober gaze. The boy's eyes were identical to Natalie's, and that uncanny likeness aroused some feelings that were extremely hard to handle. Especially now.

A tear slipped down Patrick's cheek, and Adam gently wiped it away with his thumb. "I want you to tell me why you're upset, Patrick," he said softly. "I need to know what you're thinking right now."

Patrick stared at his father for a moment, a slightly rebellious set to his mouth, then he lowered his head and nervously twisted his fingers in the front of his T-shirt. "I don't know."

Adam studied Patrick's bowed head, his eyes extremely thoughtful. Finally he asked, "Do you wish I was someone else?"

Patrick's head flew up, his eyes wide with sudden alarm. "No!" He held his father's steady gaze for a moment, then he looked down again, suddenly embarrassed. "No, I don't wish that," he whispered into his chest.

"Don't be afraid to say what you're thinking, Patrick. You have every right, you know."

The boy didn't respond, but sat huddled forlornly on Adam's lap, his misery clearly evident. After a long silence he finally lifted his head, his gray eyes again swimming with tears. "I used to think about what my dad would be like...after I went to bed and it was dark. I thought something must've been really wrong with him—or maybe he was even dead—because Mom would never talk about him. So I pretended sometimes." He wiped away the tears with the back of his hand as he hesitated, struggling valiantly to sort out his thoughts and feelings. Suddenly his composure crumbled and he started crying again, and Adam cradled his head against his shoulder. "I wished and wished you'd come. That someday, I would come home from school and you'd be there. Then I could go to school and say I had a dad, too. I wanted you so bad," he sobbed out. "Why didn't Mom tell me? Why did you have to wait so long to come?"

The angry threat Adam had flung at Natalie when he'd found out about the boy's existence, the threat about taking Patrick away from her, came back to haunt Adam now. He knew that if he wanted to turn the boy against his mother, all he'd have to say was, *She didn't tell me about you. I would have come if I had known.* Adam glanced up at Natalie, and she was watching him with naked fear in her eyes, her body rigid. They both knew he had the weapon to hurt her as much as she'd hurt him.

An eternity passed as they stared at each other across the shadowed room, but eventually Adam severed the tension-charged connection and looked down at his son. "There were reasons why. Believe me." He tried to convince himself that the desperate, fearful look on Natalie's face had nothing to do with his split-second decision to fabricate an answer. One thing he was absolutely sure of was that he'd do anything to protect this kid—it was as simple as that. "At first there were reasons she couldn't tell me about you, Patrick," he said gently. "Then later, she was afraid that I wouldn't want you, and you'd be hurt."

His hastily concocted explanation seemed to give Patrick some measure of comfort, but the effect it had on Natalie was something else altogether. The jolt she received seemed to throw her into a state of shock, and every speck of color drained from her face. Adam stared at her, wondering what was going on. It took a few moments for everything to sink in, then the significance of her reaction finally dawned on him; his invented excuse was no invention. He had unwittingly stumbled onto some answers. At least the vaguest of answers, which meant he was one step closer to the whole truth. He forced himself to drag his eyes away, an intent frown creasing his brow. The truth. But what, exactly, was that? What were the reasons that had prevented her from telling him about her pregnancy? He was still no wiser than before. No wiser, but definitely a little closer.

It took considerable self-discipline to haul his attention back to the small boy who was so hurt and bewildered. His voice had a heavily strained timbre to it as he murmured against his son's hair, "I know you're upset right now, but don't be mad at your mom, Patrick. Sometimes things happen that change our lives, and we can't do much about it."

Something compelled Adam to glance up, and his gaze locked with Natalie's. She was standing with her arms pressed against her chest as though she was experiencing excruciating pain; never in all his life had he witnessed so much anguish in another person's eyes. Fleetingly he wondered how she was able to endure it. All this emotional duress was beginning to get to him, and he could feel his resistance beginning to weaken. But he could not allow that to happen, not at any cost. From some inner reserve, he had to find the strength of will to remain detached. He tightened his arms around his son, reinforcing his resolve. Patrick was all that mattered.

Suddenly drained by the tension, he nestled his son closer, wearily leaned his head against the high back of the sofa and stared at the ceiling. His strong survival instincts were warning him he didn't dare allow his feelings toward Natalie to soften. The very last thing he needed was to let himself get involved with her again, even remotely. He had to keep reminding himself that she had messed up his life before, and she could mess it up again if he let her slip past his emotional defenses. And he had no intention of letting that happen. Ever.

Patrick stirred and pushed himself away from his father's chest, his tears finally spent. Adam experienced a kind of protective tenderness he hadn't felt for a very long time. His eyes softened as he cupped his hand around Patrick's head and drew his thumb across the boy's puffy cheek. "Do you want to talk, or do you want to leave it for a while?" he asked gently.

Patrick kept his eyes averted as he furtively slid off Adam's lap and stood between his knees, suddenly embarrassed by the arrangement. There was a knowing look in Adam's eyes and a hint of a smile around his mouth as he gazed down at the boy's lowered head. He knew exactly what had prompted Patrick to move. A boy of ten was much too big to be indulging in something so babyish as sitting on someone's knee. Now that he had a child of his own to relate to, it was surprising how clearly he remembered those same feelings from his own childhood. Adam half expected Patrick to pull out of the circle of his relaxed hold, but he remained, self-consciously fidgeting with the hem of his T-shirt.

Sensing the boy's uncertainty, Adam said quietly, "Don't sweat it, Patrick. We've got lots of time to talk later."

Patrick lifted his head and met his father's gaze with a steadiness that Adam found slightly disconcerting. He could read the reluctance in his son's eyes; he didn't want to talk. Not now, at least. Adam grasped the boy's shoulder and gave it an empathetic little shake as he nodded his head in silent understanding. Patrick lowered his head again and an uneasy silence stretched between them. Finally the boy eased out of Adam's arms and without looking at anyone, went into the other room. Adam watched him go, his eyes dark with concern, then he glanced at Natalie, who was standing in front of the window. Her back was to him, but he could tell by the stiffness in her stance that this thing with Patrick was tearing her apart.

He felt at a total loss. When he had first found out about Patrick, he had been so outraged by the injustice of what she'd done that he'd vowed to get his revenge and make her life as miserable as he could. He'd leveled some cruel and malicious threats. But now that

Patrick had actually turned on his mother, Adam discovered it was the last thing on earth he wanted.

Looking squarely at Natalie, he rested his arm on
the back of the sofa, his expression grave. "He didn't
really mean what he said, Natalie," he said firmly.
"He just needs some time to get used to the idea."

She turned and looked at him, then gave him a
bleak, twisted smile. "He means it."

"He thinks he means it because he's upset, but he'll
get over it."

She pressed her hands against her head as though
she had a bad headache, then she tilted her head back
and rubbed the back of her neck. She looked at him,
her eyes dominating her pale face, her voice filled with
gratitude. "I appreciate you . . . prevaricating for me.
It—you so easily could've told the truth."

With a penetrating stare, he waited for her reaction. "But then I wasn't really lying, was I?"

Natalie looked away abruptly. Adam saw her tense,
her eyes darkening as she stared numbly across the
room. He shifted his gaze and found that she was
staring at Patrick, who was standing at the foot of the
bed with what appeared to be a very thick photograph album in his grasp. Natalie's voice was an ago-
nized whisper that cut through the charged silence.
"No, Patrick. Not now."

But the boy never even so much as glanced at his
mother as he moved across the room, his small face
pinched, his mouth trembling. He swallowed hard,
then held the book out to Adam. "This is for you," he
whispered unevenly.

Adam cast a questioning glance at Natalie. She was
visibly shaking, but she refused to meet his gaze.

Adam looked back at his son, who was watching him with wide, uncertain eyes. It was as if he was silently begging his father to accept the gift he offered. Without saying anything, Adam took the heavy album from the boy, sensing that this was a very significant offering. Adam lifted his head to look at Natalie, but she pushed past the chair and left the room. Adam frowned, silently wondering what was going on. He felt as though he was a player in a game in which he didn't know the rules, and he felt oddly out of step.

Curiosity overcame Patrick's hesitancy and he moved closer and leaned against Adam, his fair head resting against his father's shoulder. Adam's attention was instantly dragged back to the boy and the gift he'd brought. An unaccustomed ache tightened in his throat as he shifted his position and slipped his arm around his son, deeply touched by Patrick's unquestioning recognition of him as his father. Bonds forged by blood. Only a child's unconditional trust could readily accept something like that. And only a child could forgive so easily.

Unable to speak, he tightened his arm around his son and opened the thickly padded cover. On the fly leaf, in beautiful flowery script was written, "Adam Patrick," and beneath it was neatly printed Patrick's full birth date. Adam found it increasingly hard to breathe as he turned the page and saw a photograph of a newborn baby, and mounted underneath it was the hospital nursery card. At that moment Adam knew why he had sensed this was such a significant offering. It was more than significant; it was momentous. He was holding the pictorial journal of his son's entire life.

It took a while for the stunning effects of this latest bombshell to wear off, then Adam rapidly flipped through a few pages to verify his suspicions. It was all there, even down to Patrick's old report cards. He stared at it numbly, trying to figure out what all of this meant.

His voice was very unsteady when he asked quietly, "How come you brought this, Patrick?"

The boy shrugged. "Mom had Aunt Bea put it in my suitcase. I'd never seen it before then." Patrick kept turning pages, obviously engrossed by the contents, then said excitedly, "Hey, look. Here's the page with my footprints on it."

"What do you mean, you'd never seen it before then?" Adam asked abruptly.

Patrick quit turning pages and looked up at his father. "I didn't. Not until I looked at it after Aunt Bea put it in my suitcase. I didn't even know Mom had it."

Trying to ignore the implications behind Patrick's response, Adam groped for a logical explanation. "Maybe your mother was keeping it for you."

"No. I've got my own at home. I put my old swimming badges and birthday cards and stuff like that in mine." He shrugged again and said with childlike conviction, "This is for you." With that, he calmly dismissed the issue and started leafing through the album again.

Adam's face had lost considerable color as he firmly closed the book, then turned Patrick to face him. "How do you know it's for me, Patrick?" he asked, his mouth suddenly very dry.

Patrick met his father's intense, questioning look, then lowered his head. "That's how come I knew you were...you were my dad," he whispered unsteadily. "I didn't know what was in the box when Aunt Bea put it in my suitcase, and she was so secretive about it—said it was something Mom asked her to send. And the only thing my mom ever kept secrets about was my dad. So that night after Aunt Bea went to bed, I looked." He raised his head and met his father's gaze, his eyes filled with apprehension. "I didn't know for sure what it meant until you...until you came with us." He lowered his head again, his voice barely audible. "And that's how I knew you must be my dad. Because Mom had wanted the photograph album. And because your name is Adam, too."

Adam had the funny feeling that he was getting mixed signals, and he watched Patrick intently. "Did you tell your mother all this *after* she told you about me, or before?"

"Before. She asked what was bothering me so I told her."

So the kid had put it all together. And Patrick had clobbered her with his deductions before she even had the opportunity to tell him. Adam winced as he drew his son against him in a secure embrace, trying to put everything into some sort of perspective. He rested his chin on the top of the boy's head and stared across the room. He sighed, then murmured, "Don't hate your mom, Patrick. She did what she thought was best."

Patrick abruptly pulled away from Adam, suddenly hostile and very disturbed. "I always watched your shows when they were on TV, and she knew how much I liked your books. She knew I really admir— admir—liked you, and she could have told me you were my dad." He roughly wiped his eyes. "She *should* have told me," he mumbled brokenly. "She should have told me."

Adam could feel the boy struggling to suppress his tears, and he slowly rubbed Patrick's back, trying to give some measure of comfort to his son. He felt so damned helpless. Patrick twisted his face against his father's shirt, then mumbled, "Did you know about me?"

Adam's eyes were bleak as he reluctantly answered, "No. I didn't know about you, Patrick. Not until a few days ago."

The boy burst into ragged sobs again, his small body shaking. "Why? Why didn't she tell?" There was so much hurt and bewilderment in Patrick's anguished query, and for an instant, Adam's anger flared. Damn Natalie. Damn her for making such a shambles of their lives. But then a recollection of her dark, tormented eyes took shape in his mind, and as abruptly as it flared, his anger died. Whatever her reasons, she had paid a heavy price.

Again resting his head on top of his son's, Adam stared unseeingly across the room, his face haggard. This was enough to take the heart out of anybody, he thought dully, and especially a kid. But then, he'd never once thought that Patrick would hold his mother responsible, nor did it ever enter his head that the kid could turn on her. There were too many raw wounds over all of this. Too many.

Patrick finally grew quiet in his father's embrace, and Adam gently lifted his face. "Feeling better?"

His mouth and eyes were puffy and his nose was running as Patrick self-consciously looked up and nodded. Adam's expression softened and there was a touch of amusement in his eyes as he reached into his pocket, then handed his young son a tissue to blow his nose. "Then how about us looking through the album together? You'll have to fill me in about all the pictures, you know."

Patrick gave him a wobbly grin. "Okay. If I can remember."

Looping his arm around the boy, Adam opened the large bound book. A strange poignant sensation slowly spread through him as page by page, he saw for himself the gradual development of his child. Each picture had been carefully selected and mounted, and he had the feeling that this was never meant to be a typical family album, but was intended to be a painstakingly detailed record. He wondered why she'd kept it. Patrick was convinced it was for Adam—for his father—but was it? What if it was? What did it mean? And he realized with a touch of alarm that he desperately wanted Patrick to be right, that the album was for him.

The sudden dead weight of Patrick leaning heavily against him dragged his attention back to his son. Adam smiled lopsidedly as he glanced at the child, who had dropped off to sleep, his hand resting limply on his father's thigh. Pushing the album onto the sofa, Adam gathered the boy in his arms and carried him to the bed, deriving a quiet paternal pleasure from holding his sleeping child. He could remember his own father carrying him up to bed in exactly the same way, and he could still call up the smell of pipe tobacco clinging to his father's favorite sweater. The ache in Adam's throat intensified. He wanted so badly to give Patrick those kinds of special boyhood memories.

As he laid him down, Patrick stirred and fought against the weight of sleep to open his eyes. He smiled at his father, then slipped his hand into Adam's as he whispered sleepily, "You really are my dad, aren't you?"

Tightening his hold on the small hand lying in his, Adam smiled softly. "I really am, Patrick."

"Then I can call you Dad, can't I?"

Adam had to fight to contain the fierce surge of emotion that gripped him, and his voice was very strained as he answered, "I'd like that, Patrick." The boy smiled drowsily, then with a satisfied sigh, rolled over onto his side and drifted off to sleep again. Adam gazed down at him, and there was a deep ache in his chest as he gently straightened Patrick's legs. Such a miracle, this child was. Part of himself, part of Natalie, conceived in love but born in a shroud of secrecy.

Lightly brushing his knuckles against the sleeping child's cheek, Adam straightened, then felt oddly ill at ease when he realized Natalie had been watching him from the door. He stuck his hands in his pockets as he tipped his head toward Patrick. "I think he's had it for a while."

Her voice was a soft, husky whisper. "I'm not surprised." She slipped past Adam and carefully removed Patrick's runners, then pulled the corner of the spread over him so that he was protected from the draft from the air conditioner.

Adam watched her with solemn eyes, intuitively aware that her tending of Patrick came from the basic need to touch her child. Very gently, she smoothed Patrick's tousled blond hair back from his face as she gazed down at him with immeasurable tenderness, her deep love for this child revealed in every soft, eloquent gesture. Adam saw tears well up and gather in her long lashes as she bent over and kissed Patrick softly on the temple. Struggling to contain her anguish, she reluctantly straightened, her face drawn with the kind of exhaustion that sleep would never cure. She looked so alone and so vulnerable, and Adam found himself fighting the response she was evoking in him.

As if sensing his scrutiny, she raised her eyes and met his dark, unwavering stare. Adam felt as though he was caught in some unbreakable spell, an empty ache suddenly tightening his gut. He was so close to her that he could smell her soft fragrance, and his body responded as the ache intensified. Her lips parted and he heard her breath catch on a ragged intake of air, then as though she was overwhelmed by some galvanizing emotion, she closed her eyes.

She was hurting and alone, and Adam couldn't take it any longer. He desperately wanted to pull her into his arms. He never knew he could want anything as badly as he wanted that, and the pain of that need was almost more than he could endure.

The temptation was agony. A single step, that's all it would take, and he could gather her against him. A single step, and he would once more know the feel of her body warm and soft against his.

A single step. His face looked like it was chiseled out of hard cold granite as he turned and walked out of the room.

CHAPTER SIX

THUNDERCLOUDS WERE BEGINNING TO AMASS against the impregnable palisades of the mountains, a menacing bank against the rocky peaks. The air was deadly calm and thick with heat, and not a leaf trembled as the muted rumble of thunder warned of the approaching storm.

Adam parked the Bronco in front of Doc's, then rested his arms on top of the steering wheel and watched the leading edge of the storm move closer, the dark furling clouds shadowed with ominous colors. The cumulus mass could remain there, trapped against the barrier of the mountains, or the prevailing winds could eventually roll the rain-laden clouds over the granite fortress, setting the squall free to ravage the valley.

As a small boy, Adam had experienced an untamed exhilaration each time he witnessed the awesome power of a mountain storm, and he still felt the same way. To him, it was like a shot of adrenaline, and he liked nothing better than being in the high country when a front moved in.

Exhaling a weary sigh, he dropped his hand and took the keys out of the ignition, then climbed slowly out of the truck. He felt so drained that every movement seemed to take a concentrated effort. Slamming the door, he stuffed the keys in the pocket of his jeans, then walked up the gravel driveway, his mouth compressed in a determined set. It had been one hell of a week, and he was beginning to suspect that the upcoming one wasn't going to be much better. Maybe what he needed was a pilgrimage, to head into the wilderness and find a solitary place. Except that he knew that wouldn't work. Not this time.

The week that had passed since he and Natalie had gone to pick up Patrick felt like a lifetime. Her presence was getting to him, and he was beginning to feel as though he was trying to slog his way through an endless bog. Patrick was the only bright spot. Adam made a point of having his son with him for a good portion of every day, and getting to know his child meant more to him than he could have ever imagined.

Not wanting to be confronted with any more unexpected lapses in his resistance, Adam had deliberately avoided seeing Natalie since they'd returned. But even staying away from her didn't help. He'd lie awake nights thinking about her, wondering why she'd done what she had. Then old memories would creep in, bringing with them a terrible, tormenting emptiness.

The unexplained existence of the photograph album, which was now on his bed in the trailer, haunted him, and night after night, he'd try to figure out why she'd kept it. And then he'd remember standing in that hotel room aching to touch her, yet somehow finding the strength to walk away. It was damned hard, this constant battle to shut her out.

He only hoped he could avoid her again today. He had just finished hauling the trailer to a beautiful secluded spot he'd discovered up in the mountains, and the move had taken much less time than he'd expected. Consequently, he was two hours early.

He would have waited until it was time to pick Patrick up, but with the storm moving in, he couldn't afford to take the chance. Patrick was going to be spending the next few days with him at the new location, and they planned on doing some exploring in the back country. With the poor condition of the abandoned logging road that accessed the site, Adam was concerned that a heavy rain would make it impassible. He wanted to collect his son and move out before the storm hit.

Normally, he'd phone just before he left to pick up Patrick, and the boy would be sitting on the front doorstep waiting for his father. But when he called today there had been no answer, and he had to assume that everyone was outside, trying to find some relief from the cloying heat. Attempting to dredge up some energy, Adam steeled himself against the possibility of seeing Natalie. He had too damned many weak spots as far as she was concerned, and he knew it.

But his luck finally ran out. Just as Adam rounded the corner of the house, Natalie came out the back door and started down the steps. The instant they saw each other, both stopped dead in their tracks. She stared at him wide-eyed for a second, then glanced at her watch.

His stomach twisted into a hard knot, and in an attempt to conceal his sudden edginess, Adam rammed his hands into the back pockets of his jeans. "I'm afraid I'm early," he said, his tone unnaturally gruff.

"With the storm moving in, I thought I'd better pick him up early."

It was obvious he had caught her off guard, and it took her a second to recover. "He's not here right now." He saw her grip tighten on the handrail as she took a deep unsteady breath. "He's gone with Jimmy from next door. His dad was going to pick up a Roto-tiller, so the boys went with him."

"Do you know when they'll be back?"

It was apparent that she was also feeling the strain, and her voice had a nervous quaver to it when she answered, "They left about half an hour ago, so they should be back soon."

Adam studied her thoughtfully for a moment, then turned to leave. "Tell Patrick I'll be waiting at the coffee shop in the hotel. He can give me a call there when he gets back." With that, he started walking away, and he was about to turn down the driveway when he heard his name. He stopped and turned, his tension compounding.

Her face had gone very pale and she was standing stiffly on the step, her hands clasped tightly together as she watched him with apprehensive eyes. It seemed to cost her an enormous effort when she asked shakily, "Would you like to wait here? He really shouldn't be that long."

Adam stared at her for a second, trying to gather the strength to walk away, but this time he was unable to do it. His face was heavily carved by strain as he nodded, then silently he followed her up the steps. He knew it was a big mistake, but he had no will to fight the fatal attraction. At least not now.

The shades were pulled in the living room to keep out the heat, and he paused until his eyes adjusted to the dim interior, acutely aware of her nearness. As though suddenly very unsure of herself, Natalie moved across the room. "Would you like some iced tea? I just made a fresh pitcher."

"That'd be fine," he answered, the sound of his own voice seeming oddly distant. She stood looking at him for a moment, then turned abruptly and disappeared into the kitchen. Adam moved around the room with a caged restlessness. How in hell was he going to manage to stay in the same room with her without coming undone?

"Adam."

He turned. She was standing behind him, and without speaking he took the tall glass she offered him. Needing to put some distance between them, he went over to Doc's old easy chair and sat down, stretching his legs out in front of him. Natalie sat down in the chair opposite, and an awkward silence filled the room, a silence that was oddly grating.

Several tense moments passed and then she spoke, her voice so soft he could barely hear her. "I know this won't change anything, but I don't blame you for feeling the way you do. Keeping Patrick from you was an unforgivable mistake." Her voice broke and she whispered raggedly, "I never meant to hurt you, Adam."

He looked up at her sharply, never once expecting this kind of overture from her. He stared at her for a moment, then his face hardened as he looked down at the glass in his hand. The old bitterness was fermenting inside him, and his voice was biting when he asked,

"Then why did you do it, Natalie? Not even one damned word." His anger ignited, fueled by the sense of betrayal that had stayed with him all those years. "You didn't even have the damned decency to offer an explanation. Nothing." He raised his head and stared at her coldly.

She met his hostile gaze with a kind of stoic courage, as though this ordeal of finally facing him was something she felt compelled to do. But her desolation seemed to consume her strength as she whispered, "I was wrong, Adam. I should have tried to explain."

She looked away, her thin veneer of calm taxed to the limit as she struggled to hold back tears. Adam's eyes narrowed in intense contemplation as he stared at her profile and stroked his bottom lip. He said very quietly, "Why don't you try to explain now?"

Natalie's gaze flew to his face, and it was apparent by her confused expression that this response was not at all what she had expected from him. She had expected anger. Natalie stared at him numbly, then as if it finally registered that he was waiting for an answer, she looked down at her hands. She didn't say anything for the longest time, then in a hushed tone, she started to speak. "I thought my decision was the best one—the decision not to tell you. But I was so young and so inexperienced in dealing with anything, let alone an unexpected pregnancy—" She hesitated, then looked up at him with a steadiness that said more clearly than words that she was telling the truth. "And I didn't want to drag you into something you weren't ready for," she added softly, almost reluctantly.

His face was expressionless as he stared at her. "And why did you think you'd be dragging me into something?"

She held his gaze for a minute, then she rose and went to the screen door. She stood staring out, her back to him. There was a long silence, then she said, "Do you remember Jack and Leanne Baker?"

Puzzled by her strange query, Adam frowned as he tried to think back. "Do you mean that couple on the hill you used to baby-sit for?"

"Yes, that's them." She folded her arms in front of her as she leaned against the doorjamb, her manner introspective. "I had to go over there one night—I'd left a textbook there the day before and I went to pick it up. Jack was working overtime so Leanne was home alone, and she was really upset when I arrived. I guess they'd had a fight before he went to work, and she needed someone to talk to."

"What's this got to do with you leaving?" he interrupted curtly.

Her shoulder still against the doorjamb, Natalie turned to look at him, her face grave. "Apparently Jack was a very talented hockey player. Doc said he had more natural ability and hockey sense than any juvenile he'd ever seen. He'd been scouted by several of the professional teams, and everyone assumed he'd make it in the big time."

Natalie straightened, and avoiding his gaze, came back and sat down. Thoughtful, she leaned forward, her folded arms resting across her knees. There was a peculiar quietness in her voice as she continued. "Jack was only seventeen when Leanne got pregnant, and apparently both sets of parents went wild when they

found out. It was such a mess and everyone was so ir-
ate about it that Leanne and Jack felt they had no
other choice except to get married. At that time rook-
ies had very little job security, so Jack got a job in the
mill to support his new family, and his dream of playing professional hockey went out the window.''

She met Adam's gaze, and he felt a contraction in
his chest when he saw the bleak look in her eyes. ''He
never threw up to her what he had sacrificed, and he
was a good father and he loved his kids, but he'd had
to turn his back on his lifelong dream. And both Jack
and Leanne had to live with that. He had to spend the
rest of his life tied to a job he hated. And every time
he watched a game on TV, he was reminded of how
much he'd lost.''

There was a touch of anger in Adam's voice. ''And
you thought I'd feel that way?''

She studied him for a minute, then slowly shook her
head. ''No. You would have picked yourself up and
got on with your life.'' She became intent on her hands
as she laced her fingers together. ''It was how *I* would
have dealt with it. It would've affected me the same
way it affected Leanne.'' She looked up at him again,
the pain in her eyes starkly real. ''I couldn't do that to
you, Adam. I'd have spent the rest of my life feeling
guilty for ruining a chance of a lifetime for you.'' Her
voice broke, and she abruptly looked away as she
swallowed hard. A strained moment passed, then she
continued unsteadily. ''Your success with those post-
ers was a once-in-a-lifetime chance. I couldn't take
that away from you.''

Adam's eyes narrowed and there was an unyielding
thrust to his jaw as he said tersely, ''They didn't ap-

proach me about using my photographs for the campaign until long after you disappeared.''

She met his steely gaze with unwavering directness. ''I know. Four months to be exact.''

Her response caught him by surprise, and he welded his full attention on her as he assessed everything she'd said. Something was happening here he didn't quite understand, but he sensed she was more or less leveling with him. ''Then I have to assume that something else happened to influence your decision.''

Her voice was flat and without expression. ''Yes, something else did.''

Adam remained silent as he studied her, wondering how far he could dig before she'd clam up on him. He felt as though he was on dangerous ground when he asked, ''Did it have something to do with your mother's accident?''

She gave him a startled glance, then looked away, her expression instantly guarded.

Adam could feel her withdrawing into herself, withdrawing from him, and it was suddenly imperative that he didn't let her shut him out. Willing her to look at him, he leaned forward, his voice low and urgent as he spoke. ''Talk to me, Nat.''

It had been an unconscious slip, his calling her that, a half-forgotten habit that had stuck with him after all those years. Natalie looked at him, and he could tell that his slip hadn't gone unnoticed. She was so close. So damned close. Finding it nearly impossible to speak, Adam said huskily, ''Just talk to me, Natalie.''

She raised her hand in an expressive gesture, silently beseeching him to understand. "I can't, Adam," she whispered.

There was something about how she said it, something about the tormented look in her eyes that triggered a new level of comprehension in Adam, and he experienced a flash of insight. It was suddenly all so clear. It wasn't that she was refusing to tell him; instead, it was something so emotionally shattering she was incapable of dealing with it. What, Adam reflected soberly, had exactly happened in that accident? What had scarred her so deeply?

Intent on his thoughts, Adam absently took a drink then set the glass on the table by his elbow. His expression was solemn when, compelled by the need to know, he asked a question that had been chewing at him ever since they came back from Calgary. "Was Patrick right? Was the album really for me?"

She glanced at him, then swallowed hard and quickly looked away. "Yes, it was for you."

His undivided attention was suddenly glued on her profile. Trying to ignore the disturbing sensation her barely audible answer evoked, Adam leaned forward and rested his arms across his thighs, his hands clasped between his knees. He hadn't realized until she answered him how vitally important her response was, and he found it difficult to keep his voice level when he finally spoke. "Why did you do it, Natalie? Why did you bother to keep that album for me when you made it so damned clear you wanted me out of your life?"

She met his gaze, her distress clearly revealed in her tormented eyes. "I didn't want you out of my life, Adam. But I had to get out of yours."

A current of intensity bound them as Adam stared at her, never shifting his attention for even a second. Finally he spoke. "Are you ever going to tell me why?"

She held his gaze for a moment, then looked down at her hands, her voice breaking as she whispered, "I—I don't know."

The sound of someone racing up the back steps broke the thread of tension, and Adam clamped his mouth shut, a nerve twitching in his jaw. Ten minutes. If only he'd had ten more minutes alone with her.

Patrick burst in, letting the screen door slam loudly behind him as he greeted his father. "Hi, Dad. How come you're here so early?"

It was a hard thing for Adam to do, to tear his attention away from Natalie and focus on his young son. Patrick was wearing only a pair of shorts, but his face was still flushed and his darkly tanned skin was filmed with perspiration. Adam could smell the clammy sweat that was radiating from the boy's wiry body as Patrick leaned against the arm of his chair and grinned up at his father. His freckled nose had peeled, leaving a patch of pink skin amid the golden brown. There was a smear of grease on one cheek, and his hair was tousled and clinging damply to his head. Adam experienced a surge of emotion—he did love this kid.

Patrick was looking at his father with a slightly quizzical expression in his wide gray eyes—Natalie's eyes. And a numbing realization slammed into Adam. Yes, this son of his had filled a gaping hole in his life, but not simply because Patrick was his own flesh and blood. The real truth was that he loved this child because Patrick was so very much a part of Natalie. He had her eyes, her hair, her sensitivity and warmth. This child—their son—had been created by the two of them, but he had been borne, nurtured and protected by her. It was no longer deeply significant to Adam that the seed had been his. What mattered above all else was that his seed had found fertile ground within this woman, and she had willingly harbored it.

There was a strange poignant hollowness in Adam as he forced a smile and lightly ruffled the boy's sweat-dampened hair before resting his hand on Patrick's bare shoulder. "The road up to the trailer is in bad shape, and I thought it might be wise if we made tracks before the storm hit."

"Oh, okay. I've got my stuff all packed." Patrick grinned at his father as he gave him an affectionate thump on the shoulder, then bounded off toward the hallway that led to the bedrooms. "I'll go get everything." Adam watched Patrick disappear around the corner, then stretching his long legs in front of him, he slouched back in the easy chair and glanced at Natalie.

She, too, had been watching Patrick. Adam didn't know if it was something he read in her eyes or if it was simply something that he sensed, but he was acutely aware of how much she was hurting right then. And it didn't take a genius to figure out that most of that hurt had been caused by their small son.

Adam experienced a twist of guilt. He'd been so intent on his own emotional upheaval, he'd never given much thought to what was happening between Natalie and Patrick. But with a sudden flash of insight, he was forced to admit that wasn't exactly the truth. The real truth was that he hadn't wanted to know what was happening. Because of his shaky defenses, Adam had deliberately avoided even mentioning Natalie to Patrick, let alone openly talking about her, and without realizing it, he had very likely sent some strong signals to the boy. Because of that lack of communication, Patrick probably continued to blame his mother for the years of separation.

And that was wrong. Adam knew he should have done something days ago to defuse the resentment Patrick harbored. But his ability to reason wisely had been hopelessly distorted by warring emotions, especially at the hotel when Patrick turned on Natalie. Adam had decided right then and there that it would be best if he could establish a closer relationship with Patrick before the two of them ever dared talk about Natalie, or what she'd done, or how each of them felt about it. Adam had really believed he'd been totally objective when he rationalized his decision to let things ride for a while, but now he realized he'd been less than honest with himself. It hadn't been only Patrick's emotional welfare he'd been concerned about. Not by a long shot.

The harsh lines around Adam's mouth had softened when he finally lifted his head and looked at Natalie. "I take it he's still packing a grudge because you never told him about me."

There was a brief silence before Natalie met Adam's steady gaze. She stared at him for a moment, then nodded, her expression one of concern. "He has a right to be upset." She glanced away and Adam saw her take an unsteady breath before she looked at him again. "He really idolizes you, Adam." Her voice broke and she quickly turned her head away. "All he talks about is you and what you're going to do together."

It wasn't all that long ago that her admission would have given Adam a certain amount of grim satisfaction, but now it only made him feel like a heel. It didn't seem fair that he had so easily garnered Patrick's loyalty and affection. At least not at Natalie's expense. He was about to speak to her, to try to right a wrong when Patrick bounced into the room, the expensive backpack Adam had bought him slung over his shoulders. Patrick had put on a pair of jeans and hiking boots, which Adam had also purchased for him, and in his hand he carried an old camera of his father's. Adam inwardly winced when he realized what he'd done. There was no way Natalie could compete with the money or the time Adam was able to spend on Patrick, and it must have been like a slap in the face for her when Adam had immediately become the major influence in her son's life. Now Adam realized that in some ways, he'd had an unfair and unearned advantage.

"What's the matter, Dad? Aren't we going to go now?"

Feeling suddenly even more drained, Adam leaned his head back and exhaled sharply. He looked at Patrick and nodded. "Yes, we're going now." Unable to meet Natalie's eyes, Adam stood up, and placing his hand on Patrick's shoulder, aimed him toward the door. "I'll have him back in a couple of days."

"That's fine." Natalie touched Patrick on the arm, her voice very soft. "Have a good time, Patrick."

Patrick jerkily nodded his head, deliberately avoiding eye contact. "I will," he mumbled, then bolted out the door.

Adam wanted to say something that would breach the awkward silence that Patrick's abrupt departure left, but what could he say that wouldn't make matters worse? There was a haggard look in his eyes as he rested his hand on the handle of the screen door. As if drawn against his will, he glanced at her. She was standing with her back to him, and suddenly Adam felt he had betrayed her in the most unforgivable way. His voice was very low when he said, "We'll see you in a couple of days."

She only nodded.

Patrick had already stowed his gear in the back of the Bronco and was waiting in the cab by the time Adam got there. Engrossed in the stack of maps Adam carried in the truck, Patrick didn't look up when his father climbed in. There was a stern set to Adam's jaw as he started the vehicle and put it in gear. He checked his side mirror for traffic and made a sharp U-turn, the wheels spewing a hail of gravel. But this time his anger was directed at himself. He was abandoning her, and never in his life had he felt so damned low.

They were at the outskirts of town when Patrick asked, "What's the matter, Dad?"

Adam glanced quickly at his son and swore under his breath when he saw the anxious look on the boy's face. Without giving himself a chance to reconsider, Adam pulled over and parked beside a huge shade tree. He stared at his hands for a moment, then leaning against the door, he turned to face his son. His voice was nonthreatening when he asked, "Are you still mad at your mom?"

Patrick held his father's gaze for a moment, then stared at the floor. "She should have told me. I think what she did was mean."

Adam reached across the seat and gently lifted Patrick's face until their eyes met. "Don't be mad at her, Patrick. She's been a good mother to you, and she did what she honestly thought was best." Adam studied the boy's pinched face, uncertain about how far to go. He didn't want to lay a guilt trip on the kid, but on the other hand, he couldn't allow Patrick to nurture this grudge any longer. Somehow he had to walk the narrow line in between. "Don't hurt your mom, Patrick. She's feeling very badly right now, and it must make her feel even worse when I can go out and buy you things she can't afford to get you, and we're out doing things together, and she's left alone."

Patrick tried to pull away as his mouth began to quiver and his eyes filled with tears. With his own emotions creating a tight ache in his throat, Adam took Patrick's hand in his. "Don't stop loving your mom because she made one mistake, Pat," he murmured huskily. "No matter what, she'd never stop loving you, you know."

Patrick took a racking breath, then buried his face tightly against his father's chest. His words were muffled when he sobbed out, "Why couldn't we have been a real family? Why did I have to wait so long for you?"

Adam had to swallow heavily before he could speak. "I don't know why. But I do know she loves you a lot, and I know she never meant to hurt you."

Patrick remained in the circle of his father's arms until he stopped crying, then he pulled away and looked up, his face smeared with tears. There was a stricken look in his eyes. "I never said goodbye to her, Dad. I should have said goodbye."

Taking Patrick's face in his hands, Adam tenderly wiped the last of his son's tears away with his thumbs, then smiled reassuringly. "Then I guess we'll just have to go back, won't we?"

Patrick nodded and gave him a wobbly smile. At least one hurdle had been cleared.

When they pulled up in front of Doc's, Patrick gave his dad a slightly sheepish look. "Will you come with me?"

Adam studied his son, then nodded. "If that's what you want."

Patrick grimaced, obviously embarrassed. "Yeah, I think you should come."

There was a glint of amusement in Adam's eyes as he climbed out of the truck and walked around to where Patrick was waiting for him. Neither of them spoke as they walked up the drive.

Patrick stopped short when he rounded the corner of the house, then as if seeking direction, he looked up at Adam, his uncertainty visible. Natalie was standing beneath a huge poplar tree staring across the river, her shoulder resting against the rough trunk, her arms folded in front of her. And her face was wet with tears.

Seeing her like that cut Adam to the quick. He tried to keep his face from revealing what he felt, and because of his constraint, his expression was rigid as he gave Patrick a gentle push in the direction of his mother.

The boy once again looked up at his father, his ashen face dominated by his dark eyes, and Adam nodded his encouragement. With his body stiff and his gait awkward, Patrick went toward his mother, his voice taut with anxiety. "Mom? I forgot to say good-bye, Mom."

Natalie jerked back from the tree and turned away from her son, quickly wiping away her tears with the back of her hand. By the time she faced him, she had an unsteady smile in place. "That didn't matter, Patrick," she said huskily, trying to reassure him with her smile.

Patrick stared at her, then with a muffled sob, he flung himself into her arms. "It does matter." His voice broke as he gave way to his tears. "I'm sorry, Mom. I'm really sorry. I don't want you to think I'm still mad at you."

With her son clasped in her embrace, Natalie dropped to her knees, her face twisted by pain. She squeezed her eyes against the flood of tears that slipped relentlessly down her face. It was obvious that she was going through some private hell, but she never made a sound. She contained the sounds of her weeping, contained the pain, the anguish, the grief.

Because of Patrick, because she didn't want him to know what she was experiencing right then, she somehow managed to hold it all in. As he watched her battle for control Adam grasped the depth of her feelings for their son; she'd sacrifice anything and everything for Patrick. Unable to cope with the gripping emotions that were threatening him, Adam had to walk away.

He went back to the truck to wait for Patrick. His face was carefully schooled as he braced his legs and leaned against the front fender of the mud-spattered vehicle. Hooking his thumbs in the front pockets of his jeans, he stared at the ground, vaguely aware that the storm had moved closer. No matter how hard he tried to keep his mind empty, he was unable to shut out the image of Natalie as she knelt before their son. So much pain. He felt so damned helpless, so trapped by sheer circumstance. There were too many unanswered questions, too many doubts, and no matter how much he might have wanted it otherwise, he could not pretend all that did not exist.

Adam caught a glimpse of color out of the corner of his eye, and inhaling slowly, he lifted his head. Patrick and Natalie were coming down the driveway toward him, and he watched them approach with a solemn stare. On the surface it appeared that all was well, but as the pair came closer, Adam could detect a forced brightness in Natalie that was very alien.

He tried not to think about it as he glanced down at his son. "Ready to go, Patrick?"

Patrick looked up at his mother, and Natalie smiled back. Adam could tell that her stiff smile had been dredged up to reassure her son, and apparently it did exactly that. Patrick grinned at his father and nodded. "Mom says there's gonna be enough thunder and lightning to scare even me."

Adam's own smile was forced as he opened the truck door for his son. "Is that a big deal—thunder and lightning?"

Patrick climbed into the vehicle and waited until his father slammed the door before he answered. "Mom hates storms so I bug her about it sometimes. She says someday I'll get mine."

The impact of Patrick's offhand comment stopped Adam cold. Natalie hated storms? Since when? Thinking it had to be some sort of private joke, Adam shot Natalie a questioning look. She was staring at him with a numb expression, her wide dark eyes dominating her ashen face. And suddenly Adam felt as though he had stumbled onto something acutely significant.

As their gazes locked and held, a crystal-clear recollection crowded into his mind: Natalie and him soaked to the skin as they huddled under the overhang of a rocky ledge. The rain was beating down around them in a chilling torrent, curtaining the mountainous landscape in gray. She was sitting between his upraised knees, her back pressed tightly against his chest as she shivered in the shelter of his arms, but her body taut with anticipation. Her rain-drenched face was lifted to the blackened skies as she sat transfixed with an impassioned awe, watching the jagged slashes of lightning rake the mountain peaks. As the storm raged around them, she was caught up in the savage drama. An almost sensual excitement radiated from her as the deafening thundercracks reverberated down the valley, shaking the ground with their violence. There had been no fear then, no fear at all.

In that electric moment as they stared at each other, Adam somehow knew that she was also remembering. He could see it in her eyes: the pain, the awful longing to recapture the love and laughter and happiness they had once shared. Unable to tear his gaze from hers, he found his will to resist the haunting sadness in her eyes was no longer there. And he was lost. Something gave way within him, and suddenly, in the space of a heartbeat, all the inner barriers he had erected to shut her out came crashing down. Everything he had restrained for so long broke loose, catching him undefended. All the feelings he'd ever felt for her were surging inside him, but now they were magnified tenfold. The impact was paralyzing. For all that had gone before, in spite of the hurt she had inflicted, in spite of what she'd done, he still loved her. He had never stopped.

CHAPTER SEVEN

THE HEAT SMOTHERED EVERY SOUND and trapped the usual neighborhood noises in its humid cocoon. A deep rumble of thunder rolled across the mountains, breaking the silence that was as suffocating as the heat.

"Come on, Dad," Patrick interjected as he squirmed impatiently on the seat. "Let's go. It's hot in here."

Adam had the strangest feeling as he stood there, his eyes still riveted on Natalie. It was as though he had been in a dream, trying to photograph something far off in the distance, but the image was blurred, indistinct. Then, as if released from some invisible bond, he was finally able to bring the shadowy image into sharp focus, making everything so profoundly clear.

"Are we going, Dad?"

It was all Adam could do to drag his attention away from the slender blond woman and look at his son. His elbows hanging out the open window, Patrick rested his chin on his folded arms and watched his father, squinting thoughtfully. From that look, Adam could well imagine the questions going through the boy's head—questions he didn't want to deal with, at least not yet.

Pushing away from the fender, he went around to the driver's side of the vehicle, opened the door and climbed in. The interior was stifling and the heat from the seat burned through his clothes as he put the key in the ignition. He glanced up and Natalie's face was framed in Patrick's window. Her hair was pulled back in its usual style, but some curls had slipped free of the pins and were lying damply against her neck. She looked so hot and exhausted as she stood there with that forced smile on her face.

As much as he wanted to stay, common sense told him there were other considerations. With Patrick sitting there watching, Adam didn't dare create a situation that carried the risk of emotional repercussions. He wasn't playing any more games with himself; he knew that if it hadn't been for Patrick's presence, he would have made some kind of overture toward her right there and then. He would have at least tried to talk. But he didn't want an audience, not even his son, when he finally bridged that gap of eleven years.

Even though he was aware of this, it was the hardest thing he'd ever had to do when he started the truck, put it in gear and pulled away. It was as though he was physically connected to her as he watched her diminish in the rearview mirror. He felt as if he was abandoning her, and that feeling deepened when he turned the corner and she was lost from view.

They had driven through town and across the bridge, then turned onto the old forestry road that eventually intersected the narrow trail that led up to the campsite. The dark clouds hadn't yet obscured the sun, and the long dark shadows and bright splotches of sunshine flipped by as they started to climb through the thinning forest. The fragrance of fir and cedar wafted in, and above the noise of the truck, Adam could hear the wild rush of the river that was now below them.

Patrick hooked his heels on the edge of the seat and wrapped his arms around his legs. He sat hunched in silence, the breeze from the open window ruffling through his hair as he stared out, obviously lost in thought. With his bottom lip caught between his teeth he finally turned to study his father. An anxious look on his face, Patrick tipped his head to one side and asked hesitantly, "Do you still like Mom?"

Unconsciously, Adam tightened his grip on the wheel as he tried to contend with the host of disturbing feelings that one innocent question aroused. How could he explain to this small boy that he felt as though he'd torn himself in half when he'd driven off and left her standing there? How could he explain that he had just come fact-to-face with something he'd been trying to evade for years? How could he put all that into words this child could understand?

His voice was rough and unsteady when he said, "Yes, I do...very much."

Patrick turned under the restraint of the seat belt, then rested his chin on his upraised knees. "She still likes you, too," he said, the anxious look suddenly gone. Not receiving any comment from his father, he continued, "She said you were special."

Adam's stomach nose-dived as he was hit with an electrifying mixture of fear, excitement and hope—the kind of reaction that made it nearly impossible to breathe. He cast a sharp glance at his son. "When did she say that?"

"The other night—after you took me canoeing."

His pulse pounding heavily, Adam had to fight to keep his tone casual. "How come you were talking about me?"

Patrick shrugged and leaned back against the seat. "I was telling her about all we did, and she said I was a lucky kid, that you were really special. She looked like she was gonna cry when she said it, like it made her feel bad." He turned to look at his father, a perplexed expression on his brown face. "Why would she say it like that, like it made her feel real sad? Do you know why?"

His face suddenly drawn, Adam was gripped with an intense rush of emotion, and his knuckles turned white on the steering wheel as he braked, a cloud of dust enveloping them as they slid to a stop. Bracing his arm on the open window, he clenched his jaw as he covered his eyes with his hand. If there had been room on the narrow mountain road to turn around, he would have done it. He couldn't handle this empty feeling, knowing he had left her there alone.

"What's the matter? Are you sick?" Patrick's eyes were wide with alarm, and his hands were awkward as he hastily fumbled with the buckle on the seat belt. He moved toward his father, his small face pinched with concern as he looked at Adam. "What's wrong, Dad?" he asked, a tenor of fear in his voice. "You look so funny."

Adam didn't think he could get a full breath past the excruciating tightness in his chest, but he slowly inhaled, then lifted his head and looked at his son. His voice was gruff. "Nothing's wrong, Pat." He made his body relax as he slouched back in his seat, his face suddenly very haggard. He took another deep breath, then said unevenly, "How about we go back and get your mother?"

Patrick stared at him for a second, then his anxious expression changed and lightened, as if he finally figured out the deeper meaning behind his father's words. "She won't like it up here if there's thunder and lightning," he said finally. "She gets all nervous in a bad storm." There was an air of uncertainty about him as he moved away from his father. It was obvious he was mulling something over as he sat back on the seat, raised his knees and locked his arms around them. He frowned slightly, then began absently picking at a scab on his leg. Finally he looked up at his father. "Besides, could we maybe talk, Dad?"

"About what, son?"

Patrick hesitated for a moment, then shrugged self-consciously as he deliberately avoided Adam's gaze. "You know. About you and Mom...and everything."

Adam considered that for a moment, realizing that some of Patrick's unanswered questions had to be dealt with before anything else. He switched off the ignition, then undid his seat belt and leaned back against the door, one arm loosely draped across the steering wheel. There was a note of quiet reassurance in his voice as he asked, "What exactly do you want to know?"

Patrick fiddled with the cuff of his jeans before he looked up, then squirming a little under his father's steady scrutiny, he lowered his head again. "Did you used to like each other a lot?"

Adam sensed this was something that was vitally important to Patrick's sense of security, to know that his mother and father really cared about each other. Adam's voice was very low when he said, "I loved your mom very much when we were young, Patrick." He looked out the window, waiting for the aching constriction in his throat to ease, then said softly, "And those feelings don't change easily, Pat. I still do love her."

Patrick's voice was a barely audible whisper. "I don't think she knows that, Dad. Are you going to tell her?"

The constriction became more painful. Adam leaned his head back and closed his eyes. His voice was ragged with emotion when he said softly, "Yes, I am."

IT WAS MORE THAN AN HOUR later when Adam and Patrick pulled into the clearing by the trailer. And it had been a very difficult hour. When Patrick was finally given the chance to open up and ask questions, Adam was dumbfounded by the kinds of queries the boy had made. Not only about Natalie and Adam, but about Patrick's paternal grandparents, Adam's boyhood and a range of other topics. He seemed to have an insatiable thirst to find out everything he could about his parents. And the more Patrick asked, the more Adam understood just how much this boy had bottled up.

They had climbed out of the truck and were walking through a thick stand of fir trees on their way to the lake. Patrick slipped his hand into his dad's and swung around. "What do Grandma and Grandpa Rutherford look like?"

"Well, your grandmother's tall and has hair about the color of mine. She really likes to swim and play tennis, and she and your grandfather both learned how to sail after they moved to the coast."

"Does she work?"

"She used to teach school, but now she works part-time in a craft store."

"And Grandpa?"

"Well, everybody says we look a lot alike. He was a foreman at the mill when we lived here, but he retired when they moved to Victoria. He's really big and he laughs a lot." Adam glanced down at his son and smiled reassuringly. "You'll like them, Patrick. Your grandparents always made time for kids."

"Are we going to visit them pretty soon?"

Adam considered the question briefly, then answered, "I don't see why not. We'll have to check with your mom."

Patrick scuffed his feet through the thick layer of dried needles and leaves, then looked up at Adam. "Can she come?"

Adam tried to keep his voice neutral when he answered. "If she'd like, sure."

"Do you want her to come?"

He experienced that same aching tightness in his chest when he answered softly, "Yes, I want her to come."

Reassured, Patrick squeezed his hand and grinned up at him. "Can we go fishing now?"

Relieved that the inquisition was temporarily set aside, Adam grinned back. "I think it could be arranged."

The small secluded valley where Adam had parked the trailer was particularly beautiful, and he couldn't believe his good fortune when he'd discovered it. He'd been exploring old roads, looking for good filming locations and happened on this spot strictly by chance.

A few years before, some of the locals had tried to start up a guide and outfitter's association, and this site had been part of their development. There were two small cabins, a corral and a shelter for pack animals, and a small wooden dock that angled out into the lake. The developers had also installed a septic tank and built a cistern that filled from a nearby stream. Since everything in the trailer ran off either propane or batteries, all Adam had to do was install a large propane tank and rig up a pump to get water from the cistern into the trailer. The cabins had their windows broken, the doors were missing and the roofs leaked, but it would take very little work to make the necessary repairs. The location had everything he wanted, especially the peace and serenity that was an integral part of this wilderness valley.

The cabins and trailer were situated on a slight rise of land at the north end of the lake, the natural clearing heavily dotted with clumps of alder, white birch and pine, and farther back the verdant forest crowded down the mountainside. The crystal-clear alpine lake that was cupped in the valley was the headwater for the sparkling mountain stream that bordered the campsite. At the far end of the lake, the small valley folded open to a larger one that offered a magnificent view of the rugged purple mountains. It was one of the prettiest spots he had seen in a long time.

But now there was a strange hush as the storm clouds trundled over the mountain peaks, darkening the sky and eventually covering the sun. And suddenly the ominous quiet was split by a roll of thunder, which echoed for miles along the blackened heavens.

Patrick had managed to catch one small lake trout before Adam suggested they'd better head back to shore if they wanted to beat the rain. They had just finished beaching the canoe and putting the fishing gear away when the first drops of rain fell, leaving large wet splotches on the dusty ground.

The pewter-gray lake was beginning to get rough with whitecaps, the agitation forecasting a strong wind. Adam checked to make sure everything in the camp was secure before he followed his son into the trailer, the huge drops of rain spotting his blue denim shirt. He had turned to close the door behind him when a vehicle pulled up beside the Bronco, and he frowned slightly when he recognized the car was Doc's.

Adam had ambivalent feelings about the old man. Part of him deeply resented his intrusion, and part of him recalled the hours the two of them had spent hiking these very mountains. But the resentment won out and his voice was tense as he said, "Your grandfather's here, Patrick."

Patrick let out a whoop of approval as he brushed past Adam and jumped out of the trailer, then started running toward Doc. Adam followed, his face wiped clean of any expression, an uncompromising set to his chin. Sticking his hands in the back pockets of his jeans, he nodded to the old pharmacist. "I didn't expect to see you up here, Doc."

Doc read the underlying implication beneath Adam's cool greeting, and the warm smile he'd greeted Patrick with faded as he steadily met Adam's gaze. "I need to talk to you, lad." Realizing Patrick was watching them with an anxious look, he ruffled the boy's hair as he grinned down at him. "And I had to see if the fish were biting, young Patrick. I had my mouth all set for a good feed of lake trout."

The spattering of rain was picking up momentum, and a gust of wind whipped dust and dead leaves into a blustery whirlwind. Patrick caught Doc's hand and started dragging him toward the trailer. "Come on, Grandpa. Hurry up, or we're going to get wet." With their heads bent against the wind, they crossed the clearing and entered the trailer. As Adam pulled the door firmly shut behind them, the boy scrambled up on one of the padded seats by the small table and grinned at Doc. "I only caught one fish before we had to come in, but we can share it, Grandpa. Dad said he's going to have steak instead."

Doc held back a smile as he looked at the very small fish lying in the sink, and said dryly, "Then your father is an eminently wise man."

His eyes were twinkling as he looked at Adam. There was something about the amused look in the old man's eyes that neutralized Adam's annoyance, and he found himself grinning back. "I take it I could interest you in a steak, too, Doc."

"You could indeed, lad. You could indeed."

As the sky grew darker and the wind picked up tempo, Adam set about preparing a meal for them all.

It took him back in time to watch Doc with his son. The old man still wove the same spellbinding stories that Adam remembered so well from his own youth, stories that were based on woodsmanship and a far-reaching knowledge and understanding of the wilderness. Their appeal had not lessened over the years. Adam found himself wondering if Doc had ever considered putting them on paper. Properly illustrated, they would make a fantastic children's book. It was something worth thinking about.

By the time they'd finished eating, the sky was black and the wind was gusting so strongly it was rocking the trailer, yet the heavy rain hadn't come. But Adam knew the cloudburst wasn't very far away. It was obvious that Doc had planned to stay the night, so when Patrick finally curled up in the corner and fell asleep, Adam picked him up and carried him back to the small bedroom at the back of the trailer. The table in the kitchen folded down and the seats pulled out, making another very comfortable double bed where Doc could sleep.

Quietly closing the folding door that separated the bedroom from the rest of the trailer, Adam went to a cupboard above the tiny sink and lifted out two mugs. "Would you like coffee, Doc?"

"If you please, Adam." He fished his pipe out of his pocket and nodded his thanks as Adam slid an ashtray across the table to him. Adam set both steaming mugs on the table, then slipped into the seat across from the old man. Leaning against the wall, he stretched his legs out on the long seat, then flexed one knee and draped his arm across it. Absently he took a sip of coffee, his eyes narrowing as he watched Doc go through the ritual of filling his pipe.

As the old gentleman put the flaring match to the bowl, the expression in Adam's eyes changed. There was an edge to his voice when he reminded, "You said you wanted to talk."

Doc glanced at him sharply, then fixed his attention on the match as he lit his pipe. A cloud of fragrant smoke screened his face as he drew in until the tamped tobacco glowed red, then he carefully shook out the match and dropped it in the ashtray. He took another puff, and cradling his pipe in his hand, he leaned back and met Adam's unwavering stare.

"Yes, lad, I do want to talk."

"About what?"

Doc rested his arms on the table and, avoiding looking at Adam, he fingered the elaborate carving on the bowl of his pipe. "I know it's none of my business, Adam, but I'd like to talk to you about Patrick."

That was unexpected, and Adam studied Doc, trying to figure out what the old man was leading up to. He expected him to bring up Natalie, not Patrick. "What about Patrick?" he asked flatly.

Doc's expression was grave as he stared at him for a moment, then answered, "I was wondering what arrangements you're considering for the lad."

In a stall for time, Adam took another sip of coffee, then cradled the mug in his hands as he slowly rubbed his thumb against the rough pottery texture. His mouth was taut when he finally spoke. "You think I'm planning on keeping him with me, don't you?"

Doc heaved a sigh then tipped his head. "Natalie has been deeply troubled ever since Patrick arrived, and I've wondered what's been weighing so heavily on her. I thought perhaps there had been some discussion about the boy. She hasn't that much longer before she has to go back to her job, and she's been so quiet. I thought it had something to do with him."

Adam leaned his head against the wall, his face drawn as he stared at the ceiling. "I told her I wouldn't try to take Patrick away from her." He turned and looked at his companion, his eyes revealing more than he realized. "I don't want to hurt her, Doc. And I haven't a clue what I'm going to do. I know she'll be leaving in a couple of weeks, and we haven't even talked about . . . anything." A feeling of defeat settled on Adam. What was he going to do if she decided to leave again? How in hell was he going to handle that?

Wearily rubbing his hand across his face, he straightened and looked at the white-haired gentleman sitting across the table from him. Doc's head was lowered; he was obviously deep in his own thoughts. He stroked his bottom lip with the stem of his pipe, his brow creased with a heavy frown. Suddenly it became important to Adam that he clear the air about what had happened so long ago.

"I acted pretty damned irresponsibly eleven years ago, Doc. I realize now you were caught in a bind, especially when Natalie didn't want me to find out she was pregnant."

Doc dismissed his apology with a wave. "You were hurting, lad. I knew that."

The wind rocked the trailer, and a crack of thunder sounded overhead, finally splitting the skies. The rain came lashing down, drumming heavily on the aluminum roof. The racket echoed hollowly in the trailer, and both men fell silent under the deluge, the smell of rain and wet forest seeping in through the closed windows.

Adam emptied his mug and set it back on the table, then laced his fingers around his upraised knee and turned his attention back to Doc. After a moment of deliberation he asked, "What exactly happened in the accident, Doc?"

An unusually alert expression appeared in Doc's eyes. Adam frowned slightly, and some gut feeling pushed him on. "Something happened to Natalie in that accident that left some damned deep emotional scars, and I think it had something to do with her mother finding out she was pregnant."

Adam watched Doc like a hawk, and a feeling of expectation cut through him when he saw how tightly the older man was clamping his pipe between his teeth. He'd struck a nerve. Adam pushed a little more. "I also think that the accident was no accident. I think Jean Willard drove off the cliff deliberately."

His arms still folded across his chest, Doc dropped his head and fixed his gaze on the ashtray in front of him as he puffed agitatedly on his pipe. He was carefully calculating his answer, and Adam tried to assess the real meaning of his reaction. His tone curt, Adam prodded, "I think you owe me, Doc. I want to know what in hell happened to make Natalie run. There was more to her disappearing than Patrick, that's for damned sure. She's admitted that much."

A brilliant flash of lightning sliced the darkness, followed eventually by a sharp crack of thunder that rolled menacingly along the heavens until it disappeared in a distant grumble. An unnerving tension started to build as Adam watched Doc, waiting for an answer. But as the tension grew, Adam's senses became keener. A sobering feeling of premonition sent a chill down his spine, and every muscle in his body reacted as his pulse rate increased. He was carefully disciplined as he persisted quietly, "I want to know about the accident, Doc. I want to know exactly what happened."

The silence was so thick he could have cut it with a knife, and Adam kept clenching and unclenching his jaw, fighting to maintain a veneer of calm. But it was a thin veneer. He forced himself to remain motionless, but he was poised and waiting. He sensed he was finally going to get answers to questions that had tormented him for years. It seemed like an eternity passed before the old man lifted his head and looked at him. Adam was caught completely off guard. Doc looked like he had aged twenty years in a space of moments. And it unsettled Adam even more when he realized there were tears of distress in the old man's eyes.

Doc's voice quavered. "Natalie wasn't in the car accident, Adam. She was already in the hospital in Calgary when her mother drove off that cliff."

Adam had been prepared for a bombshell, but nothing on earth could have prepared him for this. There was a moment, one split second of time before he could even think, let alone respond. He stared dumbfoundedly at Doc. "What in hell are you saying?"

"Adam, it's not a pleasant—"

"Damn it, just tell me what in hell happened to her! I need to know." He had a nearly uncontrollable urge to shake the answer out of Doc as a sickening dread started building in him. His voice carried an undercurrent of threat as he ground out, "For God's sake, answer me, Doc."

Their eyes locked, and Adam was unnerved by what he saw. Suddenly he was very cold. Like a nightmare in slow motion, he waited for the answer.

"She was raped, Adam. That bastard of a stepfather raped her."

There was a moment of frozen disbelief, then something exploded in Adam. Unable to contain all the feelings that were tearing through him, he stumbled to his feet. Like a wounded animal that was racked with pain, he started pacing back and forth in the confined area, his whole body braced against the agony of finally knowing the dark, ugly truth.

"Adam...Adam, lad," Doc soothed as he stood up and grasped the younger man by the shoulder. "Don't do this to yourself, lad. She wouldn't want it, you know that."

Adam turned away abruptly, and gripping the sink, he lowered his head, his body shaking with violent spasms. His voice was ragged when he was finally able to whisper, "Tell me everything, Doc."

There was a pause before Doc answered, his voice infinitely weary, his Irish brogue suddenly thick. "She wouldn't tell you, lad, because she was terrified you'd kill him. She didn't want you to have blood on your hands because of her. She loved you too much for that."

Doc's softly spoken words were like an injection of ice water, and Adam slowly straightened, his body trembling with shock. Numbness claimed him as he turned to stare at the white-haired man who was hunched over the table. "I would have," he whispered hoarsely. "I would have ripped him apart with my bare hands." It was no idle threat, and anyone hearing him or seeing the look on his face wouldn't have doubted him for a minute.

"She knew that, lad. She told me the night it happened. She said, 'He'd end up in jail, Doc. He'd go to jail because of me.' She couldn't bear that, Adam. She was trying to protect you, lad."

Praying that this cold, immobilizing numbness held until he heard the whole story, Adam went back to the table and sat down, his face drained of color, his hands unsteady as he raked them through his hair. "I want to know the whole story—from the beginning."

Doc puffed on his pipe then rested his elbows on the table and stared at the ashtray, quietly recalling the details. "Jean had been sent to Calgary to a specialist because of her back, and Natalie knew her mother would be gone for a few days. The lass suspected she was pregnant, but she thought that with her mother gone, it would be a perfect opportunity to find out for certain. She'd taken a bus out of the valley and went somewhere else so no one would find out. She'd been so careful not to give anything away, but somehow Carl found out."

Adam felt utter revulsion rising up in him again as he whispered, "So he went after her."

"No, he didn't—not right away. Maybe if he'd confronted her that morning when he found out, things wouldn't have turned out the way they did. But from what I gathered later, he'd spent all day drinking in the hotel and brooding about it. Being the kind of man he was, he ended up in a dirty mood. Old Mike Barnes was in the bar when he left, and he said that he'd never seen a man in such an ugly mood. It was seven o'clock when he left the bar, and it appears that he went straight home.''

''And Natalie was there alone.''

Doc leaned forward, his face heavily lined, his eyes bleak with remembering as he murmured gruffly, ''Yes, the lass was there alone.''

The muscles in Adam's face were hard and his body was rigid with restraint as he slid out of the seat, stood and opened the cupboard door above the table. He brought down a bottle of rye and a small stack of plastic glasses, then unscrewed the top and poured himself a drink. He sat back down and stared at the glass a moment, then tossed the entire contents down in one shot. His hands were very unsteady as he poured himself another drink. ''Go on,'' he said hoarsely.

''I don't know much about what happened after he got home, Adam,'' the old man continued softly, trying to ease the horror. ''She would never tell anyone what all he did to her. All I know is that he showed up in a foul rage, told Natalie he knew she was carrying your baby and that he was going to make damned sure she'd never carry it to term.''

A shudder coursed through Adam's body and his head shot up, his face white with shock. ''What are you saying, Doc?''

Doc reached across the table and covered Adam's fists with his hands, his face haggard with sorrow and compassion. "He nearly beat her to death first, Adam. I couldn't believe how battered she was when she showed up at my door. He'd smashed her jaw, several ribs were cracked, her elbow was dislocated, her pelvis was broken—" Doc wiped his eyes with the back of his hand, then clasped both hands around his empty mug as if to stop their violent shaking. His voice was so strained it was nearly inaudible when he went on. "He'd used his belt on her. Her body was a mass of welts. I hardly recognized her when I opened the door."

Adam knew a rage like he'd never known before— a still, cold and deadly rage. What kind of a bastard was Willard to do that to her? What kind of twisted mind could create such punishment? Adam felt sick to his very soul, knowing Natalie was the helpless target of a perverted bloodlust that was warped beyond rationality, the victim of the most revolting savage violation. Even though it happened so long ago, he still wanted to kill him.

And when he was finally able to speak, his voice held a deadly ring. "What did she tell you?"

Doc slowly shook his head. "She only told me what he said when he first came home. And she told me that he raped her. But beyond that, she refused to say. All the months she was in the hospital, she would freeze up and panic the instant anyone tried to uncover exactly what had happened that night. All I know is that it was seven o'clock when Carl left the bar, and it was just after nine-thirty when the lass showed up at my place."

Two and a half hours. Alone and defenseless. She was subjected to that kind of inhuman brutality for two and a half hours.

Doc's voice droned on in a weary monotone. "I called George Johnson over—he was still practicing medicine then. He said she had to have a damned good surgeon and the very best of care, so we decided to get her to a major medical center. He knew her lung had been perforated by a broken rib, so he put in a chest tube and patched her up enough so that she could tolerate the trip. It was a terrible night, storming badly and low cloud cover, but the weather was clearing to the east so Calgary was accessible. And her mother was already there. So George made arrangements for a float plane to meet us at Catherine Lake."

The old man sat back and folded his arms across his chest, his eyes solemn with this grim reminiscence. "During that drive to the airplane, George and I agreed that it would only make things more unbearable for Natalie if anyone found out what that bastard had done to her, so we decided to start laying a smoke screen. If we could help it, no one would find out what had happened that night."

The steady drone of Doc's voice had been oddly subduing and Adam was able to ease some of the rigidness in his body. In an attempt to get a grip on himself and block out the ugly images that were pressing in on him, he concentrated on the sound of the rain on the roof. It was frightening, the price she'd paid for loving him. How had she endured it all?

Adam knew the only way he could keep from losing control was to focus on the facts. He poured himself another drink and looked at Doc. "What happened when you got her to Calgary?"

"She went directly to surgery." Doc fumbled a handkerchief from his sweater pocket and roughly blew his nose, then stuffed it back in his pocket. Picking up his pipe, he clamped it between his teeth before he went on. "It was touch and go for a few hours. They wanted to take the babe, to abort him— but Natalie went hysterical when they approached her on it. She said she'd rather die than lose the babe."

Propping his elbows on the table, Adam rested his forehead on his tightly interlaced fingers, obscuring his tortured face from Doc's view. "Dammit, Doc," he whispered unevenly, "she was only sixteen. She was only sixteen."

"I know, lad. She was no more than a babe herself. But she was determined to have that child. It was the only thing that kept her going all those months. I don't know what would have happened to her if she'd lost it."

Adam's shoulders were shaking, and unable to watch the younger man's anguish, Doc slowly got up, his movements slow and stiff as he stooped and picked up Patrick's jacket off the floor. His words were somewhat muffled when he continued to speak in that same quiet monotone. "It was hard for me not to tell you the truth when you came to me, Adam. But I was afraid that her worst fears would come true if I did tell you, and she was so...fragile. And on top of everything else, there was what happened to her mother. I didn't think she could take it if anything happened to you." Bracing his hand on his thigh, he slowly straightened and looked at Adam. "I knew what you were feeling, lad. But I had to do what was best for her." He dropped the jacket on the counter, then stood in the soft glow from the light above the sink, his head lowered in reflection. "She put up a long fight, the lass did. She wasn't discharged until after Patrick was born."

Dragging his hands down his face, Adam sat back and closed his eyes. "So that explains why Patrick was born in Calgary." But then, it explained more than that. Hauling in a deep breath, he turned to look at Doc. "What about Jean's car accident? Or was it an accident?"

Doc lifted his head and shrugged. "We'll never know, lad. We'll never know. Natalie believes it was deliberate."

"What happened?"

"We had to contact Jean at her hotel so she could meet us at the hospital—she had to sign the release form for Natalie's surgery. At first, she wouldn't believe us when we told her what happened."

"What changed her mind?"

Doc came back to the table and wearily sat down. "When they were getting Natalie ready for surgery, they discovered that she had a piece of material still clutched in her hand. It was a piece of Carl's plaid shirt, and Jean recognized the pattern."

Adam felt like he'd received so many crippling blows that he couldn't react to anything else, but he reacted to that. A sudden picture formed of a nurse bending over Natalie's bruised and battered body, carefully prying open her hand. He pushed on. "What did Jean do?"

"Not much then. She sat in the waiting room, staring straight ahead, not a trace of expression on her face—frightening, in a way. It was late in the afternoon of the following day when the doctor said he was feeling fairly hopeful about the lass. Jean excused herself to go to the rest room. That was the last time I saw her."

"How did you find out about her accident?"

"George had flown back with the plane. He called me at the hospital when he got word that she was dead. That's when he came up with the scheme to tell everyone that Natalie was in the car with her mother."

Another gust of wind rocked the trailer, driving the rain loudly against the metal exterior as another crack of thunder sounded overhead. The dampness was beginning to pervade the warmth of the trailer, bringing with it a chilling clamminess.

Realizing how cool it was, Adam got up and went into the bedroom to check on Patrick. As he gazed down at his sleeping son, a strangling knot of emotion expanded in his chest. And with a sudden stab of awareness, he realized the price Natalie had paid to give him this child. His hands were unsteady and very gentle as he drew the quilt up and tucked it around the boy.

Doc had relit his pipe and a cloud of smoke was curling around his head as Adam quietly closed the folding door. Slowly rolling his shoulders to try to work out the aching tension in the muscles across his back, Adam slid into the seat. Resting one elbow on the table, he leaned back against the wall and looked at Doc. "There wasn't one leak to give your story away. And God knows, I was sure trying to dig up something. How did you ever manage to keep the lid on this?"

Doc drew in deeply, sending another curl of smoke upward, then smiled wryly. "Oh, I had a little help from my friends."

"How many people knew the whole truth?"

"Myself, George Johnson, and now you."

Adam rested the back of his hand across his mouth as he continued to watch the old man. "I take it there was never any discussion about going to the cops?"

"No. Never. Natalie didn't want it. If she was unable to bring herself to tell the doctors what had happened, she certainly could have never managed it in a court of law." His brogue was more pronounced than ever when he said quietly, "She couldna do it, Adam. It would have been an unbearable humiliation for her to face Carl *and* the town...especially without her mother. And it would have changed nothing."

The sounds of the thunder squall intensified, and in an attempt to disconnect the treadmill of his thoughts, Adam concentrated on the storm. The fir trees behind the trailer were moaning loudly as the wind cut through their heavy, swaying boughs. And he knew from the torrent outside that the narrow rutted track would already have deep trenches cut from the deluge washing down the mountain. There was another blinding flash of lightning, closely followed by a crack of thunder that shook the ground. He turned his head and listened, expecting to hear some noise from the bedroom. But Patrick slept on, unafraid. Unafraid.

Suddenly Adam remembered what Patrick had said when they'd stopped to talk. *"She won't like it up here if there's thundering and lightning. She gets all nervous when there's a bad storm.*" He had wondered why, but now he knew. It was chillingly apparent why Natalie had developed such an irrational fear of storms. Only it wasn't irrational. It was part of her nightmare. And she was all alone.

Propelled into action by that grim realization, Adam nearly knocked the table off its wall brackets, sending Doc's ashtray and the bottle of rye crashing to the floor. The old man's head jerked up, his eyebrows raised in a startled expression. "What's the matter, lad? Is something wrong?"

Adam yanked open a small storage space beside the fridge and started pulling out his gear. Determination was stamped into every line in his face. "I'm going back to town."

Doc's expression turned to one of incredulity. "Don't be daft, man. You can't go back down that road in weather like this. It isn't fit for man or beast. You'd be taking a terrible risk. You could slide into the canyon!"

Ignoring Doc's plea, Adam rammed his feet into boots, then grabbed his slicker from the hook by the door and put it on. "I'm not leaving her in there alone," he said grimly. "Patrick made a few comments about her being terrified of storms. At the time I wondered why she'd developed an aversion to them, but now I know. You said it was storming the night it happened, didn't you?"

"I did, lad. But you're daft to try to get off this mountain now."

Adam picked up a large battery-operated light, a hatchet and a thick coil of yellow rope. Slinging the rope over his shoulder, he went to the door. "If Patrick wakes up, tell him I've gone for his mother."

"Adam, wait—"

But Adam ignored the old man's entreaty and stepped out into the storm, slamming the door shut behind him. The rain felt like sleet against his skin and the wind caught his breath as he struggled through the drenching blackness, his head down against the driving force. Lightning zigzagged across the sky, and in that instant of illumination he was able to see deep puddles gathering on the ground and the trees bending and twisting in the wind. In seconds his jeans were drenched and clinging to his legs, the rain runneling down his neck. Adam shivered and yanked up the collar of the slicker, then hunched his shoulders against the gale.

But he was barely aware of what was happening around him. The only thing he could think of was Natalie and this compelling need to get to her. There was a crack of thunder, and an eerie chill crawled up the back of his neck. Damn, he wished she wasn't all alone.

CHAPTER EIGHT

THE STORM CONTINUED to assault the earth as the rain beat down, the torrent cutting deep gashes in the narrow winding road and turning the brown clay soil into treacherously slick mud. The conditions were so severe, Adam doubted if he would have even made it out of the campsite without a four-wheel-drive vehicle. Regardless of the terrible conditions, his sense of urgency drove him to the brink of recklessness as he pushed on through the slashing rain, his need to get to Natalie fueled by anxiety.

That compulsion nearly overrode his common sense when he rounded a bend and found the road blocked by a fir tree that had been uprooted by the storm, its sweeping boughs creating an impenetrable barrier. Ready to explode with frustration, Adam fought down the urge to abandon the truck and walk out. He knew rashness was the last thing he could allow to govern his actions. Swearing under his breath, he gritted his teeth and grabbed the hatchet and rope from the back seat, then climbed out of the truck into the chillingly wet night. Even at the speed he worked, it seemed to take hours to clear a path wide enough for the vehicle. And by the time he could proceed, he was soaked to the skin and nearly frantic.

The thunderstorm had moved down the valley by the time Adam drove into town. Lightning zigzagged across the sky, thunder detonated overhead with a deafening crack and the rain pounded down even harder. Water several inches deep gathered along the curbs, the downpour too heavy for the drains to handle, and branches lay broken and twisted in the deserted streets.

As Adam turned down the road that led to Doc's, the lights along the route went out, the electrical service abruptly disrupted by the storm. His anxiety escalated as the sudden darkness seemed to swallow him up, and all he could think about was Natalie alone in that house with no power. The headlights barely penetrated the gray curtain of slicing rain as he drove down the blackened street and turned into the driveway. He could feel his heart hammering wildly against his ribs as he grabbed the battery-powered light and sprang out of the mud-encrusted truck.

The thin beam of light cut through the blinding torrent as Adam sloshed through a huge puddle of water, then took the stairs at the back of the house two at a time, the rain pelting against him. His jeans were clinging to his legs and his blond hair was plastered against his head when he entered the porch. Stripping off his slicker and boots, he banged on the door leading into the main house, his apprehension growing by the minute.

Thunder rattled the windows, drowning out the sound, and he knocked again. He paused for a moment, waiting for a response, but there was none. He called out, then tried the door. With a strange feeling of caution, he entered the living room, the light in his hand creating ominously shifting shadows. The room was empty and he paused again, trying to detect some sound that would tell him where she was. But the only sounds he could hear were those of the storm and his own frantic heartbeat.

"Natalie?"

Nothing.

Drawn by instinct, he turned toward the hallway that led to the bedrooms. "Natalie, it's Adam."

He thought he heard something, but it was so indistinct he wondered if he'd only imagined it. Straining to hear above the sounds of the storm, he followed the shaft of light down the black tunnel of the hallway and paused at the first doorway he came to. Slowly he swept the light around the room. It was furnished with a single bed and a dresser, and was obviously the room that Patrick was using. And it was empty.

"Natalie, where are you?"

But the only answer was the rain pounding on the roof and the wind rattling the windows. Adam shone the light down the hall, the beam moving across a closed door at the very end. Walking silently through the darkness, he grasped the knob and pushed the door open. It was Doc's study, and for a moment, Adam thought it was empty, as well. But as he moved, the shaft of light focused on Natalie, pinning her against the far wall.

Dressed in a blue-and-white striped nightshirt, she was standing in the corner by a heavy old-fashioned wooden filing cabinet, her body rigidly pressed against the dark oak, her eyes wide with alarm. A hideaway bed was situated beside the cluttered oak desk, and from the rumpled state of the covers, he assumed she had been in bed.

Adam stood by the door, his wet clothes clinging to him. "I didn't mean to frighten you, Nat, but I was worried when you didn't answer the door." She didn't move a muscle and Adam took another step toward her. As he moved, there was a flash of light against metal, and he froze, dumbfounded by what he saw.

She clutched a long flat letter opener, the blade thin and lethal. His eyes flew to her face, and it hit him that the expression he saw in her eyes went beyond simple alarm—this was paralyzing terror. He finally grasped what was happening. Her deep-seated fear of thunderstorms had gained control, and she was reliving the horror that had been inflicted on her years before. She was so overwrought that anything—a sound, a movement, a single careless act—could push her into reacting. Adam had never felt so ill-equipped in his life, yet somehow he managed to keep his voice calm when he spoke. "Don't be afraid of me, Natalie. I won't hurt you. I just came to talk."

There was not even the slightest indication that she had heard him. Desperately trying to break through her wail of fear, he moved a step closer and cautiously stretched out his hand and murmured softly, "Give me the letter opener, Natalie. I won't touch you or come any closer, I promise. Just give me the letter opener."

Her hand moved, the gleaming blade shifting dangerously. Adam realized he dared not move an inch closer. Slowly he withdrew his hand and backed away, his eyes glued on the weapon as he frantically tried to think of some way to reach her. He thought of Patrick. He tried to keep his voice steady and nonthreatening. "Patrick was worried about you—he said you'd be afraid of the storm."

There was only the slightest response, but it was there. He saw it in her eyes. But then the fear was back and she shrank away and it suddenly hit him that her terror was magnified by the fact that she had no idea who was behind the light. He didn't even want to think of the terrifying thoughts that were going through her mind right then, but he knew he had to say or do something that would penetrate her fear.

He was still searching for solutions when the lights came back on. The lamp by the bed was small and sent out a muted glow, but it was enough to illuminate Adam's face. And with his expression taut with anxiety, he watched her, desperately longing to go to her, knowing he didn't dare. His voice was hoarse and heavily strained. "Please let me have the letter opener, Nat. I'll leave if you want me to, but just give me the letter opener."

For one awful moment, she continued to stare at him, then as if waking up from a horrible dream, her expression changed. A violent tremor shuddered through her, and she whispered his name as she closed her eyes, her knees slowly buckling beneath her.

Adam caught her before she went down. Holding her around the waist in a viselike grip, he grasped the letter opener, but she wouldn't let go. He caught her wrist and drew her arm away from her body. "Let me have the letter opener, Nat," he whispered gruffly. "You have to open your hand."

Natalie shivered again, then turned her face into his shoulder, her voice shaking so badly he could barely understand her. "I can't."

She was in such a state of shock she couldn't relax her muscles, and Adam had to pry her fingers from the carved ivory handle. As soon as he worked it free, he threw it amid the clutter on the desk, then gathered her into his embrace. An enervating rush of relief poured through him, and every muscle in his body went weak as he locked his arms around her, his heart slamming against his ribs. Suspended in the aftermath of fear, he began to tremble as he pressed her head against his shoulder, his face haggard. For a moment she remained stiff and unyielding, but then as though her strength suddenly evaporated, she melted against him.

Adam squeezed his eyes shut, and his breathing became labored. This was the first time he'd touched her, and the feel of her body against his unleashed a storm of sensations. He felt the kind of fulfillment he hadn't experienced for a very long time, and he savored that. This is what he'd been aching to do for so long—to hold her, to feel her warmth, her softness. He buried his face against her hair as he tightened his arms around her, longing to absorb her body into his.

Both of them were emotionally raw as they clung to each other, their bodies molded tightly together. But somewhere in the passage of time, Adam became aware of the fact that Natalie was still shivering. The last thing he wanted to do was let her go, but his common sense told him she should be wrapped in a warm, dry blanket, not getting more chilled from his wet clothes. Very reluctantly he forced himself to loosen his hold on her. But when he tried to ease her away from him, she wouldn't let go.

Her voice was barely audible as she whispered, "Please, Adam. Please. Don't go."

Her plea destroyed what little resolve Adam had, and with infinite tenderness, he gathered her tightly against him and murmured softly against her hair, "You're shivering, Nat, and I'm wet. You're going to get so cold." Hooking his thumb under her chin, Adam gently lifted her face. She looked absolutely ravaged, and her eyes were still haunted by fear. Only now it was a different kind of fear—the fear of what was yet to come.

He began to caress her back with long soothing strokes, his eyes bleak as he stared into the shadows. His touch was firm, yet each motion was slow and gentle. He waited until she was lulled into a state of calm before he said, "Doc told me the whole story tonight. That's why I came."

It seemed to take a second for his words to register, then she pulled away, trying to break free of his hold. Adam held her fast as her body stiffened, then a choked sound was torn from her as she twisted again. He cradled her closer and felt an awful tension build in her.

"No," she whispered brokenly. "He gave his word he would never tell you."

Adam pressed his cheek against the fragrant silk of her hair. "Don't, Nat. Don't feel that way. Nothing you can tell me is going to change how I feel about you."

He felt her tense, then she became stiff and unmoving. After a nerve-grating silence, she lifted her head and looked at him. Her eyes were dark and tormented as she met his steady gaze, searching for answers to her unspoken questions. He understood her uncertainty, her need for reassurance. Adam tenderly caressed her jawline. "I love you, Natalie. I've never stopped. And nothing is ever going to change that."

She stared at him numbly, as though unable to comprehend, then suddenly her eyes filled with tears, and she opened her mouth to speak. Adam covered her trembling lips with his thumb, afraid that she was going to say something to revoke those feelings. "Shh, Nat. Don't say anything now."

Natalie slipped her arms around his neck and clung to him as harsh sobs were wrung from her. Murmuring softly, Adam picked her up and carried her to the bed, then lay down beside her. His face was drawn as he tucked the quilt around her, holding her tightly as she finally vented the years of accumulated pain.

His hands were unsteady as he gently stroked her hair, his embrace all encompassing as he whispered, "It's all right, Natalie. Get it all out. Everything's going to be okay."

The only indication that she heard him was that she clung to him even more desperately. She wept until Adam didn't think he could stand it any longer, this tortured outpouring of a tortured soul. It was agony to witness.

The storm had moved down the valley and there was only the soft tattoo of rain against the windows when she eventually exhausted herself.

Adam held her for a while longer, then kissed her softly on the temple and murmured, "Don't be upset with Doc because he talked to me, Nat. He's been really concerned about you, and he decided it was time I knew what had happened.''

She stirred weakly in his arms, her breath warm against his neck. "I don't think I could have ever told you. I wanted to, but I didn't know how. I still don't know how.''

He stroked her hair, then let his hand rest against her neck. "Just start talking,'' he said quietly. "And tell me everything.''

She didn't say anything for the longest time, then her voice low, her expression frighteningly impassive, she told him exactly what happened that night. There were times when Adam had to fight to keep from being physically sick, and there were times when his fury was so murderous he could barely contain it, but Natalie never knew what he was experiencing as she talked about the twisted and perverted degradation she had endured. He wanted to beat Carl Willard to a bloody pulp for the atrocities he'd inflicted on her; he wanted to destroy the man who had violated her so brutally, but somehow he managed to suppress those savage feelings. He could do nothing more than hold her and listen as she dredged up the horror of that night. At long last, she was dealing with the ugliness, the pain, the sickening revulsion, the awful sense of helplessness she had suffered at the hands of her stepfather. It became an excruciating kind of purge as she finally told it all. Every ugly, brutal, sordid detail.

Natalie's story only went as far as her arrival at Doc's, and sensing she had reached her limit, Adam didn't press her to go on. When she stopped talking, he simply gathered her closer against him and kissed her lightly on the temple. Slowly, almost hesitantly, she slipped her arms around his neck and pressed her face against his shoulder, and he could tell by her ragged breathing she was struggling to contain her emotions. Gently he stroked her trembling back, aware of the fine, delicate bone structure beneath his touch. It was, he realized with sickening clarity, a miracle that she had survived at all.

The dampness from his clothes had penetrated Natalie's thin garment, and she began to shiver again. Very carefully, Adam eased her away and wrapped the blankets more snugly around her. He brushed back the loose hair that was clinging to her face, savoring the smooth texture of her skin beneath his fingertips. She looked up at him, her eyes so hollow it made his chest ache to look at her. He wanted to lock his arms around her and crush her against him. He wanted to respond to the sudden rush of desire she aroused in him, and he ached to feel her naked body beneath his—warm, soft, yielding. But he battled those feelings, knowing now was not the time.

His voice was low and very husky when he finally spoke. "You're cold, Nat, and my clothes are wet. I think maybe I should get up—"

She turned her face against the curve of his neck as she implored, "Please stay."

An ache of tenderness surged up in him, awakening a fierce protectiveness that obliterated all else. All he was aware of was Natalie. Softly, so softly, he touched her face, and it was all he could do to keep from leaning over her and covering her soft mouth with his own. He could feel his pulse quicken and become thick and heavy as he lost himself in the mesmerizing depths of her eyes. A throbbing hunger

unfolded in him. She was so lovely, and he wanted her
so damned much. His life had been so empty and
meaningless without her, and now that he had her
back, he wanted nothing more than to lose himself in
her and the galvanizing sensations she awakened in
him. But he only caressed the lines of her face. The
rest would come later.

Very gently he cupped her cheek in his hand and
whispered unevenly, "I didn't meant to frighten you
when I came in, Nat. I was in such a panic to get here,
I never thought. I'm sorry."

Tears gathered along her lashes as she shook her
head, then laid her hand on top of his. It was such a
little thing, her touching him like that, but it drove the
strength out of him. God, but he did love her.

"It wasn't just you, Adam," she whispered, her
mouth trembling. "It was the storm. I'd been sleeping, and the thunder woke me. Then I heard you come
in, and I didn't know who it was, and my imagination
got the best of me." She closed her eyes and pressed
her face against his hand. Her voice was so rough with
emotion that her words were a shaky murmur. "I can't
believe you came. It was like a dream when I realized
it was you."

Her voice breaking on a sob, she turned her face
against his shoulder, and Adam gathered her tightly to
him. In spite of the hell they had just been through, he
experienced an overwhelming sense of relief. Without
realizing she'd done it, she had let him know that he
still mattered to her, and he felt like someone had just
lifted an enormous weight off his back.

He cradled her head on his shoulder, and the hus-
kiness in his voice revealed how deeply he'd been

moved. "I love you, Nat. You'll never know how much I've missed you. There was always a part of me that was so damned empty, and I hated you for doing that to me, for ripping my life apart." Cupping his hand against her neck, he turned his head and gazed down at her, his eyes solemn. "I should have known you'd never leave unless you'd been driven to. I doubted you, and that was the worst mistake I've ever made in my life."

With a choked denial, Natalie laid her fingers against his mouth, her eyes brimming with tears. "No, Adam, no," she pleaded. "Don't blame yourself. You couldn't think anything else."

Adam could tell by the panicky tone in her voice that she was on the verge of coming apart again, and with his hand on her jaw, his fingers thrust into her hair, he nestled her head more securely against the curve of his neck. "That's all behind us, Nat," he murmured softly as he rubbed her back, his strokes firm and comforting. "We can talk about it tomorrow. I'm taking you back with me, and we can spend some quiet time together up in the mountains." Deliberately keeping his voice soft, he continued to talk to her as he slowly massaged her back. It wasn't very long before her body relaxed heavily against his, and her breathing became deep and even. With his chin resting on the top of her head, he stared into the shadows across the room, keenly aware of the woman who lay sleeping in his arms. It was going to be a long, sleepless night.

THE MORNING was clear and bright, the droplets of moisture on the rain-drenched grass glistening in the early-morning sun. Adam stood looking out the kitchen window, his hair still damp from his shower, a steaming cup of coffee in his hand. He rested his shoulder against the wide window frame as he took a sip, his eyes darkly reflective. He had managed to get a couple hours sleep, but that was about all, and he was really feeling it.

The night had been an unusual kind of ordeal. Having Natalie so close yet in so many ways unreachable, had strained his willpower to the limit. The morning sky had just started to show the first colors of sunrise when he realized he had to get away from her before he gave in to desire. It was so hard to let go of her, but he had gently eased her out of his arms, then carefully covered her. She would never know what it cost him to walk out of that room.

Adam took another sip from the earthen mug, then exhaling heavily, he straightened and turned from the window. He went over to the stove and was refilling his cup when there was a sound behind him. He turned around to find Natalie standing in the kitchen doorway. She was still wearing the blue-and-white striped nightshirt, and Adam frowned when he recognized anxiety in her eyes.

Setting his cup on the counter, he went to her. He laid his hand against her jaw, his thumb caressing her ear as he murmured softly, "Hey, what's the matter? You look like you've had another scare."

She stared up at him for a second, then weakly rested her forehead against his chest. "I woke up and I was alone . . . and I thought you'd gone."

Drawing her into his arms, he held her securely, his expression darkening when he realized she was shivering again. He held her until the trembling stopped, then caught her face between his hands as he gazed down at her, his eyes solemn. "I'm not going to leave you," he said quietly. "If there's anything in this world you can be sure of, it's that I'm not going to leave you."

"Oh, Adam—"

Shaking his head slightly, he slowly stroked her bottom lip with his thumb, his gaze tender. "We're going to see this thing through together, Natalie. Something that happened eleven years ago can't be allowed to control our lives forever."

She looked up at him, her eyes glistening, and for the longest time they stood caught in their own private space, his hands warm and gentle against her face. Finally she closed her eyes, her breath catching raggedly. "Oh, Adam, is this really happening?"

He lowered his head and kissed her closed eyes, her tears warm against his lips. "It's happening. Years too late, but it's happening."

She tensed suddenly and pulled away from him. Folding her arms tightly in front of her, she turned her back to him, her hands tightly gripping her arms. Confused by her actions, he watched her, wondering why the sudden remoteness. "What's wrong, Nat?" he asked quietly as he went to stand behind her. She only shook her head. With the awful feeling that he was losing her, Adam grasped her by the shoulders and turned her to face him. "Don't shut me out, Natalie. I need to know what you're thinking."

It was a long time before she lifted her head to look at him, and Adam felt the first stirrings of dread when he saw her expressionless face. He knew if he didn't get her talking, she would withdraw completely. His voice was harsh and edged with alarm. "Damn it, talk to me! Don't do this to me again."

She met his gaze for a moment, then with an unnatural stiffness, she turned and walked away. She went to stand before the window, her arms still clutched around her. Her voice was devoid of expression when she finally spoke. "I left because I was afraid you'd kill Carl, that you'd destroy your life because of me. If I stay, I could end up destroying you myself."

"What in hell are you talking about?"

She turned, her face so pale it appeared waxen. She met his gaze with a steadiness that made him feel even more uneasy. "I don't think you want to know."

He stared at her, trying to determine how best to deal with this alien woman standing before him. He realized he would have to stay calm if he was going to get her talking. In an effort to camouflage his tenseness, he stuck his hands in the pockets of his jeans and leaned against the cupboard. "I do need to know, Natalie," he said quietly. "It's my life at stake, too, you know."

She held his gaze briefly, then she turned back to the window, her slender body silhouetted against the morning light. Suddenly, she seemed very vulnerable and alone. He longed to go to her, but he reluctantly held his ground. She had put distance between them, and he sensed it would be a foolish move to violate it. And he didn't want to make any stupid mistakes, not when their future happiness was at stake.

Finally she spoke, and her voice had a strange quality to it, as though she was thinking aloud. "No one will ever know what it was like for me that night. And that victim's complex will stay with me for the rest of my life. My own body repulses me now, and I feel dirty and soiled. I feel contaminated, as if I'm carrying some vile disease.''

She fell silent for a moment, then she turned to face Adam. ''I feel like that all the time, Adam. I've tried to conquer that feeling but it's always there.'' She looked down and absently started breaking away the brown edges on the geranium plant that was sitting on the window ledge. When she looked up at him again, he could see the bleakness in her eyes, and he realized how hard this was for her. There was a slight tremor in her voice when she finally continued. ''But there's more to it than that. I've tried to develop a normal attitude about a relationship, but I can't.'' Her voice broke and she abruptly turned back to the window, her nails digging into her flesh as she grasped her arms. ''The minute a man touches me, I remember Carl's hands all over me, and I want to be sick. That revulsion's always going to be there, Adam. Nothing can erase it. Even an examination by a doctor is an unbelievable ordeal for me, and I can't remember the last time I had a medical.''

Feeling as though he'd just had the rug yanked out from under him, Adam stared rigidly at the floor. His anger ignited as he grimly digested this latest revelation. So the bastard had destroyed that, too—that intoxicating sensuality of hers that used to make his blood boil. She used to be so responsive, so electrifying, and now she couldn't even stand to be touched. He could kill Willard for that alone.

When her sexual self-esteem had been so debased, how could he ever convince her that she meant more to him than a bed partner? What argument could he use to make her realize she wasn't giving herself a decent chance? He stared bleakly at the floor, unaware that she was watching him. When he lifted his head, he caught a glimpse of the agony in her eyes before she quickly looked away. It was the same look she had when she was telling him the ugly details.

Feeling as though his body weighed a ton, he pushed himself away from the counter and went over to her. She resisted briefly when he tried to make her face him, but eventually, as though she dreaded meeting his gaze, she looked up. He touched her face and experienced a thin ray of hope when she didn't draw away. "How many people have you told about what happened that night?"

She frowned slightly, thrown off balance by his question. Wanting to make sure she didn't misunderstand it, he rephrased it. "Who knows exactly what he did to you?"

"Just you," she said softly.

"Why did you tell me, Nat? Why would you tell me and no one else?"

She shook her head, refusing to look at him.

Adam hooked his knuckles under her chin and raised her head. "Do you trust me, Natalie?" he asked, his eyes locked on hers.

She stared at him numbly for a second, then the dark haunted look in her eyes lightened almost imperceptibly. Her voice was trembling when she answered, "Yes, I trust you."

"Did you tell me because you trusted me?" Every muscle in his body tensed as he waited for her reply.

"Yes."

He grasped her face between his hands, his voice strained with urgency as he whispered, "Then trust me now, Natalie." He could see her waver, and his hold on her face tightened, his need to reach her vitally important. "Don't shut me out again. Needing you means more to me than just sex, Nat. And I know we can handle this if we want to. You trusted me before, now trust me about this."

There was so much longing in her eyes, but there was so much uncertainty, as well. She was a woman torn in two; her heart was pulling her one way, her mind was pulling her another. He could feel her start to tremble as she struggled with her warring emotions. She opened her mouth to speak, then closed her eyes as she took a ragged breath. When she looked at him again, he could see how close she was to yielding. "I can't do that to you, Adam. What if I can't deal with those feelings? What if they never change? I can't expect you to live the life of a monk."

Tension left his face as he gently brushed a lock of hair behind her ear, then smiled warmly. "And what if you can? And what if they do?"

"Oh, Adam...."

His expression altered and became very somber. "We'll deal with it one day at a time. And I promise you, we'll only go as far as you want—I'll never force you, Nat." His voice took on a new intensity as he whispered, "I love you, and I need you with me. I want to have my own family—you and Patrick. I want us to build a life together."

Natalie's eyes were almost black as she whispered, "I'm so scared."

Profound feelings—tenderness, compassion, love— filled him, and he found it very hard to speak. "I know," he said softly.

"I don't want to make you unhappy, Adam. I've hurt you so badly already."

Ever so gently, he caressed her face, his touch more eloquent, more poignant than words could ever be. His voice was husky with emotion when he spoke. "Nothing could hurt me more than having you leave again. Nothing could hurt worse than that."

There was a charged silence as she gazed up at him, then with her eyes brimming with tears, she whispered his name and stepped into his arms.

Adam felt as though his chest was going to explode as he enveloped her in a fiercely tender embrace, his control strained to the limit as wave after wave of emotion slammed through him. She had reached out for him, and that had been a conscious choice. Last night she had come to him out of fear, but today she'd come to him because that's where she wanted to be, and that was all that mattered to him. She was finally back. After so long she had finally come back. He felt so whole again, and so alive.

He didn't know how long they stood there, their bodies molded together in a clinging embrace, but he could have remained like that forever. But eventually he caught her by the shoulders and eased her away from him. Taking her hand in his, he silently led her toward the living room.

But as he sat down on the sofa, she pulled her hand free, and there was an anxious look in her eyes. In a nervous gesture, she pressed her hands against her thighs. Her voice was not very steady when she asked, "Why did you get up before me this morning?"

Adam stared at her for a second, then sighed heavily as he reached up and captured her hand again. He would never play games with her. It would be easier to lie, but that would get them nowhere. His expression was solemn. "You know why, Nat."

Adam watched her like a hawk. He saw her swallow and he saw the terrible look of uncertainty dull her eyes, and he could sense her shrinking inside herself. He knew she was struggling. He tried to pull her toward him, but she resisted, her face drawn. She swallowed again, then opened her mouth to speak, but he never gave her the chance. He tightened his hold as he said quietly, "Look, Nat, I said before that there was more to my needing you than sex, and I meant that. I'll admit it isn't easy not to respond, but if I have to choose between you and sexual satisfaction, it's going to be you."

Unaware that she was even doing it, she gripped his hand with a panicky strength that transmitted her fear, her guilt. "But I'm inflicting my... inability to function on you."

Ignoring her resistance, he drew her closer until her legs touched his. "Natalie, if you only knew how much pleasure I get from simply holding you. That alone gives me a kind of contentment I can't find anywhere else." His voice became very husky as he stroked the back of her hand with his thumb. "I couldn't sleep last night, partly because I really wanted you, but mostly because I wanted to be conscious of every second. I like having you in my arms." His eyes were warm and inviting as he slid his hand up her arm, then murmured, "And I really want to hold you now, Natalie." Unable to stand the vibrating tension any longer, Adam reached up and slipped his arm around her, then gently but firmly pulled her down.

Natalie melted weakly against him as he gathered her slender body across his lap. She buried her face in the curve of his neck, her breath warm against his skin. There was no need for words. Adam nestled her closer and shut his eyes, savoring the heady sensations she aroused in him.

It was a long time later that Natalie finally spoke. "I can't believe this is really happening, Adam. If you only knew how many times I thought about you holding me like this, especially when I was still in the hospital."

A haggard expression appeared on Adam's face as he opened his eyes and stared across the room, thinking about how much she had endured. In spite of how badly she was injured and how much pain she must have suffered, she still fought to have Patrick. He didn't know how to express his feelings or what words to use, so with his voice heavily strained by emotion, he simply said, "Thank you for having my son."

Bracing her arm against his chest, Natalie raised her head and looked at him, her eyes soft and misty as she whispered, "Thank you for giving him to me."

Her answer created another storm of emotions in Adam, and his eyes were smoldering with intensity as he smoothed his hand across her shoulder and up her neck. There was a tight ache in his throat as he traced the curve of her cheek. "Doc told me how you fought to have him, Nat. You could have so easily given in and had an abortion, but you didn't, and I'm so damned grateful you didn't." His voice broke roughly as he pressed the heel of his hand against her jaw. "He's such a terrific kid."

As though she was trying to erase the hard lines around his mouth, Natalie gently trailed her fingers along his lips. Her voice was just as gentle when she said, "He was the one thing I had that was yours, Adam. I was able to block everything else out as long as I could hang on to that thought."

Adam studied her face, his expression very grave. "Doc said you became hysterical when they suggested it would be safer for you if they performed an abortion." He hesitated, then went with his gut instinct. "There was more to it than simply losing the baby, wasn't there?"

Natalie stared at him, then she looked down at her hand, avoiding his penetrating eyes. In the softest of voices she whispered, "Yes."

He tightened his hold on her, trying to give her the courage to answer. "Tell me, Nat. I need to know."

A tremor shuddered through her, and Adam realized he had unwittingly confronted her with something that really upset her. He didn't expect her to answer, but she did. She kept her eyes averted, and her voice was riddled with humiliation. "It was all so ugly, but the worst was when . . . was when Carl was on top of me. I thought I was going to go out of my mind, it was so repulsive and awful, and there was so much pain. There aren't words disgusting enough to describe how filthy, how defiled I felt."

She lifted her eyes and looked at him, and a cold, murderous fury seethed in Adam when he saw how deep and how destructive her shame was. *The bastard,* he raged inwardly. *He should be tied down and castrated for what he did to her.* But he managed to keep those violent feelings from showing as he met her tormented gaze. As devastated as she was, there was still a thread of defiance in her trembling voice. "The only thing that I could hang on to that kept me sane was that your baby was growing in me, and no matter what he did, my womb was inviolate. He had the physical strength to force me to submit, he could do the most disgusting things to my body, but he could never make me pregnant."

Adam's insides convulsed into a hard sickening knot and he had to clench his jaws together to keep from reacting. His face felt numbed by shock as he stared at her, then with a low groan he hugged her tightly against him. If he had been able to keep his hands off her, if he hadn't got her pregnant in the first place, Carl Willard probably would have never assaulted her. And Adam had to live with the fact that he had been indirectly responsible for Natalie's attack.

Her touch was cool and gentle as she took his face between her hands and made him look at her. "Don't, Adam," she whispered huskily. "Don't start blaming yourself."

He had forgotten how adept she was at reading him, and he gave her a contemplative look. There was a smile in her eyes as she brushed back his hair with the same tender, maternal gesture he'd seen her use with Patrick. "Don't look so surprised," she admonished softly. "I spent too many years following you around when I was a kid not to know how you think, Adam Rutherford."

Adam found himself smiling back at her. "And a gawky little kid at that." She made a face at him, and the sickening sensation caused by her confession slowly eased as amusement lit up her eyes.

It was true. Natalie had trailed around behind him for a good many years. But Adam had never paid much attention to the girl who lived down the street. It wasn't until he'd been away at university for a couple of years and Natalie had a chance to grow up that he started taking notice. Only it was more than a simple case of noticing; it was more like getting hit by a train. The big discovery came during the annual raft races. It was just before one race was to start, and Adam and his crew were on the dock waiting to find out what heat they were in. He got their assignment and turned to go. And there she was.

His eyes alight with amused recollection, he leaned his head against the back of the sofa and stared off into space. "I'll never forget what a shock I got the first time I saw you after I got home from university that summer."

Natalie laughed and gave him a wry look. "I'm sure Mrs. Marshall never forgot what a shock *she* got, either."

"Yeah, that was great. She was such a cow—she was always giving somebody a hard time. I think the whole town cheered when she went in the drink." He looked at Natalie, his expression a mixture of tenderness and amusement. "There I was, minding my own business and I just happened to look up... and there was little Natalie Carter on another raft." His voice got husky, and his eyes darkened as he gazed at her, clearly recalling every detail. "Only it wasn't *little* Natalie anymore. She had on a sexy red harem costume and her hair was all bound in jewels, and she nearly blew my mind." The laugh lines around his eyes crinkled as he continued. "Since we were Viking warlords, I figured it would be very appropriate if we kidnapped her."

Natalie laughed and shook her head, her expression disbelieving. "Then would you please explain how Mrs. Marshall ended up in the river?"

Adam grinned. "I was so busy looking at you I didn't see her standing behind me, and I must have upended her with that big shield I was carrying. The funny part was, I was so intent on getting you off that raft that I honestly didn't realize what I'd done, at least not until I'd grabbed you and was heading to our own raft."

Natalie's eyes were still sparkling with laughter, and there was also a nostalgic glow that came from a very special reminiscence. "I couldn't figure out what you were up to when the five of you came swarming into the river. I was so surprised I couldn't even react when you grabbed me, threw me over your shoulder and carried me off."

"That's what warlords do."

"And I loved it." She became solemn, and the expression in her eyes softened as she touched his face. "And you took me to the dance that night, and you brought me star flowers to wear in my hair."

He was watching her with a heady intentness as he spoke, his voice very husky. "And you wouldn't dance with anyone else." For a moment they were caught in a spell of their own, then unable to handle the overwhelming tenderness that unfolded in his chest, Adam thrust his fingers in her hair and pressed her head against his shoulder. And for a long time, neither said a word.

Finally he sighed and combed his hand through her tousled hair. "We have so much to catch up on, Nat," he said with a touch of wishfulness. "It's been such a long, long time."

"And there's Patrick," she added softly.

"And Patrick." His expression changed as he looked at her. "Tell me about the photograph album."

She shrugged self-consciously and began toying with a button on his shirt. "I suppose it was my way of avoiding reality. As long as I was working on the album, I could keep you a part of my life." She looked up at him, her eyes darkened by the pain of remembering. "While I was in the hospital I was able to make believe that everything would be as it was before. But when I was discharged and Doc took me to live with Bea, I had to face the fact that I'd never see you again."

He frowned slightly. "If you thought you'd never see me again, why did you keep it up?"

She smiled again, her mouth trembling and her eyes suddenly brimming with tears. "Because I couldn't stop hoping."

Adam's hand wasn't quite steady as he brushed the tears from her long lashes, then kissed her gently on the corner of her mouth. He didn't know why it had become so vitally important, but he had to pick up where they had left off so many years before. "Marry me, Nat," he whispered softly against her mouth. "Marry me as soon as we can arrange it."

CHAPTER NINE

IT WAS MIDAFTERNOON when Adam and Natalie arrived at the trailer. Adam spotted Doc and Patrick down by the lake and it was apparent that neither of them heard the vehicle pull into the campsite. The old man and the young boy were standing on a rocky point just on the other side of the pier, and the way Doc was gesturing with his arms, it was obvious that either the fish were biting or he was telling one of his many fish stories. Adam grinned and glanced across the cab at Natalie. "He never changes, does he?"

She was looking toward the lake, the sunlight slanting across her face and neck. The brightness caught in the fine strands of hair that had been pulled free by the breeze whipping in from the open window, and her face was framed in a soft golden halo. There was an inflexible set to her shoulders that was unusual, and her hands were grasped together in her lap.

He leaned over and separated her hands, then laced his fingers through hers as he watched her profile. His tone was quiet when he said, "Let's hear it, Nat."

For a second she didn't respond, then Natalie turned to look at him, her finely sculpted face still showing signs of strain. She was wearing a dark blue cotton shirt and slacks, and the shade accentuated the dark shadows under her eyes. She looked exhausted. Her hold on his hand tightened when she met his gaze. "I don't know what to say to Patrick."

Leaning closer, he reached out with his free hand and brushed back a wisp of hair that was clinging to her cheek, then asked softly, "Why are you worried about it?"

She stared out the windshield, her expression bleak. "He was so upset in Calgary when he found out about you. How's he going to feel when we show up together? He's only little. He's going to wonder why it couldn't have always been this way, instead of his spending the first ten years of his life without his father."

Adam caught her chin and forced her to turn her head. His smile was warm and full of reassurance. "We've already had a talk about you, and I know for a fact you're crossing bridges that aren't even there."

The expression in Natalie's eyes changed as she watched him closely. "When was this?"

"Yesterday, before the storm."

Her voice was very strained. "What, exactly, did you talk about?"

"Everything." He turned so his legs were wedged between the bucket seats, then he hunched over and rested his elbows on his thighs. Taking both of her hands between his, he looked at her, his eyes darkening as he recalled the details of his talk with Patrick. "He asked me if I still liked you," he paused, his tone growing husky, "and I assured him I did—very much."

The intimacy between them became so charged that Adam couldn't hold her gaze any longer, and he lowered his head and began stroking the back of her hands with his thumbs. "I wanted to go back and get you right then and there, but he wanted to talk. He had a thousand questions that needed answering, but the thing that was most important to him was how we felt about each other. He needed to know that I cared about you and you cared about me. When I told him I still loved you, he said he didn't think you knew that, and he wanted to know if I was going to tell you." Adam finally looked up at Natalie, his eyes holding hers with a magnetic intensity. "When I said I was going to tell you how I felt, his whole attitude changed and he made it very obvious he wanted us together."

Natalie seemed dazed and her voice had a tremor of wonderment in it when she whispered, "You mean you'd decided on coming to get me *before* you knew what happened?"

"Yes."

Natalie stared at him for a minute, then she weakly leaned her head against his, her grip on his hands so tight that her nails dug into the backs of his hands. "Oh, Adam, you don't know what that means to me."

Extracting his hands from hers, Adam slipped his arms around her shoulders, his expression becoming grim when he felt how tense she was. She'd had about all she could take, and somehow he had to find a way to take the pressure off. Filled with an aching tenderness, Adam cupped the back of her head with his hand and nestled it in the curve of his neck. He kissed her temple, the fragrance from her hair filling his senses. "Come on, Nat," he teased softly. "You had my number when you were still practically in diapers. You must have known I'd be back."

He felt her take a shaky breath, then she raised her head and looked at him. There was laughter behind the tears clinging to her long thick lashes. "I was *not* in diapers."

He grinned at her as he dried her eyes with the side of his hand. "I had to see if I could get a rise out of you, that's all." He gave her another fleeting kiss, then said quietly, "Let's go see our son."

The sound of doors slamming carried to the lake, and Doc turned stiffly toward the small rise where he had parked his car. It was only a short space of time before Adam and Natalie appeared through the scattering of trees, walking hand in hand.

The old man felt as though a tremendous darkness had been lifted from his soul, and he experienced a profound gladness as he watched them. A hint of a smile played around Doc's mouth. Natalie looked at her companion, and Doc saw Adam lace his fingers through hers in a secure grip as he drew her closer to him. It was unquestionably a protective gesture, and Doc's expression altered as he took a closer look at her.

She looked as though she had been through a terrible ordeal. She was very pale and drawn, and Doc felt a sudden rush of concern. Perhaps it hadn't gone entirely as he had hoped. But he made sure his voice did not betray his anxious thoughts as he said lightly, "Trust the luck, Patrick. As soon as the fish are biting, we can count on someone horning in on our spot."

Adam grinned and pointed to the fishing rod Doc was holding. "If this is your spot, how come that gear looks so familiar?"

"A wee oversight," said Doc, a twinkle in his eyes as he turned to Patrick. "Shall we share our catch with them, lad, or shall we keep it for ourselves?"

But Patrick hadn't heard a word he said. He was standing stock-still, his eyes fixed anxiously on his parents. He licked his lips and nervously scrubbed his free hand against the seam in his jeans. "Hi," he said, his voice quavering.

Adam's attention was focused on his son. "Hi. So you're having a streak of luck, are you?"

"Yeah. We caught six trout already." Doc watched Adam and Patrick, realizing that the real exchange was unspoken, transmitted by sight between father and son. As though the silent message had been received, Patrick looked at his mother. "Would you like to use my rod, Mom?"

Doc could see how hard Natalie was fighting not to break down, but he wasn't the only one who was aware of her battle. Adam put his arm around her and pulled her against him. "I think your mom would rather watch for a while, Pat."

Patrick nodded and stepped back onto the flat rock he'd been standing on, his movements suddenly stiff and awkward as he cast his line. He started to reel it in, then stopped, his voice muffled. "I tangled it again."

Adam's face was showing signs of enormous strain as he gave Natalie a reassuring squeeze, then went over to his son and crouched beside him. He took the rod from Patrick and started unwinding the tangled line as the child remained standing rigidly beside him. Doc heard him murmur something to the boy, but Patrick made no response. Adam said something else, and the boy turned toward him and with a muffled sob, threw himself into his father's arms. Doc glanced at Natalie, but looked away again when he saw the naked anguish in her eyes. She had endured so much.

Adam picked up Patrick and started toward her. "It's okay, Patrick," he heard him whisper against the boy's hair. "Everything's going to be okay." As Adam crossed the rocky point with his son in his arms, he never took his eyes off Natalie, his expression taut with concern. Shifting Patrick's weight onto his hip, he reached for her, and like a magnet to metal, she went to him. Everything he was feeling was rawly exposed on Adam's face as he held them both in a crushing embrace. He was unmistakably a man shielding his own. Natalie shuddered and pressed her face against his shoulder. There was another stifled sob, and Patrick dragged one arm free and slipped it around his mother's neck. At long last, father, mother and son were united. And with his vision blurred, Doc walked away, leaving these three special people alone in this very private and moving reunion.

ADAM WAS AMAZED at the resilience of his son. Half an hour after that first emotional encounter, Patrick was acting as if it was the most ordinary thing in the world to have his mother and father together. But Adam was also aware of the many times Patrick stopped whatever he was doing and visually checked on them both, then continued on in obvious high spirits.

Natalie, however, was a different story. She was so drained she hardly had the energy to move. Remembering a hammock he had stored in one of the compartments in the trailer, Adam dug it out and strung it between two enormous poplar trees near the shore of the lake. Without giving her a chance to protest, he picked Natalie up and dumped her in it. Patrick thought that was great. The idea of someone being big enough and strong enough to put his mother to bed delighted him to no end.

Realizing that his son would soon grow bored with nothing to do, Adam decided to build a fire pit not far from where he'd hung the hammock. As they started hauling slabs of shale from the edge of the lake, Doc set about cleaning the fish for supper and a quiet harmony settled on them all.

The bright blue sky was cloudless, providing an unblemished background for the gray and purple fortresses of the distant snowcapped mountains, the dark green forests creeping densely up their granite slopes. It was such a calm, clear day that it was hard to believe there had been a violent storm the night before. Because of the location of the isolated little valley, the campsite had been relatively protected. The only evidence of the violence was a new crop of pinecones lying on the ground beneath the trees, and a few small broken poplar branches scattered across the clearing.

A light summer breeze sighed through the leaves and ruffled the surface of the lake, sending brilliances of sunlight dancing across the surface and small waves lapping at the shore. A birdcall rang clearly through the trees, the shrill notes seeming to hang suspended in the crystal-clear air. Adam noticed it all. There was nothing like it, this deep sense of oneness he had when he was in the high country.

With his hot, flushed face streaked with grime, Patrick dropped the last rock beside his father, his bare torso clammy with sweat. "Are we finished?"

"That should do it, I think."

Patrick crouched and watched his father work the flat slab into place. He absently brushed a mosquito from his forehead then scratched a bite on his arm. "Mom's asleep."

Wiping his hands on his jeans, Adam looked at the hammock, and then at his son. "I know."

"Is she sick or something? She never sleeps in the afternoon."

"Your mom has been under a lot of pressure lately. She just needs some quiet time."

That answer seemed to satisfy Patrick. He picked up a rock and threw it in the lake, then sat watching the ripples spread. "Where's Grandpa gone?"

"I think he's gone for a walk along the creek."

"Oh." Patrick pulled out a handful of grass and made a little pile, then picked up a twig and started drawing circles in the dust.

Adam leaned back and rested his hands on his thighs, a touch of knowing amusement in his eyes as he studied his son. "What is it, Pat?"

Patrick fidgeted some more, then looked at his dad. "Are you and Mom really getting married?"

"Don't you think it's about time we did?"

Grinning broadly, Patrick stretched out on his stomach, his head propped in his hand. "Yeah, well. But not many kids get to go to their parents' wedding."

"Yeah, well," Adam responded dryly.

"Will my name be Rutherford after?"

"Do you want it to be?"

Patrick let out a sigh of exasperation. "You answer questions with questions just like Mom does."

Adam grinned as he stood and reached for his shirt, which was hanging on a bush. "Well, what do *you* want?"

"Rutherford."

"Then that's what it'll be."

Patrick rolled over on his back and watched the leaves turning and twisting overhead. "Will we live here?"

"That's something the three of us are going to have to talk about, Patrick. If your mom wants to keep working, we'll settle in Los Angeles, and if not, we may go somewhere else. We might even decide to stay here." Adam did up a few buttons on his shirt and tucked it in his jeans before he asked, "Would it really bother you if you had to move away from your friends in California?"

"If we moved, we could go back for visits, couldn't we?"

"Definitely."

Patrick looked up at his dad, and it struck Adam again how much his son's eyes were like Natalie's. The boy moved his head in a gesture of approval. "Then that's okay." Patrick brushed another mosquito off his face, then pulled out a long stem of grass and chewed the end. "Will you be gone lots? Like when you go to Africa and South America and places like that?"

Adam braced his arm against the rough trunk of a tree as he gazed solemnly at his son. "I'm not going on any long shoots unless you and your mom can come, Patrick. I want you with me, not left at home."

Patrick's eyes lit up. "Hey, you mean I might get to go to Africa?"

"Very likely."

"Wow," he breathed, his eyes wide with wonder. He fell silent as he watched the sunlight dancing across the lake, a faraway look in his eyes. Several minutes passed, then he sat up and drew up his knees. Grass and dead leaves were clinging to his damp skin and tangled in his blond hair. With jerky little movements, he started pulling single blades of grass from a clump of sod that had been dug from the hole for the fire pit. "Dad?"

"What?"

He wouldn't look at his father as he continued to pluck nervously at the grass. "I'm really glad…about you and Mom and everything."

There was a brief silence before Adam spoke, his voice very husky. "So am I, Patrick."

As if he were trying to avoid any more awkward conversation, Patrick scrambled to his feet and picked up the small collapsible spade they had used to dig the fire pit. "I'll go put this back with your backpack."

Adam smiled knowingly as he ruffled his son's hair. "If you bring me back my big brown camera case and the camera I gave you, I'll teach you how to use the telephoto lens."

"Oh, boy," Patrick exclaimed, and he raced off toward the trailer.

Adam watched him dodge through the trees, then sticking his hands in the back pockets of his jeans, he went over to the hammock. Natalie was still asleep, her chest rising and falling shallowly, her lips parted. She had her head turned toward him, the side of her face resting on her hand, her long lashes fanning out against her cheeks. Her fair hair was pulled back in the usual chignon, but the movement of her head against the coarse weave of the hammock had loosened the pins and strands had pulled free.

Sunlight winked through the fluttering leaves, dancing across her face in patches of light and catching in her hair. She looked very delicate as she lay sleeping, a soft flush coloring her cheeks. Adam's gold-flecked eyes absorbed every detail. Drawn by a need to touch her, he gently traced the long scar along her jaw and wondered what other scars her body carried. As he lightly brushed the back of his knuckles against her neck, she stirred and slowly opened her eyes.

For an instant she stared at him, then she smiled sleepily and covered his hand with her own. "Hi," she murmured drowsily.

It was all Adam could do to keep from responding to a sudden rush of desire. Her mouth was so damned tempting, and he ached to lean over and cover it with his own and experience the intoxicating moistness. He could remember her clinging to him and moaning softly, her mouth hot and yielding, and he could remember how she'd move beneath him, her body seeking the rhythm of his. He could remember it so vividly....

"What's the matter?" she whispered, her eyes suddenly alert.

Curling his fingers around her hand, he forced himself to smile down at her, his voice slightly gruff.

"Nothing's the matter, Nat. I was just remembering, that's all."

"Remembering what?"

His expression softened as he gazed at her. "You," he said simply. And unable to resist any longer, he bent over and cupped his hands around her face, then kissed her softly on the corner of her mouth, the contact testing his endurance to the limit. Adam didn't know if he would have had the strength to draw away if he hadn't heard Patrick coming. But he doubted it.

His heart was pounding violently, and he inhaled very slowly, then straightened. "I was going to turn Patrick loose with a camera. Would you like to come?"

Natalie's voice was unsteady. "I'd love to." Grasping Adam's outstretched hand, she let him pull her out of the hammock and onto her feet. She straightened her shirt, then raised her arms to tidy her hair.

Adam caught her wrists and held them. Loose wisps of hair framed her face and curled against her neck. It was soft and feminine and utterly appealing. "Don't," he whispered huskily.

She stared at him blankly for a moment, then looked away, a light blush coloring her cheeks.

Patrick came tearing across the small clearing, the camera bag slamming against his legs, another small case around his neck, and a plastic bag clutched in his hand. "I got it, Dad. I brought my camera case, too." His chest heaving and his breath coming in deep gasps, he stopped in front of his father. He set the larger case on the ground, then he lifted the other strap over his head and set that case down beside his father's. He wiped the palm of his hand on his jeans as he looked up at his mother. "Are you coming too, Mom?"

Natalie nodded, then indicated the large bag of shelled sunflower seeds he was holding. "Where did you get those?"

Patrick grinned as he held the bag up for his father to see. "Grandpa was in the trailer making tea, and he said you'd lash him to death with your tongue if you caught him eating these. He made a mistake and got the salted ones, so he said I'd better take 'em." He opened the bag and took out a handful, then funneled them into his mouth. "He said the chipmunks and squirrels would like them."

Natalie raised her eyebrows in skepticism, then commented dryly, "Not to mention yourself."

With a look of utter innocence, Patrick held out the bag toward her. "Want some?"

Biting back a smile, Natalie narrowed her eyes at him as she reached into the bag. Patrick offered the seeds to his father, then squatted and opened the Velcro fasteners on the camera cases, removing a camera from the small one.

Wiping his hands on his jeans, Adam crouched beside the boy and took the camera Patrick handed him, then opened a padded compartment in the large case and lifted out a long-barreled lens. Patrick watched intently as his father removed the regular lens from his camera and placed it in the compartment. Adam attached the telephoto lens, then handed the assembled equipment to Patrick. "I think that's going to be too heavy for you to hold steady, Pat. You'll likely have to use a tripod so your pictures aren't blurred."

Patrick nodded, then listened intently as his father explained the basic mechanics and showed him how to use the lens. The boy asked a few questions, then tried to focus on a weathered stump that was sticking out of the water. Leaving Patrick to do some experimenting, Adam lifted out another camera from the case, then picked up both bags and slung the straps over his shoulder. "You'd better stick that insect repellent in your pocket, Patrick, and put on your shirt. With the rain last night, the mosquitoes will be thick in the bush."

"Oh, okay." Patrick did as he was told, then held the bag toward his mother. "Will you carry this, Mom? I'll need both hands."

She took it from him, then shook her head ruefully as she brushed his sweat-dampened hair off his dirt-streaked face. "You certainly are not the cleanest kid I ever laid eyes on."

Patrick gave her a pained look and groaned. "Aw, Mom. It's summer holidays."

Adam was laughing as he held out his hand toward Natalie. "Give it up, Mom. A little bit of dirt gives him character."

"Yeah, Mom," echoed Patrick, an impish grin splitting his face as he danced along the trail in front of them. "It gives me character."

Taking Adam's outstretched hand, Natalie gave him a loaded look. "I hope you remember this when his ears rot off."

"If they haven't rotted off by now, I think he stands a good chance of hanging on to them."

Patrick's eyes were sparkling mischievously as he turned around to look at them. "And I really need 'em if I ever have to wear glasses, right, Dad?"

Adam laughed again. "Among other things."

"Does all this mean you're going to wash them?" Natalie asked, trying not to smile.

"Oh boy," said Patrick, woefully shaking his head.

The deer trail emerged from the trees and ran along the lakeshore for a short distance. Patrick picked up a small rock and threw it in the lake, the ripples radiating along the smooth surface of the water.

Adam squinted and gave Natalie a calculating look, a definite gleam in his eyes as he said very casually, "Speaking of washing, how about the supper dishes?"

She gave him a puzzled look, then a light began to dawn in her eyes as he bent over and picked up a smooth flat pebble. He handed it to her. "Supper dishes?" he said again.

Her face lit up and she took the pebble from him. "Supper dishes," she agreed with a grin.

Patrick had been watching his parents, a totally confused look on his face. "What? What do you mean 'supper dishes'? I don't understand."

"A long time ago, your mom and I used to have contests skipping stones. We'd make certain deals, and if I lost, I had to do whatever she'd challenged me to do, and if she lost, she had to do whatever I'd challenged her to."

"Hey, that's neat."

Adam thought so, too. That was how he'd finally managed to get Natalie to go skinny-dipping with him the first time. And as he'd recalled, he'd never skipped stones like that before, and he certainly had never done it since. That was some afternoon.

He was smiling to himself as he remembered that episode in living color. Natalie's soft laugh interrupted his musings. He glanced at her and found her watching him with an amused, knowing look. And he could tell by the gleam in her eyes that she had tuned in to his thoughts. "But then, Adam," she said heartlessly, "there was the time that you ended up painting three hundred feet of fence."

He laughed, positioned the pebble on his fingers and made a smooth side-arm pitch. The stone skipped five times. "Beat that lady, or you do dishes."

"That's not fair," she protested. "I haven't done this for years. I need a warm-up."

"No dice. Put up or shut up."

She gave him a menacing look, then carefully selected a rock. Aiming for the best reflecting angle, she bent to the side, and the pebble kissed across the surface, disappearing after six hits. Natalie laughed and clapped her hands, then made a doleful face at him. "Poor Adam. Has to do the dishes."

Undaunted, Adam picked up another pebble and slammed it into her hand. "Supper."

"Supper," she agreed.

Patrick straddled a piece of driftwood, an impish look on his face. "Popcorn," he challenged.

Adam and Natalie laughed, and his father handed him a rock. "You're on, kid."

They skipped stones until they lost track of who was to do what for whom, and the grand finale was a niner by Adam, who asked Natalie if she felt like a swim.

She gave him a pithy look, and he laughed. Firmly clasping her hand in his, he drew her beside him as they started walking again, wending their way through the trees.

Like most small boys, Patrick was enthralled with bugs. With the help of his father, he managed to photograph a colony of ants, a spider weaving a fragile deadly web between some slender reeds, and two water beetles walking across the still water of a small stagnant pond, their hairlike feet leaving minute dimples in the water. Patrick was fascinated as his father explained the role each insect played in nature, and was obviously awed by how much his father knew.

They had happened on a secluded clearing where the stream burbled into a clear mountain pool and the soft golden sunlight filtered through the trees in shafts. A thick growth of ferns spread beneath broad trunks of giant fir trees, the delicate fronds rimming a small lea that ran along one side of the creek. The grass grew lush and green in the shallow hollow, the humus soil retaining moisture from the spring flood. Wild lupine grew thickly, their stocks of blue flowers swaying lightly in the breeze, and just beyond the grass, before the ferns dominated, a path of yellow violets grew among their shiny heart-shaped leaves. On the other side of the creek, a thicket of wild dogwood bushes crowded against a rocky outcrop.

Adam showed Patrick where the long grass in the middle of the thicket was flattened, explaining that some wild animal, probably a deer, had lain there. Dragonflies flitted through the clearing, their blue gauzy wings glinting opalescently in the rays of light.

Patrick squatted and watched intently as one lit on a branch near the ground, its fragile wings outstretched. "What do they eat, Dad?"

"Mosquitoes, mostly." Adam checked the light meter attached to his camera strap, then pulled the tripod from the side strap on the camera case. "With the angle of the light, the colors in the wings should show up. Do you want to try it?"

Patrick nodded, and he and his father prepared to photograph. Natalie watched them for a moment then wandered deeper into the clearing. Adam noticed her move away and thought how perfectly she fit into this enchanted little dell in the wilderness. He could have watched her indefinitely, and a little reluctantly, he dragged his attention back to his small son.

Patrick had photographed the dragonflies and was focusing his attention on a furry caterpillar when a familiar sensation crept up the back of Adam's neck and he turned his head.

Natalie was standing motionless at the edge of the clearing, her hand outstretched. Downwind, and camouflaged in the shadows, were a doe and her fawn. All eyes and ears, the deer watched Natalie as she started talking to them in soft singsong tones, coaxing them toward her with the hypnotic lure of her voice.

Adam had forgotten her rare gift to instill trust in animals. Ever since she was a small child, she seemed to possess some magical power that enabled her to communicate with them, and tame or wild, they seemed to know she'd never harm them. It had amazed him the first time he'd seen her do it, and it amazed him now. Moving cautiously, he reached over and took the camera with the telephoto lens from Patrick's hands. Adam's actions caught his son by surprise, and Patrick turned to protest. Adam clapped his hand over his mouth to silence him, then pointed toward Natalie.

Patrick turned, his mouth dropping open. Adam caught him by the shoulder and held him immobile. "Watch, Patrick," he said in a barely audible whisper. "She'll get the doe to come right up to her." Patrick glanced at his father, not quite believing him, then he looked back at his mother. She was standing very still, her hand outstretched, and Adam realized she was holding a handful of sunflower seeds. She kept talking in the same quiet tone, and slowly the adult deer came a step closer, then another, and another. The doe hesitated, then stretched out her neck and very daintily nuzzled the sunflower seeds from Natalie's hand.

Patrick's eyes nearly fell out of his head. He stood rooted to the spot as the animal licked the salt from his mother's palm. Adam shot several frames, then wanting to get a close-up of her, he zoomed in on Natalie's face. Intent, expressive and so lovely. And carrying a long jagged scar along her jaw.

Adam's insides twisted into a hard knot as he suddenly recalled one particularly sordid and graphic description Natalie had numbly related the night before. He clenched his teeth, fighting to contain his anger, his frustration, his bitter sense of helplessness. He grimly wondered what he would do if he ever came face-to-face with Carl Willard. Would he be able to keep from killing him? He doubted it.

That grisly thought stuck with Adam for the rest of the day, and he became quiet and withdrawn. At supper he was aware that Natalie was watching him, her eyes anxious, but he couldn't snap out of the dark introspective mood that had settled on him.

He knew he needed some time alone, so as soon as Doc and Patrick were ready to go to bed, he took his bedroll out to one of the cabins. But sleep eluded him as his mind focused on one particular realization; he had to face some hard cold facts about himself. He was the kind of person who did not forget easily. And because of this characteristic, he now had to face the fact that the anger, the frustration, the sense of helplessness he felt about Natalie's assault would always be there, and those feelings would rise up to haunt him at the most unexpected times. Like this afternoon. She had been stuck with the horror and brutality, the pain and suffering; he had been stuck with the haunting aftermath.

The sounds of night filtered through Adam's bleak thoughts. The dilapidated cabin was near the lake, and through the paneless windows he could hear the gentle lap of water against the rocky shore. The leaves rustled softly overhead, and an owl hooted in the distance. There had been a threat of rain when he had left the trailer, but now the night sky was sprinkled with a canopy of stars, and a spectral wisp of cloud drifted across the moon.

The chill of the alpine air touched his skin as Adam stared out the rectangle of the door, the solitude of darkness laying an eerie stillness on the forest. He lay on his back, his fingers laced behind his head as he peered into the night, trying to ward off disturbing thoughts of Natalie. Today was the first time he'd really seen her as Patrick's mother. He had caught glimpses of her in that role when they'd gone to Calgary, but the situation had been so strained and unnatural, he hadn't seen the true picture.

It could not have been easy for her raising a son on her own. Especially a son like Patrick, who had an endless store of energy. Adam was aware that the boy could have easily ended up being one of those kids who approached everything at full speed without taking the time to follow through on anything. But Natalie had used the boy's natural curiosity to channel that energy, and consequently he had turned out to be a bright, intense kid who had been encouraged to develop a broad range of interests. She had done a remarkable job of raising him. And Adam wished like hell he'd been a part of the process.

Feeling suddenly very empty, he stared unseeingly into the darkness, trying to block out other images of Natalie that threatened to inundate him. Images he didn't dare let develop.

HE DIDN'T KNOW how long he'd been asleep. The night was still smothered in darkness, but something, some foreign sound had penetrated his sleep. With his senses suddenly alert, he opened his eyes and turned his head toward the door. His voice was thick with sleep as he said softly, "Natalie?"

The shadow at the door moved and slipped soundlessly into the cabin and dropped to his side. He reached out toward her, his hand touching her bare arm. He could feel her shivering. "What's the matter?" he murmured as he raised up on one arm.

She exhaled slowly, as though she was trying to make herself relax. "Nothing. I—I just wanted to make sure you were all right. It got so cold."

Adam slid his hand up her arm and across her back. "Come here, Nat. Let me hold you." He could feel her resist as he threw back the sleeping bag that covered him. "I just want to hold you," he said softly as he overrode her resistance and drew her down. He pulled the sleeping bag around her, then lying back down, he cradled her tightly against him. "Now tell me what's wrong," he whispered against her hair.

"Nothing's wrong, Adam," she said as she pressed her face against his neck, her breath warm against his skin. "I woke up, and for a minute I didn't know where I was. And I had this awful feeling that I had been dreaming this."

Quietly savoring the feel of her in his arms, he started to massage her back. "But there was more to it than that, wasn't there?" he asked astutely.

She lay so still he couldn't even feel her breathing, then she moved her head, and he knew she was staring off into the darkness. "Yes, I guess there was."

"Like what?"

She didn't say anything for a moment, then she answered quietly—too quietly. "So much has changed, Adam, and I know that nothing will ever be as it was."

There was an undertone there that made him uneasy, and his own voice was strained. "What are you driving at, Natalie?"

Again she hesitated before she answered, only this time he could hear the apprehension. "What if we can't work things out, Adam? What if I never get over my . . . inhibitions?"

Relieved that her fears were not his own, he cuddled her closer and whispered, "I told you before not to cross bridges, Nat. Given enough time, I know we can overcome anything."

"But how much time?" He detected a thread of fear as she continued, her voice so taut it was trembling. "You can't be expected to stand around waiting while I decide whether I can come to terms with my problems or not. It's too much to ask."

"Don't doubt my feelings," he admonished gently.

"Oh Adam, I don't. But what scares me more than anything is that you could end up loathing me."

He slid his hand up the nape of her neck, his fingers tunneling into her hair as he pressed her head against his shoulder. "That isn't going to happen— ever," he said, his voice low and sure.

Raising up on one elbow, Natalie laid her hand against his jaw, her long slim fingers caressing his neck. The moonlight from the door make it possible for him to see the shadowy outline of her face as she leaned against him. Her voice was husky and soft. "I know you, Adam. I know how much you need the physical aspects of a relationship." Her hand pressed against his face and her voice became very uneven. "I knew exactly what you were feeling this afternoon when you woke me up. I could feel that sexual tension in you the minute you touched me. And how long can I expect you to go on denying your own masculinity because of me?"

Adam didn't know. He really didn't know. And now was a hell of a time to consider it. With her so soft and warm against him, with him fighting to clamp down on the hunger she aroused in him, with his body responding to the nearness of hers.

He inhaled slowly, trying to calm his laboring heartbeat, then whispered raggedly, "We'll work it out, Nat. We have to. I need you in my life." And somehow, he had to keep believing that they could work it out. Because he didn't know how he would survive if they couldn't.

CHAPTER TEN

ADAM CAME OUT of the office at the back of the drugstore and started walking up the side aisle between the display racks of greeting cards and paperback novels. He was wearing tight jeans, hand-tooled cowboy boots and a plaid shirt that was open at the neck. His tawny sun-streaked hair was windblown and he was darkly tanned, and his heavily tinted sunglasses added a touch of mystery to his very masculine face. Moving with the saunter of an athlete, he came toward the front of the store, a preoccupied look on his face as he rolled back the cuffs of his sleeves.

Stella had been busy restocking the supply of cigarettes at the front counter, but she stopped what she was doing and watched him come toward her. Her eyes narrowed with appreciation. Here was a man who bloody well knew what being a man was all about. His masculinity was so blatant, he may as well have had Virile stamped on his forehead. With a dramatic sigh, she took the gum out of her mouth, dropped it in the wastepaper basket and shook her head in awe. "Gawd, you should be flexing your muscles in underwear ads. Give us poor underprivileged women a chance to drool over your body."

Adam gave her a suspicious look, as if he thought she'd just lost her mind. There was a wicked gleam in her eyes as she raised her gaze to the ceiling, beseeching some greater power. "Why wasn't he born twenty years sooner? I ask you . . . why?"

Adam grinned and took off his sunglasses. "You know somebody always screws up the logistics, Stella." He was standing with his feet apart and his legs locked, and his shirt pulled taut across his shoulders as he folded his arms across his chest.

She gave him another wistful glance, then sighed again and raised her hands in a gesture of futility. "Ah, well. Maybe next time around." She broke open another carton of cigarettes, then crumpled up the wrap and threw it in the garbage. She started filling the slot in the showcase. "Did you finish your phoning?"

Adam nodded and dropped a handful of bills on the counter. "Yeah. This should cover the long-distance charges."

Stella eyed the money then gave him a cynical look. "Where did you call—China?"

His smile didn't quite reach his eyes as he shook his head. "Not quite."

She studied him. "Where *did* you call?"

Adam was straightening the rolls of breath mints that were displayed in a rack on the front of the counter, the sunlight from the window highlighting the blond hair on his darkly tanned arms. "I phoned Vital Statistics in Alberta to find out how we go about getting Patrick's name changed."

"And?"

He glanced up at her, his expression relaxing slightly. "It's a lot less complicated than I expected. Both Natalie and I have to make a statement in writing that Patrick's my son. Once the bureau receives that, the existing records are changed, registering me as his natural parent. After the legalities are completed, a new birth certificate is issued in the name of Adam Patrick Rutherford.''

Stella frowned as she leaned against the counter. "You mean Natalie didn't list you as his father?"

"She wasn't allowed to unless I had acknowledged in writing that Patrick was mine."

Stella raised her eyebrows in an expression of mild surprise. "I didn't know that." She squinted as she watched Adam's face, then she casually tidied the countertop. "And who else did you call, Adam?" she asked a little too innocently.

He looked at her sharply, his expression guarded. Stella took a calculated guess. "By any chance, you didn't try to track down Carl Willard, did you?"

Adam stared at her, then he glanced away, his jaw rigid. "As a matter of fact, I did."

She snorted. "I take it it wasn't a social call to invite him to the wedding." Adam made no comment, and Stella studied him intently as she absently tapped the glass top of the display case with her long scarlet nails. "So," she said very softly, "Natalie wasn't in the accident after all."

Adam's gaze riveted on her. She gave him a mirthless smile. "Don't look so stunned, Adam. Something never sat quite right with me when Jean died, but I had no choice but to take the whole story at face value. But ever since you blew back into town, it's been bugging the hell out of me. The whole thing just seemed too . . . tidy."

Adam's eyes were flashing as he looked away. Stella continued, her attention focused on his profile. "After both you and Natalie turned up, I started thinking about it again. The more I thought about it, the more holes I could see. There seemed to be only one logical explanation, and I thought I'd better do a little quiet digging so I could head you off at the pass if I had to." She hesitated for a moment and glanced down, mulling something over. When she looked up, her eyes were very sober. "I found out Carl Willard's in a nursing home in Ontario," she said quietly. "He had a bad stroke six years ago that left him partially paralyzed and unable to speak."

It was a long time before Adam turned to face her, but when he did, his eyes were cold and his voice was harsh as he ground out, "I could kill him, Stella. I could break his neck with my bare hands."

Stella's tone was caustic. "And put that son of a bitch out of his misery? Don't be stupid." Her expression softened as she came around the counter and went over to him. Laying her hand on his arm, she said earnestly, "Leave it, Adam. A higher power has already dealt with him. He could spend the next twenty years locked up in that body, unable to speak, unable to move. Just think about it—it's a punishment worse than death. So leave it be. Get on with your life."

Adam still wouldn't look at her. "How did you figure it out?"

"Gut instinct, I guess. He always bothered me, and then there was the way he dropped out of sight after the fire. He wasn't the type to walk away from a good job. And Doc would get so riled if anyone mentioned his name.'' She gave Adam's arm a little shake, trying to snap him out of his grim mood. ''Don't dwell on it, Adam. He can't ever hurt her or anyone else again, and that's all that matters.''

Adam looked down at her, his eyes bleak, then sighed heavily. ''I don't know if I'll ever be able to think about him without wanting to kill him.''

''You will. In time, you will.''

Tipping his head back, he wearily massaged the back of his neck. ''I sure hope you're right.''

''Of course I'm right.'' She gave him another pat, then went behind the counter. ''Now wipe that hang-dog look off your face and look sexy. Natalie's coming across the street.''

Adam gave her a rueful grin. ''Lord, but you're bossy.''

Stella waved her hand in an airy gesture. ''It's from working with Doc all these years. It just doesn't seem right without him in here every day, giving orders.''

''I thought he'd retired.''

Stella shook her head. ''Not really. He still owns the business, and he wanders in here from time to time to make sure I haven't run it into the ground.''

The bell on the door jangled and Natalie entered. Stella would have dropped dead before she'd ever admitted it, but underneath her cynicism and flippant manner, she was a dyed-in-the-wool romantic. And seeing these two people together left her feeling very misty-eyed, especially when she noticed how the expression on Adam's face softened when Natalie smiled up at him.

Blinking furiously, Stella blew her nose then plastered a bright smile on her face. "Well it's about time you got here. I'm going to take you two to lunch."

Natalie grasped her chest and grimaced. "You mean you're going to make us eat at the coffee shop?"

Stella pursed her lips and gave Natalie a very dry look. "Serves you right. I've had to put up with Mick's cooking for years. You can stick it for one lousy meal." Mick and his brother owned the hotel, and Mick ran the coffee shop. He was an excellent chef, but for some reason, both Natalie and Stella had always got some sort of perverse delight out of giving him a hard time.

Adam was grinning as he held the door open for the two women. "I think I'm going to clue poor old Mick in on how you two deride his cooking."

Stella sniffed. "Ha. I could teach him a thing or two."

"Oh, I'm sure you could," Adam said smoothly. "And not just about cooking, either."

The redhead gave him a long narrow look, then directed her attention to Natalie. "Any change in plans for the wedding?" she asked hopefully.

Natalie slanted an amused look up at Adam, then turned to her old friend, a tone of warning in her voice. "There aren't going to be any plans, Stella."

Stella let out a heavy sigh. "Damn, I wish you kids would let me organize a do. It doesn't seem right, just five of us at the church, especially when you both grew up here. I don't know why you won't go along with an open house at least."

"It wouldn't be right without Adam's parents here," Natalie responded.

"I hope they disown you both when they find out you got married without them," Stella said peevishly. "They lived in this town for most of their life, and they have so many friends here. And you know how Hilda loves weddings. And to think Gordon has given the toast to the bride to half the married women in this town. They will be so disappointed about this." Stella really would have liked to organize something for them, but she did understand. Adam's parents were on a fishing trip in the Northwest Territories, and there was no way of reaching them. And she suspected that Natalie was using the Rutherfords' inaccessibility as the excuse for a very private ceremony.

Adam, she guessed, was using his family's inaccessibility for entirely different reasons. This way, there was no delay; if he couldn't contact them, he wouldn't have to wait for them to arrive. And he had made it very clear that he did not want to wait.

Gordon and Hilda Rutherford had thought the world of Natalie, and Hilda especially had been very upset when Natalie had left town without so much as a goodbye. Stella couldn't help but wonder what their reaction would be when they found out that Adam and Natalie were married.

And that they already had a ten-year-old son.

THE FOLLOWING DAY, at seven o'clock in the evening, Natalie and Adam were married in the old stone church. It was a simple ceremony with no bridal march, no organ music, no flowers at the altar. There was only Doc, Stella and Patrick to watch them exchange their solemn vows and their plain gold bands.

Outside the open door, the long shadows of early evening fell as robins twittered in the still, clear air of dusk, and the soft breeze carried a fragrance of stocks, roses and freshly mown grass. The last golden blaze of sunlight slanted through the stained-glass window behind the choir loft, the diffused rays glancing across the altar in muted shafts of light.

With the soft sounds of dusk infiltrating the old church, Natalie and Adam made their eternal commitment to each other. Natalie, with dainty starflowers in her hair, stood beside Adam, the floating blue chiffon of her dress brushing against his slacks as she placed her right hand on his. The contours of Adam's face became even more pronounced as he closed his hand around hers and looked down at her. His intense gaze never wavered and his voice was filled with conviction as he made his pledge. He promised to love and comfort her, honor and keep her. The depth of feeling in his quietly spoken words overwhelmed Natalie, and she held his compelling gaze, her eyes brimming with unshed tears. And with her voice trembling with emotion, she repeated the vows that would bind them together. The rings were exchanged, and after years of separation and heartache, they were finally proclaimed husband and wife.

As the tears spilled over and slipped down her face, Natalie whispered his name. Adam's eyes darkened as he raised her hand, then solemnly kissed the gold band he had just placed on her finger. Wordlessly they stared at each other, then drawing a deep unsteady breath, Adam took her face in his hands and whispered unevenly, "Natalie. My Nat."

Drawn to her by the enraptured glow in her eyes, he lowered his head and kissed the corner of her mouth. Her whole body shaking, Natalie moved her head until their mouths met, and with a tremor coursing through him, he gathered her into his arms. For the space of that brief, galvanizing embrace, the overpowering storm of emotions was so strong it broke down the dark barriers in her mind. For that one senseless moment, Natalie's fears were overridden by sheer need. Adam held her, wondering how he was ever going to let her go.

It was twilight when Adam and Natalie returned to the trailer. The sky still held the fading colors of sunset, the jagged outline of the mountains silhouetted against a muted orange. As though the setting sun was drawing the color from the darkening sky, the orange diminished through a spectrum of shades until finally it blended with the faded light of dusk. Each vibrant shade was perfectly mirrored in the still, silvery surface of the lake, the reflections adding to the subtle hues. The stillness seemed to magnify the eerie spell as the melancholy cry of a loon echoed across the water.

Adam leaned against the fender of the truck, his arms folded in front of him as he watched Natalie. She had been very quiet during the drive up the mountain, and he had sensed she was dreading arriving at the campsite. He couldn't really blame her; he had been dreading it himself. He didn't know how he was going to handle being by themselves tonight, especially after that one staggering encouter in the church. That had rocked him . . . badly. It was one thing to exercise control when she was distressed. It was an entirely different thing to exercise control after she'd blown his discipline to bits.

But now that they were here, he hoped she would be temporarily distracted by the haunting beauty and the peace that surrounded her. The air was cool, and he saw her shiver. Feeling as though every muscle in his face had petrified, he stripped off his jacket and draped it around her shoulders. "Come on, Nat. We'd better go in before you freeze."

The ground was uneven, and the fading light made it difficult to see. Adam took her hand in his, his grasp firm as he led her silently toward the angular shape of the trailer. He could feel her shaking, but he wasn't sure if it was from the cold or from nerves.

Once inside, he turned on the small light mounted on the wall by the door, then moved away from her, determined not to touch her. He couldn't touch her; he didn't dare. Feeling as though he was suffocating, he roughly stripped off his tie and undid the top buttons of his shirt, his expression inflexible.

"Adam?"

He dropped the tie on the table, then turned to face her. She was watching him, her body so stiff she appeared almost breakable, the anxiety in her eyes dominating her face. Suddenly her shoulders sagged and she clutched her arms in front of her in a gesture of anguish. "Oh, Adam, what have I done to you?"

He reacted. She closed her eyes, her breath catching a tortured sob as he pulled her against him, encircling her slender form. He cradled her head against his shoulder, his face pressed against her hair as he whispered hoarsely, "Shh, Nat. Don't cry. It's okay."

"Adam—"

"Don't try to talk," he interjected raggedly. "Just let me hold you."

It helped—being able to hold her. Her warmth soothed the hollow ache in him, and the firmness of her body against his helped dull his unsatisfied hunger. She filled up the emptiness, and that eased the tension that gripped him. He closed his eyes, savoring the delicate scent of her perfume, the sensuousness of her silky dress against her bare back, the weight of her arms around his shoulders. Yes, it did help.

He held her for a long time, unaware of the deepening night or of the breeze eddying in through the open door or of the moths fluttering around the dim light. He held her until his heartbeat steadied and until her trembling stopped.

Finally she stirred in his arms, and easing away from him slightly, she looked up. Her eyes darkening, she took his face in her hands and drew his head down, her mouth moving lightly against his in a tormentingly gentle kiss. It was all Adam could do to keep from crushing her against him.

With a sigh, she slowly opened her eyes as she pulled away, her hands still warm against his face. There was a misty glow in her eyes as she whispered, "I do love you, Adam."

Moved beyond words, he swallowed against the ache in his throat as he caressed her back, his eyes absorbing every detail of her. When he was able to speak, his voice was painfully husky. "I've been waiting all my life for today, Nat." Feeling raw and exposed, he closed his eyes and tightened his arms around her. "I need you so damned much."

Holding him tightly, she slid her hand into his hair, her embrace protective. When she felt his tension ease, she began to slowly stroke his head, her touch soothing and gentle. "Just think, Adam," she whispered, her words tinged with quiet wonder, "today is the beginning of a whole new life."

Adam kissed the curve of her neck, then raised his head. He trailed his finger across the fullness of her bottom lip, his expression softening. "Then maybe we should break open a bottle of champagne to launch it."

Natalie narrowed her eyes in a very skeptical look. "Is that a genuine invitation or merely an idle thought?"

The fine laugh lines around his eyes deepened as he grinned. "A genuine invitation."

Not quite convinced, she asked suspiciously, "Is this some of Doc's dreadful potato champagne, or is it the real stuff?"

"Definitely not the best, possibly not even very good, but certainly the real stuff."

Natalie laughed, and Adam was completely captivated by her. She looked so lovely standing there with flowers in her hair and her eyes so full of life and laughter.

"What's the matter, Adam?"

She was watching him with a puzzled look, and he smiled softly as he caressed her cheek. "Do you know how much I love to hear you laugh?" he asked gruffly.

She laid her hand on top of his and met his warm gaze. "Do you know how happy I am?"

There was an amused gleam in his eyes. "Patrick's right. You do answer questions with questions."

She smiled, then sighed and shook her head. "He's going to run wild at Doc's, especially with Stella indulging him."

"Good. Every kid should have a chance to run wild and be indulged once in a while."

"That's easy for you to say."

He grinned. "You're right. It easy for me to say." Adam lost all sense of time and place as he gazed down into her wide gray eyes, her physical closeness testing him to the limit. Knowing he had little resistance left, he caught her shoulders and eased her away. "I'll get the champagne," he murmured unsteadily.

Adam had brought a small suitcase of Natalie's with him when he had come back to get dressed for the ceremony, and he had laid it on the settee at the end of the trailer. He heard her open it as he took the chilled bottle out of the fridge. Closing the refrigerator door with his elbow, he picked two glasses out of the cupboard and went over to her. He knew something was wrong when she didn't look up at him.

"What's the matter?"

She nervously fingered a garment still packed in the suitcase, then turned to look at him. All the vibrancy had drained out of her face.

Sensing she did not want him to touch her, he very carefully set the bottle and glasses down, then stuck his hands in the pockets of his slacks and leaned against the cupboard. His expression was solemn as he encouraged her, "Talk to me, Nat."

Her voice was weak. "My feelings are all over the place. One minute I'm so happy I can't believe it, and the next minute I'm so scared I can hardly think. And mixed up with that is so much guilt, it seems I'll never get out from under it."

"What happened just now? What frightened you?"

She averted her gaze and folded her arms stiffly in front of her. There was some inner struggle going on; that was evident by the look on her face. And it was evident by the brittleness in her voice when she finally spoke. "It's obvious that we didn't make arrangements to be here by ourselves so we could sleep in separate beds."

It sounded so harsh, but he recognized the sharp undertone as one of self-contempt, and Adam waited, a heaviness settling in his stomach. She gave him a taut smile. "When you went to get the champagne, I wanted to say something a new wife would say, like 'Why don't we take it to bed with us.' I wanted to be able to do that, but the minute I started rehearsing it in my head, I started freezing up. And I remember—" She turned away abruptly, her body rigid as she gave a forced, bitter laugh. "Isn't this a wonderful, unforgettable experience, Adam? A honeymoon with a paranoid wife?"

Adam had never felt quite so impotent in his life, but he knew he had to make her say it all. "Why the guilt, Nat?" he asked quietly. "What makes you feel guilty?"

At first he thought she wasn't going to answer, then she turned, stared at him for a long time and finally whispered, "You make me feel guilty."

She may as well have slapped him. The muscles in his face stiffened. "How?" he asked tautly.

"Because, Adam," she answered. "Because I sometimes feel as though I've trapped you. If it hadn't been for finding out about Patrick, would you have ever come back after you talked to me that first time? And if it hadn't been for Patrick, would you be stuck with a woman who is so sexually warped she panics when somebody touches her?''

Adam suddenly felt as though he didn't know this slender woman with the haunting eyes who stood before him. His voice was cold as he said, ''So you resent having him.''

''No!'' Her face went white with shock as she caught his arm, her eyes beseeching him to understand. ''Heavens, no. I don't resent him, Adam. He's my son, and I love him.'' Her eyes suddenly filled with tears and she turned away. ''Don't you see? If you hadn't found out about Patrick, you would have left town and never looked back.''

And finally, Adam did see. Somehow he was going to have to make her understand. ''I might have left town, Nat,'' he said solemnly, ''but I most certainly would have looked back.''

Natalie faced him, her brimming eyes revealing the look of someone desperately wanting to believe. He met her gaze with a steady stare. His tone was without censure as he said softly, ''I told you once before not to doubt my feelings. I'm here because I want to be.''

Brushing away the tears with her fingertips, she clasped her arms around herself and whispered, more to herself than to him, ''But are you going to want to stay?''

It annoyed him that she had so little faith in the sincerity of his feelings, and his voice had a steely edge when he demanded, "And what in hell is that supposed to mean?"

She was struggling to hold back tears and she tried to swallow. Unable to speak, she shrugged her shoulders in a helpless gesture, and he felt like a bastard for hurting her. He wanted to stop this ordeal, but he didn't know how. It wasn't something he could simply walk away from. Not now. Deliberately avoiding her eyes, he slowly undid the cuffs of his sleeves and rolled them back. "How else do I make you feel guilty?"

It took her a moment before she could answer, and even then he could barely hear her. "I know you so well, Adam. We spent so much time together, and I know—" Closing her eyes, she tipped her head back, as though she was utterly spent. "You said there was more to a relationship than sex." She looked at him, her expression solemn. "Those are fine words, but how long can a relationship last under that kind of strain?"

She stopped him as he opened his mouth to answer. "No! Don't say anything," she pleaded. "Let me finish. Please let me finish." She made a gesture of frustration with her hands then clenched them into fists, her expression tormented. "I think I've relived every moment we spent together at least a thousand times. And if I learned anything that summer, it was what a very physical person you are." She hauled in a deep breath and pressed her hands tightly against her thighs. Her voice became very strained as she whispered huskily, "I know how much pleasure you derive from that intimacy, and I know how little it takes to arouse you. And I know what you were feeling in the church, and I know what you were feeling a few minutes ago. I know these things, Adam.'' Her voice broke, her desperate unhappiness apparent. "And do you know how much I want to give you that pleasure again, and what I'd give to be able to lose myself in that incredible passion we used to share? Do you know?'' Tears were slipping down her face, and she had her arms clutched in front of her.

Adam was rooted to the spot, his own face haggard as her unbearable pain became his. But somehow he managed to speak, his voice ragged. "Have you any idea how empty and meaningless my life has been? Do you know the times I would have endured anything just to be able to wake up in the middle of the night and find you sleeping beside me?''

She kept her distance for a moment, then with a low sob, she was in his arms, clinging to him with desperate strength. Clenching his jaw against the strangling ache in his throat, Adam crushed her against him. "If I have to choose, I'll take the frustration over the emptiness anytime,'' he murmured hoarsely. "Anything is more tolerable than that.''

"Adam—''

"No. No more, Nat,'' he said firmly, gently. "No more self-recriminations or doubts. I know it isn't going to be easy, but we're damned lucky to even be together.'' He closed his eyes and rested his head against hers, waiting for the ache in his chest to ease.

Neither of them spoke again, and he stroked her back until he felt her body relax. Finally he eased her away from him and smiled down at her. "I have this bottle of questionable vintage and even more questionable quality, and I have every intention of getting you slightly drunk."

He could sense her inner struggle to hang on to her shaky composure, but like sunshine through the rain, she smiled at him through her tears. "It sounds wonderful." The tears spilled down her face, but the smile stayed as she suggested unevenly, "Why don't we take it to bed with us."

The lights went on in Adam's eyes, and his face creased into an engaging grin. "Sounds like one hell of an idea." He gave her a quick hug then caught her by the wrist. "Come on."

She resisted and he glanced down at her. She looked just the way she did when she was sixteen—shy, uncertain, a little scared—and he suddenly felt the loss of the intervening years. "What?" he asked softly.

The pulse in her throat was fluttering wildly, and it was obvious she was nervous as she slipped her hand out of his. "You go ahead. I'll be in in a minute."

He gazed at her for a moment, then nodded, and picking up the bottle and glasses, he went into the minuscule bedroom and quietly closed the door.

The room was stuffy from being closed up all day, and Adam set the bottle and glasses on the shelf at the head of the bed, turned on the small lamp mounted on the wall, then cranked open all the windows. A soft night breeze wafted in as Adam stripped off his jacket and shirt and hung them on a hook. His expression was very thoughtful. He had a number of silent conversations with himself as he removed the rest of his clothes, but none of them got him anywhere.

She had to change clothes; that was obvious. And because she wouldn't want to provoke him by wear-

ing something soft and feminine, she would put on
something practical. Adam wished it could have been
different, but that's the way it was. Leaving his underwear on as a concession to her, Adam threw back
the covers and climbed into bed. With an air of
preoccupation, he stacked the pillows behind his back
and drew up the sheet. His face still solemn, he
reached for the bottle and began peeling off the foil
wrap.

The folding door opened, and Natalie came in.
Adam froze, his full attention glued on her. What she
had on was anything but practical. Seductive? Yes.
Provocative? Absolutely. But practical? Not even
close.

He could feel his heavy pulse accelerate as he scrutinized her. She still had her hair up, exposing the long
column of her neck and her naked shoulders. But that
was only half of it. She had on a deep mauve negligee
that accentuated every curve, and the lace bodice revealed tantalizing amounts of cleavage and bare skin.
The long skirt molded to her and when she moved, it
seemed to erotically caress her.

His heart was hammering so hard he could barely
breathe, and it felt as if it would slam through his chest
as he absorbed every intoxicating detail of her. When
he was able to speak, his voice was low and velvety and
textured by a smoldering sexuality. "Nice. Very nice."

She was trembling and uncertain, but her gaze was
riveted on him, her eyes dark and smoky. Leaning
forward, Adam caught her wrist, his expression serious as he drew her to him. It cost him a heavy price not
to touch her the way he wanted to, but he simply
pulled her down and gathered her against him. Hold-

ing her like that felt so good, but he wanted so much more. Every nerve in his body was on fire, but he clamped down on the heated excitement that was pounding through him, determined to control the incredible fever of wanting her.

It seemed to take an eternity for that initial burst of desire to pass, but eventually his pulse steadied and the ache abated. Still very shaken, he smoothed his hand across her back. "Thank you," he whispered, his lips moving against the soft curve of her shoulder.

Raising herself on one elbow, she looked at him. "For what?"

He caressed her neck with the back of his hand, his eyes dark as he slipped his fingers under the strap of her negligee. "For trusting me enough to wear this."

A light flush colored her cheeks and she shrugged self-consciously. "If we hadn't talked before I never would have had the courage." Her expression changed as she absently combed her fingers through his hair, her eyes deeply troubled. "What's wrong with me, Adam? Why can I go this far but no farther? Why—"

"Don't, Nat. Tonight we simply enjoy being together." He loosely wrapped his arms around her back, and there was a glint of amusement in his eyes as he looked at her. "Don't worry about it. It takes me a while to calm down, but my grandmother used to swear that denial was good for the soul."

There was a smile in her eyes as she propped her head on her hand, her other arm resting on his chest. "That sounds like a lousy way to develop character."

He laughed. "I always thought so." He shifted his hold on her, and the silky material of her negligee moved against her skin. The expression in his eyes softened as he smoothed his hand up her back. "It does feel so damned good to hold you."

A gleam of mischief appeared in her eyes and she grinned down at him. "What you really mean is that under the circumstances, holding me is only slightly less trying than throwing yourself in front of a moving train."

His smile was lopsided and he gave her a wry look. "Something like that." He shifted his shoulders to a more comfortable position, then adjusted his hold on her as his smile broadened. "Besides, I want to talk."

She laughed and gave his chest a playful slap. "Now that's a new twist. And such a *good* line, Adam."

He grinned up at her. "Glad you like it."

The sparkle in her eyes softened as she slowly trailed her finger across his bottom lip. "Do you know how much I love you, Adam Rutherford?"

He kissed her fingertip as he tightened his arm around her. "I think I could stand to have you tell me, Natalie Rutherford."

Her tone was teasing as she said, "I thought you were going to get me drunk."

"I think I'm drunk already," he said, his gaze smoldering.

She wove her fingers through his hair and laughed softly. "Cute, Adam, but definitely clichéd."

"Married three hours and a critic already."

Her eyes dancing with laughter, Natalie caught his ears and gave his head a shake as she groaned in frustration. "Just pour the wine, Adam. Pour the damned wine."

Adam laughed and hugged her hard, then hauled himself into a sitting position. With Natalie sitting cross-legged beside him, he opened the bottle, the plastic cork leaving a dint in the roof when it exploded, before ricocheting off the walls. The champagne fizzed down the side of the bottle onto his bare chest, and Natalie made some smart comments when it collected in his navel. It set the mood for the rest of the night. They emptied the bottle, they talked, they laughed, and they talked some more. There were no shadows, no grim reminders. Instead, it was a time of incredible closeness; it was a time of a very special kind of sharing. The sky was starting to lighten when Natalie finally drifted off to sleep, her head on his shoulder, her arm draped across his chest. And as he watched her sleep, Adam didn't think it was possible for him to love anybody more than he loved her.

CHAPTER ELEVEN

IT WAS THE THIRD NIGHT in a row that Adam had quietly left his bed, leaving Natalie alone as she slept. He had gone down to the lake, trying to find relief from the agony of wanting her, but fighting his natural instincts was a hopeless battle. Especially at night.

During the day, he could discipline himself to a certain degree, and he made certain he tested that discipline as little as possible. But at night, when she was lying so close to him, his mind rebelled and he'd lie there in the dark, trying to ignore the consuming hunger that inflamed him. He'd hit a point where he had to leave, the fever of desire finally unbearable. And he was beginning to wonder how much longer he could maintain the facade of calmly coping with the situation when he was, in fact, quietly going out of his mind.

A log in the fire charred through and the burning wood shifted, sending a shower of sparks skyward. Adam was lying in the hammock with his hands behind his head, staring unseeingly at the black canopy of densely interwoven branches. The fire snapped and crackled again, sending up another eruption of sparks, and he turned his head to watch the dancing flames, his expression solemn. The night sky had lightened slightly and he could see the lake, its surface mirror smooth in the stillness of approaching dawn, the jagged outline of the mountains barely visible against the fading blackness.

The firelight cast flickering shadows against the trunks of the trees, and Adam watched the play of light and darkness, trying to focus his thoughts on something other than the unsatisfied ache that was gnawing at him. Unable to remain motionless any longer, he swung out of the hammock. He checked the fire, then turned toward the lake. His boots echoed hollowly on the wooden dock, then he reached the end and stood staring out. There was a raft anchored a short distance from the shore, and he could just make out the dark outline of it against the faint gleam of water. He hesitated a moment, then started stripping off his clothes.

The water was so frigid it knocked the wind out of him, and he had trouble catching his breath when he surfaced. He finally hauled in some air, and with dogged single-mindedness, set out toward the raft in a clean fast crawl. Adam did laps from the end of the dock to the raft until his body was nearly paralyzed with cold, but he continued to push himself on, trying to dull his senses with sheer exhaustion.

He was on his way back to the dock when he caught a soft glimmer of satin and realized that Natalie was standing on the weathered wooden structure watching him. The mauve nightie shimmered as she moved toward him, and she looked like some shadowy illusion emerging from the darkness. As she stopped at the end of the pier, a sudden breeze billowed through the lustrous fabric, swirling it around her, and her hair whipped across her face, the faint light touching it with a silver sheen.

Placing his hands on the wooden surface, he hoisted himself out of the frigid water, the muscles across his shoulders rippling. Water sluiced down his naked body as he stood up, his skin gleaming. Silently he reached for his jeans, which were draped over one of the air mattresses leaning against the pilings.

Her presence disturbed him, and he was even more disturbed when she reached out and touched him—a touch that was like liquid fire as she slowly brushed beads of moisture from his chest. As though scalded, Adam reacted. Catching her wrist, he pulled her hand away. "Don't, Natalie," he said, a taut edge to his voice.

"Let me," she whispered unsteadily.

Adam felt as if his chest was caving in, and he clenched his jaw against the rush of heat that pumped through him. He loosened his hold on her slightly, keenly aware that he could feel her rapid pulse beneath his fingers. His voice was hoarse when he spoke. "Don't, Nat. Don't make it worse than it is."

She moved closer, and her hair feathered across his chest with tantalizing lightness as she smoothed her other hand up his torso. "This time you have to trust me, Adam," she murmured. Then very lightly, she moved her hand downward.

Clamping his teeth together, Adam tried to choke back a groan as the intimacy of her caress set off an explosion of white-hot heat, a surge of desire searing through him. He couldn't breathe, and an incapacitating weakness slammed into him as she lightly stroked him, driving him senseless with her touch. He ground out her name and roughly grasped her wrist. "Please, Nat. Stop. For God's sake, stop."

Weakly she leaned against him, her face against his chest. "Hold me."

Adam felt as if every drop of his blood was engorging his groin. Shaken and fighting for breath, he released his grip on her wrists, then gathered her against him, his face buried in her hair. Natalie was trembling as she slipped her arms around him, and when she spoke her voice was low. "I want so badly to touch you the way I used to. Please let me, Adam."

He tried to think, tried to regain some control over his scorching desire that had sensitized every nerve, but he was lost. The only thing he was conscious of was Natalie, and the unbearable ache of wanting her. She turned her head and slowly brushed her mouth against his. "Please, Adam." She caught his arms and pushed them away, then she sank to her knees in front of him.

But before she could touch him, he grasped her head and held her immobile. The last of his strength deserted him, and with his legs too weak to support him any longer, he sank down in front of her. Tightening his grip on her face, he spoke, his voice raw and unsteady. "I love you, Nat. And I don't want you to do anything simply because you think you should."

She didn't answer. Instead, she caressed his jaw, then leaned forward and kissed him softly. With his heart slamming against his chest, Adam opened his mouth and responded hungrily, urgently, his body famished for the sustenance of hers. He felt her tense, then she tightened her hold on him and pulled away.

Taking a ragged breath, she whispered unevenly, "Let me love you, Adam. Let me do it my way."

He understood what she was asking, but he didn't know how he was going to keep from responding. But somehow, he had to. Closing his eyes, he turned his head and kissed the palm of her hand, his voice chocked. "I won't do anything to frighten you, Nat. I promise."

The air mattress was cold and damp, but Adam was unaware of everything except the weight of her on top of him and the soothing hardness of her against his groin. His breathing became more labored and his pulse went wild as she began to work her spell. Adam thought he was going to go out of his mind. Her mouth was warm and moist against his skin, and her hands slowly explored the planes of his wet body, as though she was committing every inch of him to memory. He wanted to move against her, to find the driving rhythm that would bring relief from the torment, but he remained immobile, his body braced against the throbbing agony she aroused.

A low sound was wrung from him as Natalie eased her weight off him, the thick heavy ache no longer soothed by the pressure of her body. Unable to endure it, Adam was about to roll over on his stomach, but she gently grasped him, and he had to grit his teeth to keep from crying out. He was so inundated with fevered sensations that he didn't fully comprehend her intent when she straddled his body, but when she guided him into her, he reacted. Roughly clasping her arms, he pulled her down against him, his voice ragged and weak. "Nat, you don't have to—"

But she moved against him and he was unable to go on, his body paralyzed with wild excitement. She bracketed his face with her hands and kissed him softly, then whispered huskily against his mouth. "I want to, Adam." Her weight shifted, and Adam's breath caught as shock waves of heat ripped through him, every movement tormenting him even more. She disengaged his grip and pressed his arms down, then tightly lacing her fingers through his, she slowly started to move against him.

She stroked him to a frenzy, slowly drawing away, then engulfing him, her body moist and tight around his. The hunger in him continued to build to an agonizing pressure, and he felt as if she were dragging him inside out each time she drew away. Finally he hit the peak of his endurance, and he groaned and twisted under her as the liquid heat finally erupted from him with a devastating force. The scalding release was so violent, so exquisite that he was senseless to everything else. Everything except the woman who lay trembling in his arms. And turning his face into the tumble of her hair, he held her with immeasurable tenderness, a dull ache suddenly encasing his chest.

ADAM AWOKE THE NEXT MORNING to sounds of rain on the roof and an outside world that was shrouded in a gray drizzle. He was lying on his stomach, a sheet draped loosely across his hips, his body drugged by a warm, languid sensation. But the drifting sense of contentment was roughly dispelled when he recalled what had happened on the dock only hours before.

And he became wide awake. The encounter had shaken Natalie badly, and she had really gone to pieces afterward. She had trembled as though she was in shock, and he had carried her back to the trailer and put her to bed, a sick feeling twisting in the pit of his stomach when she continued to cling to him, yet refused to talk.

Now, in the cold light of day, that same sick feeling hit him. Adam closed his eyes, his face drawn. How was he going to face her, knowing that she'd forced herself to do what she had because of guilt. His eyes flew open and he stared at the empty pillow beside him. And where was she? Suddenly apprehensive, he pushed himself out of bed.

Just then the folding door slid open, and Natalie came in carrying two mugs of coffee. Adam's attention was instantly riveted on her face. She seemed unwilling to meet his gaze as she came around the end of the bed and set the cups on the ledge by his head. There were taut lines around his mouth as he caught her wrist. "I know it doesn't really help much, but I am sorry about last night."

Natalie looked at him, her eyes glistening with unshed tears as she turned her wrist and slipped her hand into his. Her grip was tight as she murmured, "Don't be sorry." Her mouth was trembling, and she looked so vulnerable. But suddenly she smiled through her tears, and with a soft sob, she slipped into his arms. "Don't be sorry, Adam. If you only knew how special last night was for me."

With his hands tangled in her hair, Adam caught her face and gently raised it until he could see her eyes. His expression was grave. "But was it, Nat, or was it just an exercise to please me?"

She pulled away from him, and brushing aside her tears with the back of her hand, she gazed down at him, her eyes dark and misty. "I was so scared, Adam. I wanted so badly to touch you, to make love to you the way I used to. But I didn't know how far I could go. But knowing how much you needed me—" She glanced away and swallowed with great difficulty, fighting hard to suppress her raw emotions. It took her a while to regain control, but finally she drew in an unsteady breath and continued, her voice even more husky. "Knowing you needed me somehow gave me the courage to go on."

Adam slowly caressed her face, his eyes troubled. "But it wasn't that good for you, was it?"

Sitting up, she took his hand between hers, and he sensed the emotional upheaval she was struggling with as she stared down at their joined hands. She finally looked at him, her voice breaking beneath the stress. "I know you won't really understand it, but whether it was good for me or it wasn't didn't really matter. It wasn't important."

"It's important to me, Nat," he said quietly.

Her eyes intent, she whispered, "Do you know how special it was for me to be able to give you that kind of pleasure? I was so afraid I couldn't follow through, but I did, Adam, and that meant so much." Fresh tears slipped down her face. "The fact that I didn't have a climax *wasn't* important, but the fact that I could share something like that with you was. Don't you see, Adam, that I took an enormous step forward?"

Adam studied her, then looked down at her hands as he toyed with her wedding ring, an odd tenor to his voice. "But in other words, I still have to keep my hands to myself."

Pulling free of his grasp, Natalie lifted his chin, forcing him to look at her. "Don't feel that you're cheating me out of anything, Adam. Please, don't feel that way. It meant so much to me."

His gaze was penetrating. "If that's true, why were you so upset afterward?"

Her eyes clouded and her uneasiness was apparent. She looked away, the pulse in her neck beating wildly. He touched her cheek to turn her face toward him. "Why, Natalie?"

Her breath caught, and she nervously clasped her hands together, her expressive eyes revealing her distress. "I don't know how to explain it."

"Try."

She stared at him for a moment longer, then she looked away, her face pale. "For the first time in eleven years, I felt clean inside. That awful tainted feeling was gone, and I don't think I can ever find the words to explain how good that feels." His hand was still against her cheek, and she covered it with her own as she looked at him again. "I know you're having trouble with what happened," she whispered, "but if you only knew how vitally important it is to me to simply feel touchable again, you wouldn't question what happened last night."

A painful contraction tightened Adam's chest, and without speaking he slipped his hand to the back of her head and pulled her down. Closing his eyes, he wrapped his arms around her and gathered her securely against him, his face set in somber lines. He should have been more than satisfied with her explanation, but for some reason it left him feeling very hollow.

The soft patter of rain on the roof filled the silence as he held her and stared off into space. Finally he dragged his thoughts back, and sighing softly, he began to stroke her hair. "I don't want you doing anything, especially going to bed with me, simply because you think you owe it to me, Nat," he said quietly.

She raised her head, her eyes smoky. "I love the feel of your body, and I like to touch you. And just because I didn't experience the same thing you did doesn't mean it wasn't enjoyable for me." Her voice became unsteady as she softly caressed his lips. "You gave me the space I needed last night, and that made me feel so special."

Brushing her tousled hair back behind her ear, Adam let his hand rest against her neck, his eyes serious as he stroked her jaw with his thumb. His voice was husky when he murmured, "If only you knew how hard it was to keep from touching you. You arouse me until I can hardly think, and it's so damned incredible and exciting. I just want to be able to arouse the same feeling in you."

Her trembling fingers against his mouth, she struggled to contain her feelings. "Don't," she whispered brokenly. "Don't think about something that might never be. I might never be able to put the entire nightmare behind me."

"Nat—"

But she didn't give him a chance to speak. She caught his head, her fingers buried in his hair as she covered his mouth in a soft pliant kiss. His response was instantaneous, and he shuddered as the heat of desire rushed through him. Hauling in a ragged breath, he twisted his head free, his pulse pounding as he murmured hoarsely, "Nat . . . don't."

But she found his mouth again, her hands curved around his neck, her hold on his face secure. "I want to, Adam," she whispered against his mouth. "Don't fight me."

And Adam felt as if he was paralyzed as she moved on top of him, her body molded tightly against his, her softness inflaming his senses. He was lost, trapped in the fire that she aroused in him.

THE NEXT WEEK was almost perfect. There were times, though, when Adam was deeply bothered by the feeling he was using her, but for the most part those days were truly golden ones. They had the time and the privacy to redevelop the special closeness they had once shared, and each savored every minute of it.

Even the weather was perfect, but it turned scorching hot, and in an attempt to beat the heat, they had gone for a swim. The mountain lake was freezing, and they only managed a few laps to the raft and back before Natalie decided she'd had enough and hauled herself onto the dock, the water from her hair cascading down her back. She picked up a towel and dried her face and arms, then started toweling her hair.

Hooking his arms on the edge of the pier, Adam watched her. "Don't tell me you're quitting already."

Her lips blue with cold, she confirmed, "I'm quitting already."

He laughed as he hoisted himself onto the dock, then wiped the water from his face. "I told you not to tell me that."

Natalie shivered, her teeth chattering. "I think you're trying to do away with me, Adam Rutherford. If that water was one degree colder, it would be ice."

He grinned at her as he took the towel out of her hands. "What a baby."

She made a face, then checked the position of the sun before she moved one of the air mattresses. "I don't care if I'm a baby or not. It's still going to take me at least two hours to thaw out."

She stretched out on her stomach, then resting her head on her arms, she turned her head toward the sun and closed her eyes. Adam tossed the other air mattress down beside her. Lying on his back, he, too, shut his eyes.

Her voice was slightly muffled. "Why, may I ask, are you lying here? I thought you intended on swimming another eight or nine miles."

"Don't get smart," he warned, "or I'll throw you in again."

"I'd sink your canoe."

"You can't sink that canoe, Natalie."

There was amusement in her voice. "Why? We've done it before."

Adam started laughing. "I'd forgotten about that. Dad's brand-new canoe and we rip the bottom out going through the rapids." Squinting against the blinding sun, he turned his head to look at her, his face creased with a grin. "Lord, did I catch hell for that."

She opened her eyes and gave him a reproachful look. "You did not. Considering he lost his new canoe and we nearly drowned in the whirlpool trying to find it, your dad was really decent about it."

"He might have been decent about his canoe, but he sure in hell wasn't decent about my taking you through those rapids in the first place. Even Mom got into it. For days afterward, every conversation was peppered with pointed little references about assuming responsibility."

Dragging her hand from under her head, Natalie reached over and patted his shoulder. "Poor Adam," she said without a shred of sympathy.

"You could show a little remorse, you know. Especially since it was your damned idea in the first place. 'Take me white-water canoeing, Adam. It'll be so much fun,'" he mimicked.

She grinned and slapped his chest. "It *was* fun." Bracing herself on her elbows, she leaned over and kissed him on the cheek. "And you were an angel not to tell your parents I pushed you into it."

He gazed up at her, his eyes dancing with amusement as he softly caressed her shoulder. "They wouldn't have believed me anyway. As far as they were concerned, you were a blameless innocent. Their only concern about us spending so much time together was the four-year difference between us. They felt it was such a big gap at that age." His eyes developed a wicked gleam as he added, "And they were concerned their golden-haired boy would lead you astray."

Natalie slanted an amused look down at him. "And who says parents are blind." Her expression grew pensive as she began tracing invisible patterns on his darkly tanned chest. "It was funny, but just before Patrick was born, it was your mom I wanted with me most. I was so scared, and she was always so calm and unflappable. She always seemed to know what to do or what people needed." Natalie looked at him, her expression troubled. "I really missed them when I left. In fact, if they'd been home the night it happened, I would have gone to them first."

Tightening his hold on her shoulder, he said softly, "They thought a lot of you. I know you're worried about facing them, but I know for a fact they're going to be so glad to have you back." He smiled with affection as he trailed his finger down her cheek. "Come on, Nat, can't you picture it? Mom will have a little cry, and Dad will get all blustery and gruff and overprotective."

She shrugged self-consciously, a touch of apprehension in her eyes. "I guess the big thing is Patrick. What are they going to say?"

He gazed at her for a minute, then grinned. "I *know* what they're going to say. Dad's going to give me hell for leading his blameless innocent astray, and every conversation will be peppered with pointed little references about assuming responsibility."

That made her smile, and she shook her head at him. "You're awful, do you know that?"

"I know."

Propping her head on her hand, she began to trace patterns on his chest again, not quite sure how to approach him. She finally looked at him and said unevenly, "How would you feel about me getting pregnant right away?"

He watched her intently. "How about defining 'right away.'"

She gave him an anxious little half smile. "Like maybe already."

He stared up at her, feeling a little like she'd dropped him in the lake with that one. When he finally surfaced from the jolt, he realized she had a very worried expression on her face. Shifting his position, he slipped his arms around her, his gaze tender. "I think I could learn to live with it," he said gently. "As a matter of fact, I kind of like the idea."

She exhaled in a rush and relaxed against him. He slid his hand around her neck and hooked his knuckles under her chin, then lifted her face. "Hey, Nat," he admonished gently, "I'm not the only one to be considered here. How about you?"

She gazed down at him, and when she assured herself he was being completely honest, her face lit up with gladness. "I'd love it."

The warm expression in his eyes held a hint of amusement. "How do you think Patrick would feel about us having another kid?"

"I think he'd love it, too. He's totally sick of being an only child. He'd see a new baby as the big liberation. I'd have somebody else to fuss over, and maybe I'd get off his case."

Adam grinned. "Sounds like a hell of a deal." There were beads of water from her hair clinging to her shoulders, and Adam wiped them away with his hand. Unable to resist the texture of her skin, he lightly caressed the nape of her neck, then tunneled his fingers into the wet tangle of her hair.

Natalie's eyes darkened and she slowly smoothed her hand across his chest, her touch deliberately provocative. He caught her hand and kissed her palm, then said gruffly, "It's too hot, Nat."

"But I'm cold, Adam," she whispered as she cupped her hand beneath his head and leaned over him.

She was still chilled from the swim, and her wet swimsuit was cold against his skin as he turned to face her. Gathering her against him, he began to stroke her back. Right then, he would have sold his soul to be able to strip off the wet barrier of fabric that separated them and experience the intoxicating sensation of her naked body against his. Natalie began to caress his shoulder, and Adam braced himself on his elbow as he gazed down at her. The warmth in her eyes hypnotized him as she caught him by the back of the head and pressed him down.

It was a gentle searching kiss that knocked the wind out of him, but he felt even more breathless as she opened her mouth under his. With his senses drugged by a rush of desire, he responded with a blistering, thirsty kiss. That contact completely shattered his control, and without thinking, he crushed her against him, his arms like a vise as he pulled her beneath him. For a split second Natalie remained pliant in his fierce embrace, then suddenly she was twisting frantically, trying to fight him off.

Jerking her head away, she pushed against his chest, her voice filled with panic. "No! Don't!"

Her reaction stunned him, and Adam froze. His face was suddenly expressionless as he stared down into her terror-filled eyes, then averting his gaze, he stiffly withdrew his arms and rolled to his feet. His eyes were steely and the muscles in his jaw were twitching as he stood at the end of the dock and stared rigidly across the lake. The fault was his; he knew that, but even recognizing that fact, her reaction had still stung. Maybe what wounded his pride more than anything was the fact that she had, for that brief flash, replaced him with the ugly recollections of her stepfather. And that realization left him cold.

He heard her get up, and every muscle in his body tensed as she paused beside him and laid her hand on his arm. Her voice was shaking and very weak. "I'm sorry, Adam. That was an unforgivable thing to do to you."

He turned his head and stared down at her, then answered tautly, "Yes, it was." He snatched the other towel off the piling, then turned and left her standing there.

He knew he was handling this all wrong, but he couldn't stop himself. Realizing that she reacted to him the same way she must have reacted to Carl Willard filled him with a sickness he couldn't describe. He felt as though she'd stabbed him in the back.

Entering the trailer, he flung the towel on the counter, then opened the top cupboard and took out a bottle of rye. He picked a glass out of the sink and went into the bedroom, his face like stone as he slammed the folding door shut behind him. He poured himself a drink and tossed it back, then changed into his jeans.

Adam had just finished pulling on his boots when he heard Natalie enter the trailer. He poured himself another drink and stood with his back toward the door, his mouth compressed into a hard line.

The door slid open, and a soft breeze stirred the curtains. There was a tense silence, then Natalie spoke. "I don't blame you for being angry, Adam. What I did to you out there was the worst insult I could have ever leveled at you. I know it's not enough to say I'm sorry, but I am."

He took a stiff drink, then turned to face her. "Under the circumstances, I can't see any point in discussing it."

Natalie was standing in the doorway, her hair hanging down her back in a wet tangle, her swimsuit damp against her body. There was an air of inevitability about her as she met his hostile gaze. "Would it be better if I left?"

He responded coldly, "Do you want to leave?"

She had seemed so self-possessed, but it wasn't until she looked away that he realized how stark her expression was. "What I want, Adam," she said carefully, "is to not hurt you anymore." She cast him a quick glance, then turned and walked out of the tiny room.

Swearing in frustration, Adam slammed his glass down and went after her. He caught her by the arm and whirled her around. "Where in hell are you going?"

She tried to pull free of his grasp. "Just let me go," she said brokenly.

He eased his grip on her, but his expression was still uncompromising as he stared down at her. "I have no intentions of letting you go," he snapped.

"Anybody home?"

Adam tensed, and Natalie weakly closed her eyes. "It's Doc."

Adam swore under his breath, then let go of her arm. "Go change," he said curtly, "and I'll go talk to him."

Doc was almost at the trailer when Adam went to the door. But he was not alone. There was another man with him who was wearing the uniform of a park ranger.

Doc raised his hand in greeting when he saw Adam. "Sorry to intrude, lad, but we have a wee bit of an emergency on our hands."

Adam opened the screen door and stood back as the two men entered the trailer. Doc turned stiffly to introduce the man who had followed him in. "This is Doug Clifford, Adam. He's the park warden at Andrews Lake." As they shook hands, Adam scrutinized Doc's companion. The warden was in his early fifties and had the weathered look of a man who had spent most of his life outdoors.

Andrews Lake was the name the locals tagged a nearby provincial park that covered several hundred square miles of some of the most rugged terrain in the province. This year, the area had been extremely dry and there was some concern about the wildlife. Adam wondered if that problem had something to do with the warden's visit.

He motioned them toward the settee. "So what's this emergency?"

Doug Clifford sat down wearily, then took off his hat and wiped his brow. "We have a group of five young hikers who are trapped in the box canyon at the south face of Hoodoo Mountain. We had a fire break out in that area last night. There wouldn't have been too much to worry about, but we had a wind change early this morning, and the fire's moving across the mouth of the canyon."

Hooking his thumbs in the loops on his jeans, Adam leaned against the cupboard. "Can't you get in there with helicopters?"

The warden shook his head. "The visibility is zero with the smoke, and the winds are really gusting. And you can count on strong downdrafts there even at the best of times. That canyon's hell to get into even in perfect conditions. We could put somebody on the top of Hoodoo, but there's no way we can get in at the bottom."

Doc picked up an ashtray off the counter, then sat down at the other end of the settee. "Doug heard that I knew of a route down the west face that bypasses the overhang, and he came to see me about it." He scraped out his pipe and emptied the ashes in the ashtray, then looked up at Adam. "As you remember, lad, that area below the overhang has been off limits to hikers for the past fifteen years. But Doug says the erosion has deteriorated that whole base even more during the past few years, and everyone knows it's dangerous. Consequently, no one among the park staff is very familiar with that side at all." Clamping the stem between his teeth, he leaned back and folded his arms across his chest, his expression earnest. "Unfortunately, the only way they can get those boys out of there is either straight up the south face or bring them across base and hike them up the west side. The south face is out of the question because none of them are experienced climbers." He paused and pursed his lips, then fumbled in his pocket for his pouch of pipe tobacco. "The problem is, lad, that we need somebody who knows that old route."

Adam was very thoughtful as he stared at the old pharmacist. "That's a long time ago, Doc, and how old was I? Thirteen or fourteen? I don't know if I can remember it that well."

Doc nodded his head in complete confidence. "You knew that whole canyon like the back of your hand, lad. You'll remember once you're there."

Adam narrowed his eyes in contemplation as he looked at the warden. "You're certain you can get a helicopter to the top of Hoodoo?"

Doug nodded. "That won't be a problem, but whoever goes in is going to have to dangle. That fire's traveling damned fast, and if it gets into the canyon, we could be in big trouble."

Adam lifted his head, and he felt oddly disquieted when he realized Natalie had been standing in the narrow entrance to the bedroom. It was obvious by her expression that she had been listening for some time, and she was more than a little concerned. That didn't make Adam feel any better, and he looked away, his face inflexible.

Doug leaned forward and rested his arms across his legs, then thoughtfully rubbed his chin. "How much time would it take to go in that way?"

Adam made himself concentrate on the warden. "It's a good six-hour hike down the west side, and then probably another two hours to get to them. There's no way we can make that climb out of there in the dark, so it'll be the better part of two days. I can cut some time off that going in, but the climb back out will take longer. And if the fire moves into the canyon, the wind will be against us, and we'll be fighting smoke the whole time."

Doug Clifford was watching Adam closely. "Then you'll go in?"

Adam gave him an intent look. "Didn't you want me to?"

Doc chuckled and started tamping his tobacco into his pipe. "Of course they want you to, lad. We wouldn't have driven in over that terrible excuse for a road just to have a little chat. But one of the senior bureaucrats with Parks was a tad disturbed that we were going to ask the famous Adam Rutherford to head up a rescue mission. He felt that we had an uncommon amount of cheek to even *think* about asking you. Said something about it being like asking a brain surgeon to paint the town hall."

Adam grinned wryly as he straightened. "Well, if I had a choice, I'd rather paint the town hall."

Doug Clifford rose and tucked his hat under his arm. "How soon can you be ready to go? I don't know how the reception will be from here, but I can try to radio out so there's a chopper waiting for us in town."

"Twenty minutes. I need to get my gear together."

Doc stood up slowly, his legs obviously stiff, then his face lit up. "Well, Natalie, I didn't see you standing there."

Her smile was slightly forced, and there was tension in her shoulders as she came forward and kissed the old man on the cheek. "Hello, Doc. Didn't Patrick come with you?"

"No, lass, he has better things to do. Stella's put him to work at the drugstore and he's having a grand time."

A strained awkwardness still stretched between Adam and Natalie, and Adam's manner was slightly aloof as he introduced her to Doug Clifford. Feeling more disturbed about the rift between them than he liked to admit, he deliberately avoided looking at her as he went to the door. "I'll get my gear together. I have everything stored in one of the cabins, so it'll take me a few minutes."

Doug Clifford followed him. "And I'll see if I can scare up somebody on the radio."

"While you're at it, see if they can scare up a good topographical map of Hoodoo and the immediate area. I'd like a chance to refresh my memory." Adam glanced up as he was about to leave the trailer, and his gaze connected with Natalie's. For one tense moment, they stared at each other, then with his mouth set, Adam stepped out into the blinding sunshine.

He had his gear laid out and was kneeling on the rough floor of the cabin packing a small backpack when a shadow fell across him. He looked up and his face tightened when he saw Natalie standing there.

She sat down beside him. "I brought you a change of clothes and the first-aid kit."

He continued to pack, his tone deliberately impassive. "I want to travel with a small pack, so I won't have room for the clothes."

She went through the stack of folded garments she had laid on her lap, then handed him a pair of socks. "At least take these. You'll need a dry pair."

Natalie was experienced enough to realize that this venture was no hike in the woods, and he could tell by the strained quality of her voice that she was concerned for his safety. And in spite of everything, he did not want her worrying about him. Nor did he want to leave her with this air of restraint hanging between them. His expression softened, and he stopped what he was doing and looked at her. "Don't worry, Nat," he said quietly. "It isn't going to be that risky."

Natalie looked up at him, her eyes dark with distress. She didn't say anything for the longest time, then she murmured unsteadily, "It's not just the rescue mission, Adam. I am so sorry about what happened earlier. I know it doesn't change things, but it wasn't a conscious reaction." She swallowed hard and looked away.

Adam's anger evaporated and he gazed at her profile, his expression grave as he reached across and slowly brushed her hair back. "I'm sorry, too," he said softly. He smoothed his hand along her cheek as he stared at her with obvious concern. Very gently, he turned her head so he could see her face, then he leaned over and kissed her lightly on the mouth.

With a choked sound, she slipped her arms around him and held him tightly. "Be careful, Adam. I don't know what I would do if anything ever happened to you."

Adam closed his eyes and pressed his face against the soft skin of her neck. "I'll be back before you know it," he whispered huskily. "And that's a solemn promise."

CHAPTER TWELVE

THE SILENCE WAS STIFLING. Natalie was completely motionless as she stood beside Doc's leather chair, her face drained of color. The jolt had been so traumatic, she felt as though every ounce of breath had been driven out of her body. With a weird detached sensation, she watched Doc fumble for support, then grasp the arm of his chair and slowly lower himself into it, his skin suddenly an unhealthy gray. Agitated, he looked at Doug Clifford and said sharply, "What do you mean—Adam never made it back?"

Dropping his hat on the table, the warden slowly sat down, his face showing the effects of long grueling hours with very little sleep. "When the helicopter went to pick the bunch of them off Hoodoo, there were only four hikers there. Seems that one of the kids fell and broke his leg pretty bad. They'd made a stretcher and were carrying him out, but the fire moved into the canyon and it looked like their route to the west could be cut off. Adam found a cave that he figured would give them some protection, and they were all going to hole up there. But the kid who was hurt was no dummy and he realized the fix they were in. He told Adam to leave him there and get the others out."

"My God," Natalie whispered, her eyes wide with alarm. "You mean Adam's down there alone—with no help, and an injured man to bring out?"

Leaning back in the chair, Doug Clifford dragged his hand through his thinning hair in a gesture of weariness, the worry lines deepening. "I'm afraid so, ma'am. I guess Adam was concerned about the direction of wind, and he figured he had to make a choice. Either get four out for sure, or stay and maybe take a chance that they'd all be trapped. So he brought the four out, then went back for the one they'd left behind. One of the kids we rescued was able to pinpoint the location of the cave. We've had the water bombers hitting that area pretty heavy, but it's so dry it's like a pile of kindling down there. With the mountains so close, the planes don't have much room to maneuver, but they're trying their damnedest to get as close to Hoodoo as they can. Your husband had a hand-held portable radio with him, but in this terrain, you can almost spit farther than they'll receive and send. Unless a plane is right overhead, they won't pick up a signal. The only reason he had it with him in the first place was to bring in the chopper once they hit the ledge on Hoodoo."

Natalie looked at Doc, then swallowed against fear, she turned her attention back to Doug Clifford. "I take it you've picked up no transmission?"

There was a disturbing somberness about him as he answered quietly, "No, ma'am. Nothing." His exhaustion seemed to weigh him down as he drew his hands across his eyes. When he raised his head to look at Doc and Natalie, his expression was bleak. "I'm afraid it looks pretty bad, Mrs. Rutherford. We're making every effort we can to locate them, but the fire's right at the base of Hoodoo, and there aren't a whole lot of places he could have gone.''

Still in a state of shock, Natalie numbly turned and went to stand before the window, her arms clasped tightly around her. Staring out, she tried to fight through the numbness of disbelief. Like a tormenting dream, she suddenly remembered Adam giving her his solemn promise that he would be back soon, and with a cold shiver, she dragged her mind back to the grim present. ''Have you considered sending someone down the west side?''

There was an air of defeat about him as the warden stared at her. ''No, ma'am, we haven't. If you know Hoodoo at all, you'll remember that the ledge where we land isn't that wide. The smoke is heavy, in fact it's sitting in that canyon like soup, and we need good visibility so the chopper pilots can get in under that flat ridge on the upper part of the mountain.''

''How long do you think it will be before you can?''

Doug Clifford picked up his hat and began turning it around and around in his hands as he considered her question. ''It's hard to say. Unless there's a radical change in the wind or we get a gully washer of a rain...two, maybe three days.''

She turned to look at him, her face drawn. ''Are there facilities at Andrews Lake where I can stay?''

He stared at her briefly, then leaned forward and rested his arms on his legs. ''There's not a whole lot there right now, but we could put you up in one of the staff quarters. We're moving in a trailer camp for the extra men.'' There was a heavy frown on his face as he began fidgeting with his hat again. ''You may want to reconsider about going up to Andrews, Mrs. Rutherford. Somehow word leaked out that your husband had gone in on a rescue mission, and the place is swarming with reporters. We even have some from a TV network out of Los Angeles. They could make it pretty tough on you."

Who cares, she thought frantically. *Who gives a royal damn about reporters.* Aloud she assured him, "I'll manage."

The warden pursed his lips and shook his head, then heaved himself to his feet. "I can take you with me now if you like."

The shock was beginning to wear off, and Natalie suddenly felt very unsteady, and her voice revealed what she was feeling. "Thank you, but no. I want to talk to our son before I go, and I'd prefer to have a vehicle there." She went to the desk and made a notation on a slip of paper. "Adam has a phone in his truck, so you can either reach me here or on the radio telephone." She went over to him and handed him the paper. "Here's the mobile-call sign."

Doug Clifford took it, his manner preoccupied as he carefully folded the paper and tucked it in his breast pocket. "I want you to know that we're going to do our damnedest to get him out."

Natalie clasped her hands tightly together as she forced a tight smile. "I know you are, Warden."

Doc stood up and wearily clapped the warden on the back. "We have to keep faith with the lad, Doug. He uses his head, Adam does. And he'll come through this, you can be sure of that."

The warden sighed heavily, his expression anxious. "I hope so." He put his hat on as he went to the door.

"We have the area sealed off, but I'll leave word at the gate that you're coming in, Mrs. Rutherford. And if something changes in the meantime, I'll get word to you."

Natalie nodded. "That will be fine."

He stared at her for a moment, as though he wanted to say something else. But he shook his head instead and opened the door. "The damned weather is against us, that's for sure. We had such a dry fall last year, and we haven't had much rain up there yet. Seems strange. Only eighty miles from here to Andrews Lake and it's as different as night and day. But maybe we'll get lucky and have a downpour tonight." He shook his head again, then touched the brim of his hat in a gesture of farewell. "We'll see you later, ma'am."

Doc followed him into the porch and as soon as the two men disappeared, Natalie sank into a chair, her strength suddenly gone. She felt strangely disconnected, as though her body were somewhere else. The sensation added to her growing alarm, but as fearful as she was for Adam's safety, she was determined not to give in to panic. She simply had to believe that he was still alive.

"I don't think it's a good idea for you to go up there, lass. The reporters could become an enormous drain on you."

Natalie looked up at Doc, her ashen face set with determination. "I can deal with it."

He sat back down in his chair, his shoulders even more stooped than usual. "You'll serve no purpose by being there, Natalie," he reasoned gently.

No purpose. She met his worried gaze with an unyielding stare, her voice low and inflexible. "I will personally walk every square foot of that canyon if I have to, but I will not leave until we find him."

It was obvious by her tone that absolutely nothing would change her mind. Doc had seen her like this once before, and that was when she was sixteen years old and the doctors had tried to convince her to terminate her pregnancy. She had not given in then, and he knew she would not give in now. Feeling very tired, he rubbed his temple with his fingertips. "What are you going to tell Patrick?"

"The truth—that his father has gone back in to bring an injured hiker out." She met Doc's gaze square on, the look in her eyes daring him to challenge her. "He'll understand why I want to be there."

"Natalie, lass, you have to be realistic about the possibility that—"

"No!" Her eyes were flashing as she abruptly stood up. "No. Don't even think it, Doc. He's going to be all right. He has to be." She turned away quickly, and Doc saw her shoulders start to shake. "He has to be," she said again. And the undercurrent of sheer panic he heard in her voice was also grimly familiar. It was too much the same, this ordeal she was facing, and there was little he could do to give her comfort. Especially when he was well aware of just how critical the situation was. He slowly rose, then went over and patted her shoulder. "I'll go for Patrick, lass, while you pack your things."

THE COMMAND POST at Andrews Lake was bedlam. Men and equipment were being moved in, along with the supplies and services to support them. The fire, which was raging out of control, was consuming hundreds and hundreds of acres of prime forest, and if not contained, would consume thousands more. That in itself was tragic enough, but to make matters worse, a well-known wildlife photographer was missing on a dangerous rescue mission, and the media were having a field day with that.

Doug Clifford was right about them. They had latched on to Natalie the moment she arrived. But their persistence only made her more determined to maintain a calm, confident front, regardless of the fact that with each passing hour, her fears for Adam's safety mounted.

The sky was unnaturally murky and the sun burned like an eerie red globe through the smoke, the outline of the mountains barely visible through the gray haze. The water bombers reloaded on Lake Andrews, and the drone of them taxiing across the lake as they took on water seemed almost continuous. The smell of burning timber insinuated itself on her senses, and the acrid odor of smoke clung to her clothes and hair.

The first night in camp was never-ending for Natalie. Camp units had been hauled in for accommodations, and she had been put up in the trailer provided for the women. But she never closed her eyes. During the day, as long as she didn't have time to dwell on it, she could keep her confidence up.

But it was a different story at night. As she lay staring into the darkness, she tried to battle the awful realization that there was every possibility that Adam was already dead. And as some sort of masochistic punishment, her mind turned on her, and she was tortured with grisly mental scenarios of Adam trapped in the fire. The stark horror of knowing those scenarios could be deadly accurate awakened a cold sickening feeling in her, and she experienced a new level of fear. As she stared into the darkness, she tried not to think about what life would be like without him. Instead, she tried to call up the warm secure feeling of going to sleep in Adam's arms, but it eluded her, and only the smell of smoke infiltrated her senses.

As soon as the sky started to lighten, Natalie left her bed. She had a shower in the campgrounds' shower and bathroom facilities, then went over to the kitchen to help with breakfast. Shortly after her arrival, Natalie realized they were desperately shorthanded in the kitchen. Needing something to do to take her mind off the endless waiting, she had volunteered to help. The cook had put her to work, and Natalie had spent hours making sandwiches and packing lunches.

The warden came in just as she was pouring herself a cup of coffee. She poured a second cup and took them over to his table.

He glanced up as she set the mug before him. "Why thanks, Mrs. Rutherford." He watched as she sat down, a worried look in his eyes. "You're sure not expected to help out here, you know. You're going to be dead on your feet if you keep that up."

She gave him a small smile. "Keeping busy helps, Warden. You don't have so much time to think." Avoiding his eyes, she tidied the arrangement of salt and pepper shakers, napkin holder, then moved the cream and sugar to the side. "Have you had any reports yet this morning?"

He hunched over his coffee as he stirred in the cream, then raised his head. His eyes were red-rimmed, and he looked as though he hadn't slept in days. "Only by radio, and those reports aren't going to give us anything about your husband. Another hour and it'll be light enough for the water bombers to take off. We'll know more then."

Natalie's expression was carefully schooled as she looked at him. "You said last night that one of the helicopters would make a sweep over Hoodoo this morning."

"Yes, ma'am, as soon as it's light enough."

"I want to go."

He stared at her for a moment, then looked down at his coffee. "I think maybe it would be better if you stayed on the ground, ma'am," he answered gruffly.

Reaching across the table, she laid her hand on his wrist as she pleaded with him. "Please, I have to go. I need to see it, Warden. For my own peace of mind, I have to see that canyon."

He raised his eyes and looked at her, his expression grim. "It isn't going to do a hell of a lot for your peace of mind, ma'am. I can assure you of that."

Three-quarters of an hour later, Natalie was a passenger in the Bell helicopter that was making the reconnaissance flight. The noise in the machine was deafening, and Doug Clifford had given her headphones so she could hear the conversation between him and the pilot.

They were skimming along a few hundred feet above the ground, the rocky surface slipping dizzily below them. Suddenly they crested a ridge and the earth dropped sharply away, and spread below them were miles and miles of burning timber. The pilot's voice crackled hollowly on the intercom. "We'll be turning north in a minute here, Mrs. Rutherford. We have to fly around that ridge to the west before we have a clear shot of the canyon.''

They swept around the ridge, and their destination came into view. It was a long narrow canyon that was hemmed in by mountains, the far end blocked by the eerie, looming fortress of Hoodoo. And it was a trough of flames. There wasn't a square inch that had escaped the inferno. At the throat of the canyon, there was the charred, smoldering remains of a virgin forest, and at the other end, there was a raging wall of fire licking at the base of Hoodoo. Squeezing her eyes shut, she weakly leaned her head against the window as a cold sweat hit her. Not even in her worst nightmares had it been this bad.

The warden had been watching her over the back of his seat, and he shook his head when he saw the expression on her face. "I think she's seen enough, Mike. You'd better head back."

Natalie was vaguely aware of the return flight, but she felt numbly disoriented when she realized they had landed. Her senses dulled by shock, she went through the motions of taking off the headset and undoing her seat belt like a robot. The minute she emerged from the doorway, TV cameras focused on her and reporters moved closer. Realizing that she was functioning in a daze, Doug Clifford pressed her head down as they ran out from beneath the whirling blades.

Somehow she got through the cluster of reporters, and somehow she made it back to the camp. Once clear of any onlookers and Doug Clifford's deep concern, she stumbled into the bush like a wounded wild animal going to ground. Her numbness cracked like crystal as the reaction set in, and she was violently sick. She could play all the games she wanted to, but sheer logic told her that no living thing could have possibly survived that canyon fire. She desperately wanted to run, but there was no place for her to go.

The rest of that day passed in a numb blur. By the following day, she was so exhausted she could barely stay on her feet.

On the third morning, relief finally came when the winds changed, and the fire was driven back on itself. And Natalie knew with a deep cold dread that it was only a matter of hours until her waiting would be over.

That end came early the next morning. The helicopters had taken off at first light, and it was just midmorning when Doug Clifford appeared in the cook house. One of the men turned to speak to him, but he held up his hand and shook his head, then quickly scanned the room. He stopped looking when he spotted her, and Natalie's stomach dropped sickeningly as he wound his way through the tables to her, his expression tense.

Tightly grasping the edge of the counter, she watched him approach, her body braced for bad news.

"One of the choppers has something, Mrs. Ruthford, but we don't know what. The pilot's been having trouble with the radio the past couple of days, but the transmission was really breaking up bad today. We could only make out the odd word. All's we know for sure is they found something and they're headed back. They should be on the pad in twenty minutes." He took his hat off and ran his hand through his hair, then looked at her, his eyes very solemn. "I wouldn't get my hopes up if I were you," he warned gently. "You know what that area was like."

She swallowed hard, then looked away, her voice strained. "Yes, I know."

A sudden hush fell in the kitchen, and for an instant, all eyes were riveted on Natalie. Then as though they didn't want to intrude on her private hell, they averted their eyes. The only sound came from the far corner as two photographers quietly eased away from the table, collected their equipment and left the room. The silence became oppressive, and finally Natalie broke it. "I'll be down at the landing pad if you want me," she said very quietly.

The sky was heavily overcast and there was a mugginess in the air that warned of an impending storm. Natalie stood removed from the others, unable to endure the claustrophobic confinement. Her mind was a jumble of disjointed thoughts as she stared numbly at the leaden sky.

She heard the approaching helicopter before she saw it. Then it shot out from behind a ridge, skimming above the trees, and Natalie experienced a flurry of dread as she watched it come closer. The aircraft made a sweeping turn into the wind, then briefly hovered, the pitch from the turbine changing as it slowly lowered to the ground. The downdraft kicked up a flurry of dust, and Natalie shielded her eyes and turned her head from the machine-made whirlwind. The minute it settled on the gravel pad, Doug Clifford and two other uniformed men headed for the plane, ducking to miss the whirling rotor blades.

They slid open the side door and Natalie experienced a frightening heaviness in her chest as the warden climbed in. It was as though she was looking through a long thin tunnel, her attention welded on that open door. For one agonizing moment there was nothing. Then a rescue cradle was lifted out.

The warden crouched beside the stretcher, and Natalie felt as if every drop of blood suddenly drained from her body as she saw him shake his head. Her view was blocked as some photographers moved in, and panic started to build in her when she couldn't see. Desperate to find out who was in the stretcher, she started to run. The ground was rough and she stumbled, her muscles anesthetized by fear. A photographer turned and let out a whoop of excitement, and a cheer went up from those waiting at the sidelines. It took a minute for it to sink in that the person in the cradle was alive. Her heart started slamming frantically in her chest, and she could hardly breathe as she was hit with an incapacitating mixture of fear and hope. Just then, one of the flight crew who had been standing in the doorway stepped aside, and Natalie could see the other passenger.

Adam Rutherford ducked through the helicopter door.

There were no words to explain how she felt. She couldn't think. She couldn't breathe. She could barely absorb the fact that he was there. Aware of no one but him, she stared across the space that separated them, feeling as though she was finally waking up from a long and horrible dream. He was back, and he was safe. Then the aftermath of fear hit her, and she knew if she moved one single muscle, she would start to shake so badly she wouldn't be able to stand. He had somehow managed to escape that scorching fury.

And from the look of him, it had been a vicious struggle. He was filthy and caked with mud, and every inch of exposed skin was blackened by soot. His smudged face was streaked with sweat and a rough beard covered his jaw. His eyes were bloodshot and glazed with exhaustion, and he moved as though he was ready to drop. He looked as if he'd been to hell and back.

Orders were being shouted, and the warden pointed to the stretcher, then motioned to the helicopter, and the reporters started moving away from the aircraft. Adam crouched beside the cradle, his expression intent as he spoke to the injured hiker, then patting the young man on the shoulder, he slowly straightened. He helped reload the casualty on the helicopter, then spoke briefly to the medic who had followed the stretcher on board. As he closed the door, the warden shouted at Adam, and Adam turned abruptly and looked in Natalie's direction. The pitch of the rotors changed and the engine's whine accelerated as Adam ducked and headed toward her.

Natalie started to shake, but somehow she found the strength to move. He reached for her and she stumbled blindly into his arms, unable to contain the unbearable surge of relief any longer. When they came together, Adam's arms were like a vise clamping her against him. He turned his face into the curve of her neck and whispered hoarsely, "God, Nat, I'm so damned glad to see you."

He smelled strongly of smoke and sweat, and Natalie squeezed her eyes shut as she inhaled the living essence of him. She was trembling badly and her voice was ragged. "Adam . . . Adam—I was so scared."

"I know, love," he whispered roughly. "I know."

His hand in her hair, he pressed her head against his shoulder, cradling her body in an enveloping, protective hold.

"We'd like a shot of Mr. Rutherford if you don't mind. Could you turn for the camera?"

Adam swore. Drawing a deep shuddering breath, Natalie lifted her head and he gently eased her away from him. His throat was raw from smoke, and his voice was very hoarse when he asked, "Are you okay?"

Not trusting herself to speak, she nodded and wiped her eyes with the side of her hand.

He touched her face and said softly, "Just a few more minutes, and we can get the hell out of here, Nat. Can you hang in there for a little longer?"

She answered with a shaky smile. The expression in his eyes softened, and he lightly touched her face. He gazed at her a second longer, then assured she was able to deal with the final hurdle, he slipped his arm around her shoulders and turned to face the cluster of reporters.

Natalie felt him sway slightly, and she looked up at him, her expression suddenly anxious. He was so exhausted he was on the verge of dropping in his tracks. Slipping her arm around his waist to give him what support she could, she matched her stride with his as they started walking toward the camp.

A reporter who had a reputation for being pushy hurried ahead of them, then turned to face them. Walking backward, he held out the mike of his tape recorder and started quizzing Adam. "Tell us how you felt being trapped down there."

Adam gave him a cutting look and answered dryly, "Unhappy."

Natalie looked up at him, the worried look in his eyes giving way to a glint of amusement. He winked at her and she grinned, and suddenly he didn't feel so damned beat.

"And how did you finally manage to get out?"

The reporter's manner started to irritate Adam and he stared at him coldly. "Luck," he answered tersely.

Realizing he'd get nowhere with Adam, the pimple-faced young man made the grave mistake of shoving the mike at Natalie. She stumbled as she tried to avoid it, and with lightning speed and his eyes flashing fire, Adam knocked the mike out of his hands. "Stick that in her face again," he said through clenched teeth, "and I can assure you you'll eat the damned thing."

With the main attraction obviously in no mood for interviews, everyone quietly faded away, and Adam and Natalie covered the rest of the distance in silence. It was all Adam could do to keep putting one foot in front of the other. His eyes felt as if there was gravel in them, his throat was burned raw from smoke, his tongue felt like leather, and he was so tired he could go to sleep standing up.

When they got to the kitchen, Doug Clifford was waiting for them at the door. "Sorry I had to take off down there, but I had to let the other units know we got you out."

Too weary to answer, Adam nodded in acknowledgment, then reluctantly withdrew his arm from around Natalie so she could precede him. Once inside, he sank into the first chair he came to, tipped his head back and closed his eyes. Somehow he would have to find the energy to tell the warden what happened.

"Adam?"

He lowered his head and slowly opened his eyes. Natalie was standing beside him with a large glass of water in one hand and a frosty glass of milk in the other. Feeling as though his arms weighed a ton, he took both glasses from her and managed a feeble smile, "You're reading my mind again."

The water was ice cold, and he downed it thirstily. Natalie took the empty glass from him and set it on the table. She stood behind him, her arms draped loosely around his neck. Her hands were cool and soothing against his skin as she pressed him back. Experiencing a poignant rush of gratitude, he wearily leaned his head against her abdomen.

Doug Clifford pulled out a chair and sat down. "I know you're wiped, but I'm afraid I have to bug you for a couple details. We have these damned reports that have to be filed."

Adam took a long drink of milk, then fixed his bleary gaze on the warden. "What do you need to know?"

The warden gave him a warped smile. "How the hell you walked out of that inferno."

Adam finished the milk, then covered one of Natalie's hands with his. "If it hadn't been for the accuracy of those water bombers, we would have been fried three days ago. They gave me the time and the room I needed to get from the cave to the base. And from there I packed the kid up onto the overhang." Adam managed a weak grin. "Then I prayed that the erosion at the base of it wasn't really as bad as it looked."

The warden appeared stunned. "Dammit, man, that's one hell of a climb."

Adam nodded, a spark of humor in his eyes. "It sure in hell is."

"How did you ever lug that kid up there?"

"I piggybacked him. Fortunately he was small and light. I never would have made it if he'd been any heavier. As it was, my legs nearly gave out on me."

The warden shook his head, his expression dazed. "I don't know how you managed it. I really don't."

Adam's tone was dry. "A forest fire licking at your heels gives you plenty of incentive, Warden."

The man shook his head again, then looked at Adam. "So you holed up on the overhang," he said, his voice tinged with amazement.

"When the wind turned, I decided I'd better move out while I had the chance. We were on the ledge when the chopper spotted us."

Doug Clifford mulled that over for a moment, then frowned as he studied Adam. "How bad is the kid?"

"He has a bad fracture in his ankle, and I suspect he has some torn ligaments in his knee. He was in a lot of pain, and four nights on a mountain with no shelter doesn't do anyone much good, but he's young. He'll come out of this okay."

Leaning forward, the warden stared at the floor for a moment, then he raised his head, his expression grave. "It doesn't seem like enough to say how damned much we appreciate what you did for us here. Five young kids can thank their lucky stars you were around."

Adam met his serious gaze. "Anytime," he answered quietly.

There was a silent exchange between the two men, then the warden slapped his knees and stood up. "I think you'd better hit the sack before you fall asleep right here. There's some empty beds in the bunkhouse."

Adam managed a weak grin and shook his head. "If you don't mind, I'd just as soon get the hell out of here."

The warden frowned. "The minute you step out that door, those media guys are going to be all over you."

Natalie smoothed her hand across Adam's shoulder. "I'll take him out the back." There was a touch of cynicism in her smile. "None of them would be caught dead in a kitchen."

"Well, if you're smart, you won't go back to Doc's. That pack out there will follow you to the ends of the earth." He paused and rubbed his chin thoughtfully. "If I were you, I'd head for that trailer of yours."

Natalie glanced down at Adam, who was leaning heavily against her, and a deep ache tightened in her chest when she saw that he was already asleep. The warden was right. Adam needed a few hours of undisturbed rest, and the trailer would be the only place he'd get it. She gently stroked Adam's coarsely bearded face, her voice suddenly husky, "Would you contact Doc and explain? Tell him Adam's fine but I'm taking him back to the trailer for a while."

"I'll have to radio, so I'll give you a half hour head start before I contact him just in case a wise ass is monitoring the radio channels." He tipped his hat back on his head and motioned to Adam. "Now let's get him out the back door."

Adam was out like a light the minute he settled into the comfortable reclining bucket seat in the Bronco. The next thing he was aware of was Natalie bending over him, a cool breeze against his face. "Come on, Adam," she said softly. "We're home." It took him a while before he could fight his way through the heavy fog that clogged his mind. When he was finally able to focus, he realized that Natalie had driven the truck right down to the trailer instead of parking it where they normally did. He rubbed his face, then looked at her. The front of her pale pink shirt was smeared with dirt, and there was a smudge of soot along her neck and across her jaw. He realized the grime was from him, and he also realized just how damned filthy he was. Suddenly he desperately wanted a long hot shower.

He wearily climbed out of the truck and closed the door. "By any chance, did you leave the propane on when you left?"

She grimaced guiltily. "I'm afraid I did. I never even thought to shut it off."

He gave her a lopsided grin as he laid his arm across her shoulders. "A wise mistake, Nat. That means there's a whole tankful of hot water."

"Don't you want something to eat first?"

There was a flicker of humor in his eyes. "Not if it's anything I have to chew."

Natalie opened the door, then looked up at him, a smile pulling at her mouth. "Can you manage something really taxing, like swallowing?"

"Maybe. And maybe not."

The trailer was hot and stuffy from being closed up for so long, and Natalie opened all the windows and vents, then went to the fridge. While Adam was shaving, she fixed a tall mixed fruit drink with crushed ice, and Adam doubted if he'd ever drunk anything that tasted so good. He was badly dehydrated after five days in that heat with closely rationed liquids, and his throat was so sore, something cold and wet was all he wanted.

Natalie stood by the cupboard as she watched him drink. "Are you sure you don't want anything to eat? I can fix you something light, like an omelet."

He handed her the empty glass as he shook his head. "Maybe later. Right now all I want is a long hot shower and a bed."

Adam stayed in the shower until he drained the hot water tank. When he finally got out, the heat had sapped what little strength he had. He made a halfhearted effort to dry his hair, then wrapping a towel around his hips, he went into the bedroom. Natalie had folded the bed down and there was another tall glass of fruit punch on the ledge behind the bed.

"Is there anything else I can get you?" she asked softly.

Adam turned. She was looking up at him, her eyes so dark they seemed almost black. He reached out and slowly caressed her cheek. "All I need right now is a few hours' sleep."

She looked down quickly but not quick enough, and Adam caught the gleam of tears. He hooked his knuckles under her chin and gently raised her face. "What's the matter?"

"I saw that canyon," she whispered unevenly. "And to think you walked out of that...."

He wanted to put that ordeal behind them, and he tried to lighten the mood. "Didn't Doc ever tell you that close calls don't count, Nat?" he said softly.

She stared at him for a moment, then with her breath catching on a choked sob, she was in his arms. He hugged her tightly against him, his cheek pressed into her hair. "I'm sorry, Natalie," he murmured huskily. "I shouldn't treat it lightly. It's just that there were too damned many hours when I really wondered if I'd ever see you again." He tightened his arms around her and his voice became even more gruff. "There was one point when it looked really grim, and I would have given anything to have one last chance to tell you how much I love you."

Hauling in a ragged breath, she caught the back of his head, and with a low sound, she covered his mouth with her own. There was a staggering amount of emotion in that kiss—fear, relief, but beneath it all, there was a fire of passion. And Adam's response was instantaneous. Like a starving man, he moved his mouth against hers, famished for the warmth and moistness she was giving him. An incredible energy flooded through him, the feel of her body against his washing away the utter exhaustion. He couldn't move; he couldn't think. All he could do was feel, and galvanizing sensations coursed through him with a blinding intensity.

But suddenly a sliver of sanity penetrated the fever and he realized what was happening. Grasping her by the shoulders, he pushed her arms away, roughly severing the scalding contact. He was fighting for breath as he buried his face in the curve of her neck and whispered hoarsely, "God, Nat. I'm sorry."

She seemed almost frantic as she caught his head, her mouth hot and liquid against his neck. "Don't, Adam. Please, don't stop. Don't stop." She found his mouth and moaned against it, her desperation tearing at her. "Please, Adam . . . please."

A groan was wrung out of him, and widening his stance, he locked her against him, his need out of control. She responded to every move he made, and a searing passion possessed them, welding them together in a white-hot heat. And much as he wanted to be gentle with her, he could not relax his hold on her. He felt as if he would go out of his mind if he severed that electric contact, even for a second.

Natalie made a low throaty sound of protest as he caught her hips and held her motionless. Then with shaking fingers he undid her slacks, and slipping his hands against her naked skin, he pushed her jeans down. As though she couldn't stand the separation, she clasped his head between her hands and kissed him with a blistering heat as he unbuttoned her shirt.

Groaning against her mouth, Adam experienced the agonizing pleasure of their naked bodies locked together, and from somewhere he found the strength to drag her down on the bed beside him. Natalie cried out as he drew her beneath him, her body moving frantically against his, searching for the rhythm that would carry them even higher. He took her, and she arched against him, her body convulsing around his and drawing from him a hot, liquid eruption that paralyzed him. And they clung to each other, fused by a blinding release.

IN THE FIRST DRIFTING STAGE of consciousness, he felt oddly displaced. Slowly he became aware that he was lying on his stomach and there was a cool breeze against his skin. The sound of a light drizzle on the metal roof penetrated his sleepy stupor, and he slowly opened his eyes. The curtain on the open window lazily billowed, and drops of rain slid down the foggy windowpane. And it was so unbelievably still.

The heaviness of sleep weighed him down, but somehow he summoned up enough strength to turn his head and look at Natalie. But she wasn't there. Instantly awake, he levered himself out of bed. He swayed slightly, his body still drugged by the residue of a very deep and heavy sleep, and shaking his head to clear the fog, he went to the bedroom door.

The trailer was empty and silent, and Adam suddenly had a very hollow feeling in the pit of his stomach. He turned to get dressed, intending on going after her. But before he could move, the door opened and Natalie came in, wearing nothing except his yellow slicker. He felt welded to the floor as he watched her, his apprehension nearly suffocating. How would she react to him after the blaze of passion? Had that encounter dredged up ugly memories, or had it overpowered them?

Pulling the door shut, she kicked off her shoes and looked up. Adam felt as if his life were hanging by a thread. For a split second, they simply stared at each other, then she smiled and brushed the rain from her face. "I remembered I left the windows of the truck open." She grimaced a little sheepishly. "I thought I might get away with one goof over the propane, but I would never get away with two."

Adam had a hard time easing a breath past the strangling ache in his chest. Most of her hair had pulled free of the pins, the loose strands framing her face, and tiny beads of moisture were caught in the disheveled tangle. The slicker hung open, exposing a long narrow strip of her naked body, and the whole combination was totally alluring and very, very sexy. But what captivated him more than anything else was the soft glow in her eyes.

It took a tremendous effort for him to speak, and his voice was very husky as he murmured, "If that's what you wear to roll up windows, you can leave them down in a hurricane if you want."

Her eyes darkened and she moved toward him, holding his gaze with a mesmerizing intensity, her mysterious half smile very provocative. She stopped in front of him, seducing him with her eyes as she slowly smoothed her hands across his pelvis and up his chest. "I like that, Adam—a man who knows his priorities."

Her touch set off shock waves of sensation, and closing his eyes, he crushed her against him. The smell of rain clung to her hair, and he breathed deeply as he pressed his face into the silky tumble, his deep feelings for her nearly overwhelming him. "God, Nat," he whispered hoarsely, "when I woke up and you weren't there, I thought for sure I had come on too strong."

She caught his head and forced it up so she could see his face, then with trembling fingers she stroked his mouth. "Nothing can ever equal the kind of cold paralyzing dread I had when you were missing, Adam. And my other fears were so insignificant compared to that." Her voice became more strained and her eyes darkened. "You overpowered my senses, Adam, and I couldn't think of anything but what was happening between us."

Feeling raw and exposed, Adam lowered his head and kissed her softly. Her mouth slackened beneath his, and became hot and yielding as the kiss deepened into a scalding explosion of desire. Running his hands across her shoulders and down her arms, Adam stripped the slicker from her slender body, then picked her up and carried her to the bed. Her eyes were glazed with passion as he leaned over her, then with a soft sob, she tried to pull him down on top of her.

Resisting the pressure, he thrust his fingers into the tangle of her hair and slowly stroked her cheek with his thumb. He smiled softly. "No, Nat," he murmured huskily. "I've waited a damned long time to really make love to you, and I want to make it last. I want to savor every sensation, and I want time to savor every inch of you." He smoothed his hand along her thigh and let it rest on her midriff, his smoldering gaze locked on hers. Then in an agony of tension, he slowly moved his hand higher.

Her reaction was explosive, and her breath was driven out of her by the force. Twisting her head to the side, she closed her eyes as a heavy tremor coursed through her. A galvanizing hunger spread through him while he caressed her, his senses reeling as he watched her respond. Another tremor shuddered through her, then she slowly opened her eyes and looked at him, her fevered gaze intoxicating. Her eyes locked on his, she reached up, caught his head and drew it down. Moaning softly, she arched against him as he touched her sensitive flesh with his mouth, and as she responded to his intimate caress, his rigid control caved in around him.

The agony of the past was finally behind them. He had led her out of the shadows, and now he would lead her into the light.

EPILOGUE

A VIBRANT AUTUMN SUNSET lit the western sky, tinting the cloud formation a blaze of colors, and each vivid shade was perfectly mirrored on the smooth surface of the lake. The smell of burning leaves drifted up on the crisp autumn air, and sounds of laughter echoed across the still water.

Adam leaned back against the trunk of a tree, the rough bark penetrating the thickness of his heavy fisherman-knit sweater. Flexing one knee, he rested his arm across it, lazily watching the dancing flames of the bonfire through half-closed eyes.

Just three days earlier he had finished filming the main background material for his documentary about the cougar, and this chance to relax was a treat. He still had to get more close-up footage, but that would have to be done in the spring and summer months so he could record the development of the cubs, providing, of course, that the female he'd been tracking did him the favor of having some. It had been a good shoot, and he was experiencing the deep satisfaction he always did at the end of a project. But then, he had a lot to feel satisfied about.

It was the Thanksgiving weekend and Stella and Natalie had organized a massive buffet that was both Thanksgiving dinner and a windup bash. They had packed everything Friday afternoon, and as soon as Patrick got home from school, they moved out to the lake for the long weekend. Adam's parents had driven in from the coast in their motor home, and Pete, the sound man, had somehow managed to wheel the huge network remote unit up the mountain road.

Adam had fully restored one cabin, and Doc, Patrick and three of Patrick's friends had moved into that. Stella had scandalized Doc by closing the drugstore Saturday, stating very loudly that she had no damned intention of missing all the fun. And Stella, being Stella, spent the night wherever she had her last cigarette. It had been a fantastic weekend so far, and Adam was glad they still had another day.

Shifting his shoulders to a more comfortable spot, he grinned as he watched his father and Doc whipping the pants off two members of the film crew in a game of horseshoes. Stella and his mother were sitting in lawn chairs on the other side of the fire, and Natalie was on the ground in front of them, her arms locked around her knees.

His expression became sober as Adam considered his parents. They had been terrific about everything. When he had taken Natalie and Patrick out for the first visit, Adam's mother had welcomed her new daughter-in-law as though Natalie had never been away. They had been absolutely enthralled with Patrick, and he with them. Natalie had really surprised Adam the first night they were there. They had been sitting around the kitchen table having coffee, recalling the time Natalie and Adam sank Gordon's brandnew canoe. They had laughed about it, and a few other episodes were remembered.

There had been a comfortable silence, then Natalie had spoken up, her voice shaking. "I want you to know that the reason I left had nothing to do with me being pregnant." And then in an unsteady voice, she told them, without getting into the sordid details, what had happened. It was almost eerie to watch his father's reaction. It had virtually been a duplicate of his own.

"Are you sleeping or are you just hiding behind your eyelids?"

Adam opened his eyes to find Natalie crouched beside him, a steaming cup of coffee in her hand. He grinned as he took it from her. "I'm hiding. I had a hard day."

"What you had was too much turkey and pumpkin pie," she said succinctly.

Adam took a sip and choked, his coffee slopping over the edge of the cup. Biting back a grin, Natalie shrugged, her tone almost reproving. "It's only a little brandy."

"A little!" he rasped, his eyes watering. "And whose 'little'—yours or Doc's?"

"Actually, it's Stella's. But I'm just trying to keep your blood circulating."

He gave her a long steady stare as he said suggestively, "There are other, much more satisfactory ways of keeping my blood circulating, Natalie."

There was laughter in her eyes as she leaned over and gave him a quick kiss. "You can tell me all about them later." Adam caught her around the waist and pulled her on top of him, then shifted her weight so she was sitting between his legs with her back against his chest. "Let's talk about them now," he murmured against her ear.

She was smiling as she leaned back against him, and Adam tightened his arm around her and snuggled her closer. "What we need to talk about," she said firmly, "is the fact that Pete and his gang are now at the picnic table teaching Pat and his gang the fine art of playing poker."

Adam took another sip of coffee, then laughed softly. "Don't worry about it. By the time Pete finishes explaining the rules, Patrick and his gang will have graduated from high school."

Pete's soft Louisiana drawl came out of the shadows. "Oh, I think we could move that projection up a year or two. That kid plays poker just like his old man." Squatting beside them, he took a long pull of his beer, then started picking at the label. "I just thought about something I meant to ask you when we first came up. I heard you had a bit of a run-in with Deek McCarthy."

Adam frowned and shook his head. "I don't know a Deek McCarthy."

There was a devilish grin on Pete's face. "Sure you do. That pimple-faced mouth that does locations for the network."

"Never laid eyes on him."

The grin broadened. "Well that's not how he tells it. Seems that you pitched a five-hundred-dollar mike of his over a cliff because he crowded your little lady here."

Adam's tone was cryptic. "He was damned lucky I didn't pitch him over a cliff."

Pete studied the two of them. "Yeah," he said thoughtfully "I'd say he was." Pete had worked with Adam Rutherford for a good many years and he knew him pretty well. And knowing Adam Rutherford the way he did, he wouldn't give two cents for anyone who ever laid a hand on Natalie.

Patrick came tearing up and dropped on his knees in front of his parents. "Hey, Dad, can I have your Buck knife? Aunt Stella has a big bag of marshmallows for us to roast, and Grandpa's going to take us to some willow sticks. And we need a sharp knife."

Holding Natalie securely, Adam twisted and undid the leather case he wore on his belt, then handed the knife to Patrick. "Which Grandpa's going with you?"

Patrick scrambled to his feet. "Both Grandpas. Grandpa Patterson is going to show Grandpa Rutherford where he caught that big trout." He smiled broadly as he scrubbed his nose with the back of his hand. "Grandma says that scales will start popping out on their arms any day now."

Natalie took a Kleenex out of her pocket and handed it to him. "I hope you'll remember that, Patrick. Your grandmother is a wise woman."

He gave his mother a long-suffering look then blew his nose. "Grandpa Rutherford is going to teach me how to play chess. He says he's going to get me some books to read so I can learn all about it." Patrick wiped his nose again, then wadded up the tissue and dropped it on the ground.

"This isn't a garbage can, Patrick," his father said quietly.

Patrick picked up his litter, a sheepish tone in his voice. "I *know*, Dad. The only thing I'm supposed to leave behind are my footprints."

Smiling, Natalie shifted so she could look at Adam. "I am impressed. Now if you can only house-train him."

Patrick grinned and made a face, then darted away when Doc called him. Adam watched his son run up to Doc, and as he handed him the knife, the old man affectionately ruffled the boy's hair. A very strong bond had developed between the two, and nothing could have pleased Adam more. It reminded him of his own youth, and how he had become Doc's shadow when he wasn't much older than Patrick. And he had a hunch that his son's presence had as much to do with Doc's improved health as Natalie's care.

Pete had been watching Patrick, and he turned to face Natalie and Adam. "I don't think I've ever run across a kid that's so keen on learning. Is there anything he isn't interested in?"

"Yes," said Natalie dryly. "Washing."

Adam laughed as he looped his arms over her shoulders. "What a nag."

Stretching out on the ground, Pete propped his head on his hand and gazed out across the lake. "This is really beautiful country. I can sure understand why you've decided to use this as a home base, especially with that house you're building down there beside Doc's. And this place here—man, it's fantastic."

Adam rested his head against Natalie's as he stared into the deepening dusk, his expression suddenly sober. "Yeah, Pete, it is. It feels pretty damned good to put down roots after being on the move for so long.''

Grinning broadly, Pete looked at Natalie. ''You talk about house-training—I'd say you done a fair to middlin' job on ol' Adam here. A wife, a house, a kid. Next thing, you'll have him changing diapers.'' He glanced over at the bonfire, an almost embarrassed look on his face as he got to his feet. ''Think I'll try my hand at those marshmallows—haven't roasted one in years. Second childhood, I guess.''

''Ah,'' said Natalie gravely. ''What you need is a wife, a house, a kid.''

Pete nodded, his eyes glinting with humor. ''I think I could just about handle that.'' He turned and started to walk away. ''But I think I'd better wait and see how ol' Adam hangs in there.''

Natalie's voice was rich with amusement as she asked quietly, ''And how *is* ol' Adam hanging in there?'

''I'll survive,'' he responded, a husky tone in his voice.

She turned to look at him. ''You haven't told him yet, have you?''

Adam gently lifted a loose curl off her face and tucked it behind her ear. ''No, not yet,'' he answered quietly, his touch lingering as he slowly smoothed back her hair. ''This is something that's very special for me, Nat. And telling a bunch of freewheeling single guys that we're going to have another kid seems so out of context with what I'm feeling.'' His eyes darkened and became even more solemn, his tone reverent. ''It's such a miracle, and this time I'm going to be around to watch it happen.''

The depth of feeling in his words made Natalie's throat ache, and her voice was uneven as she whispered, "Being able to share all this with you this time makes it so special, Adam. I missed that so much when I was pregnant with Patrick—having you there."

Adam's arms tightened around her, his voice taking on a new intensity. "I can't wait for the house to be finished. The day we can move all your stuff out of storage and into our home can't come soon enough."

Natalie smiled as she rested her head on his shoulder, a faraway look in her eyes. "It's going to be so nice to be able to stay home with this one. I'm going to love every minute of it."

"Come on you two. Enough lollygagging around. Your mother and I are challenging you to a game of horseshoes."

Adam smiled at his father. "You can't even see the pegs. How can you play horseshoes in the dark?"

Gordon Rutherford chuckled. "The way your mother plays, it may as well be dark."

Natalie laughed, then gave her father-in-law a narrow look. "I'm going to tell her what you said, Gordon, and then you'll be in big trouble."

"Now Natalie. You know for a fact I spend half my time in trouble with that woman already."

"Sure, Dad. Sure," Adam said, without an ounce of conviction.

Hilda Rutherford came up behind Gordon and slapped him affectionately on the rear, then grinned. "Be nice to me, Father, or the next time they come to visit, I'll lend them your brand-new boat."

He chuckled again. "You're a terrible woman, Hilda. Terrible."

Getting to her feet, Natalie dusted off her jeans, then reached down and caught Adam's hand, her eyes dancing. "Come on, Adam. Don't just lie there like a big lump. Show these people what you can do in the dark."

He shot her a loaded look, then came smoothly to his feet, his own eyes flashing. "You're a terrible woman, Natalie. Terrible."

Hand in hand, they followed the senior Rutherfords. A gas lantern was suspended from the branch of a tree, casting a soft light on the group at the picnic table. Stella and Doc had joined them, and Stella had a pile of small pebbles heaped in front of her. Adam laughed. "You've just about got enough to start a gravel company, Stella."

"Wouldn't you know it. I get hot and the ante is a bunch of damned rocks."

"You're always hot," Doc said slyly as he puffed on his pipe.

"Cute, Doc. Real cute. Now ante up. I'm going to win that damned drugstore off you tonight or die trying."

His eyes were twinkling. "I don't know why you want it, lass. It would never be open with you off gadding around the country playing poker."

"Such a nice friendly little game," Adam said.

Natalie spoke just loud enough for him to hear. "I *like* friendly little games."

He had been standing behind her, and he slipped his arms around her waist and drew her back against him. His head against hers, he laughed softly. "If that's the case, why don't you let me show you what I can do in the dark?"

She laughed and leaned her head against his shoulder. "Later, Adam."

Patrick propped his head on his hand as he gazed contentedly up at his mother and father, a tone of satisfaction in his voice. "I really like it here. It makes me feel—I don't know—fuzzy inside."

And Adam and Natalie knew exactly what he meant.

Harlequin Superromance

COMING NEXT MONTH

#198 SEARCHING • Robyn Anzelon
Helping Mac Kincaid with his article on adoption
seemed simple enough to Carrie Prescott, but in the
end she is left with two choices: give up her own
search for her natural mother or give up Mac. Either
way she stands to lose....

#199 STORMSWEPT • Lynn Erickson
When Amy Slavin accompanies a rescue team to
Pearl Pass, she becomes caught up in a complicated
web of intrigue and deceit. Falling in love with a man
she can't trust is just too risky!

#200 BEYOND COMPARE • Risa Kirk
Television hosts Neil Kerrigan and Dinah Blake
disagree about everything—except the growing
attraction between them. Dinah quickly learns that
one doesn't have to like everything about a man to
fall in love with him....

#201 TWIN BRIDGES Sally Garrett
Best-selling author and recluse Laudon Brockman
and horse-breeder Michelle Innes are opposites. Yet
drawn together in the Montana Rockies they begin to
see the world with new eyes, the eyes of love....

What readers say about
HARLEQUIN SUPERROMANCE™

"Bravo! Your SUPERROMANCE [is]... super!"
R.V.,* Montgomery, Illinois

"I am impatiently awaiting
the next SUPERROMANCE."
J.D., Sandusky, Ohio

"Delightful... great."
. C.B., Fort Wayne, Indiana

"Terrific love stories. Just
keep them coming!"
M.G., Toronto, Ontario

Take 4 novels and a surprise gift FREE

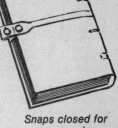